THE
WIND
STONE

BOOK THREE
THE REIGN OF THE ELEMENTS

RILEY CARNEY

Illustration © 2010 by Riley Carney

First Edition

Printed in the United States of America

Library of Congress Control Number: 2011901969

ISBN 9780984130740

Summary: Malik is on the move and Matt must face new enemies, as Matt and his friends must race against time to unravel the mystery of Matt's past and the location of the Wind Stone.

Visit www.booklightpress.com

This book is dedicated to Mom, Dad, and Nick.

A portion of the sales from this book will go to Breaking the Chain to help eliminate the bonds of illiteracy and poverty.

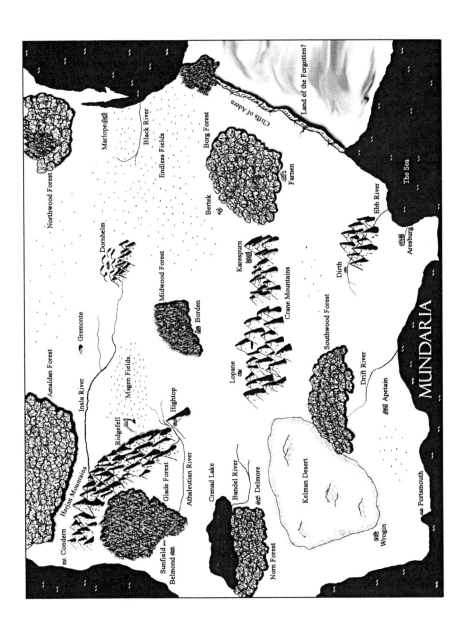

SAMSIRE

PROLOGUE

The Commander of Shadows was angry again. Kerwin could feel the waves of rage radiating from his master's body. Kerwin wrung his hands together in agitation. He was not usually one to be nervous, but his favor with his master had fallen considerably as of late. And it was all because of the boy. An unseemly sneer formed on Kerwin's pale face. The boy had caused all of this.

"What do you have to report, Kerwin? I am not in a patient mood. Speak quickly."

The Commander leaned forward in his chair. His uneven limbs stretched against his sides and his charred, crusted skin swirled into a grotesque gray across his hairless head. His bat-like ears were keen and attentive, but the most frightening aspect of the Commander was his eyes. The shiny black pupils were enormous, and the undersized irises were a fusion of colors: red, orange, blue, gray, and green. His gaze was menacing and calculating as he clasped his long hands together in front of his disfigured body and stared at the elf standing before him.

Kerwin dropped his gaze to the floor, knowing that his master would not be pleased with what he had to say. He stood as tall as he could and took a breath.

"Barrum has reported from Hightop," he said slowly. "He claims that there has been trouble with Rellin, the previous duke. It seems that he, or one of his family members, may have had communication with outsiders. Barrum has locked the duke and his family in the dungeons and-"

The Commander of Shadows jumped to his feet so quickly that Kerwin barely registered the movement, and he was completely unprepared for the arm that streaked through the air and rammed into his chest. He skidded across the cold marble floor on his back where he lay momentarily stunned, gasping for breath. Slowly, he pushed himself onto his knees, bowing his head. He glanced up. The Commander was once more hunched in his chair, as if he had never moved.

"Do not trouble me with such petty, unimportant reports, Kerwin," the Commander said, his voice dangerous. "You are avoiding the issue that matters. I don't care about Duke Rellin. I care that your man failed and that now our situation has been compromised. I have become further weakened. Just tell me where the boy is."

"The boy is in Gremonte, my lord," Kerwin replied, unable to keep the dread out of his voice. "He now has…possession of the Water Stone."

Kerwin cringed, anticipating his master's anger. The Commander did not attack again, but his multicolored eyes flashed hatefully.

"It is just as I have already guessed. It is not too late, though. He may have two of the Stones, but it will not be long before he is overpowered. I have been weakened by recent activity, Kerwin, but I will regain strength soon. It is time for us to move on to the next stage of the plan. We must prepare to move to a more suitable location. You now have the opportunity to redeem yourself."

"Yes, my lord," Kerwin said quickly.

"I await the arrival of my Aguran. I sent a shadow to speak to it days ago.

"I believe the Aguran is on its way, my lord."

A troubling silence filled the room. The Commander regarded Kerwin carefully before speaking.

"What of the Scroll? I greatly desire to know of its location."

Kerwin wet his dry lips. "No more news, my lord."

"Then we must focus on the task at hand. Have you ordered Vivona to make the necessary preparations?"

"I will do so, my lord."

More silence followed, but Kerwin was reluctant to risk speaking more than was necessary. Fortunately, at that moment the large doors were flung open to reveal a hideous, gray-skinned creature.

"So you have returned, my Aguran," the Commander declared, and Kerwin could detect a hint of excitement in his voice. "Come here."

The doors shut loudly as the Aguran slunk silently into the cavernous room. It sidled up beside Kerwin, towering over him, and stood motionless before the Commander of Shadows.

"What do you have to report?"

The Aguran brought a long, bony hand to its throat. It did not have a voice.

"Must I do everything?" the Commander spat.

Kerwin spoke tentatively, "If you would allow me, my lord-"

"No! I will do it."

The Commander once again leaned forward in his chair and held his hand up to the Aguran's throat. There was a barely perceptible flash of light as the creature fell to the ground and the Commander of Shadows crumpled beside it.

"My lord!"

Kerwin ran to his master's side and grabbed one of his gangly arms. The Commander held up a hand.

"I am fine, Kerwin. Step aside."

Kerwin stepped back. His master was weak. Vivona would be needed immediately.

"Now, Aguran, tell me, have you done what I have asked you to?"

The Aguran spoke, its new voice rough and gravelly. "It has been done. Her mind has been tampered with effectively. There will be no recollection of the incident."

"Good. Your work has been most valuable, Aguran. Kerwin, relieve it of its voice."

Kerwin nodded briskly and held up a hand to the Aguran's throat just as the Commander had done and quickly dismissed the creature's voice. It groped at its throat, then straightened and waited for the next command.

"Go. Watch over the garans."

The Aguran slid silently out of the room, leaving Kerwin and the Commander of Shadows alone again.

"I have been weakened, Kerwin. The past few weeks have been taxing. Fortunately, there are only a few necessary adjustments left to make. The army here is strong and the men of

Marlope are loyal to me. It is time to leave. Notify the weapon makers and trainers to set to work as soon as we depart."

"I will do so, my lord," Kerwin replied.

"Leave me."

Kerwin bowed his head and turned his back on the disfigured Commander of Shadows. He let the heavy doors slam shut behind him. His confidence returned as he left his master behind. He walked briskly until he reached a winding, marble staircase and stopped at a plain door halfway down the hall. He flung it open without knocking. Inside, a woman with jet black hair and pale skin sat on a stool, stirring a dark liquid in a giant pot. The small room was filled with shelves laden with bottles, strange plants, and other sinister-looking instruments. She blinked as Kerwin entered the room, annoyed by his ill-mannered entrance.

"Kerwin," she said icily. "What do you want?"

"The Commander is weakened, Vivona," Kerwin spat. "You are not making it strong enough."

"You did not tell me to make it stronger, Kerwin," Vivona snapped back.

"I am telling you now. Both the Commander and I need more. It must be made stronger. We will be leaving soon, so make enough to take with us."

Without waiting for her response, he swept abruptly from the room.

It was time for the plan to go into effect.

CHAPTER ONE

A brisk wind whipped through Matt's cloak as he waded through the knee-high, dead grass. He pulled it tighter around his body and glanced up at the gray sky. It was still autumn, but the dark clouds and cold air threatened winter storms. Matt wandered through the field alone, his mind preoccupied. It was nice to be outside of the underground cavern in the open air. He let his thoughts wander, enjoying the feeling of freedom. He kicked at a loose stone, watching it roll into a small stream that snaked through the grass.

There was a roar in the distance and Matt looked up to see Samsire soaring leisurely above him. The alorath's blue, green, and red feathers still shimmered sleekly even in the dull light of the gray day.

Matt watched him for a moment, marveling. He had seen the alorath fly hundreds of times, but it always amazed him. Sam spotted him, tucked his wings in close to his sides, and streaked down toward Matt with such speed that Matt involuntarily stepped backward. Spreading his wings, Sam pulled to an abrupt stop and dropped gently to the ground next to Matt.

"Scared?" the alorath asked playfully.

"Terrified," Matt replied with a grin.

Sam nudged him forcefully with his snout, nearly knocking Matt off his feet. He laughed and tried to push Sam back, but the alorath merely looked down at him in amusement. Matt shook his head and patted Sam's neck.

"Come on. Let's go back. I'm getting cold."

They walked through the grassy field, Samsire's large body comfortably shielding Matt from the wind. They soon reached the enormous stone gates of the city of Gremonte. The doors were charred and crooked with a gap between them large enough for a man to fit through. Matt smiled slightly. He had blasted the doors with magic so he could save its inhabitants from a plague with the magical water of Oberdine, the mythical dwarf city. The doors had not yet been repaired.

As they approached, a lean figure appeared in the gap, carefully maneuvering himself between the doors and stepping lightly onto the ground outside.

"Hey, Matt!" Galen called, smiling. "I've been looking for you."

"Hey, Galen," Matt said. "How are you feeling?"

Galen shrugged. "Better every day."

He did seem to be recovering well from his near-fatal duel with Rock Thompson. The Water Stone and the water of Oberdine had worked wonders.

Galen turned to look up at Samsire. "Hello, Sam. Enjoying the cold weather?"

"Couldn't ask for better," Samsire replied.

"So what's going on? Why did you come looking for me?" Matt asked.

"Lucian wants to see you," Galen told him. "He's waiting in the library."

"Right," Matt said, feeling slightly anxious.

Usually, when Lucian specifically asked for Matt to meet with him, it meant something was about to happen – lessons and unpleasant news were common, but Matt never knew what to expect.

He turned to Sam and gave him a final pat. "I'll see you later, Sam."

Sam snorted, flapped his wings twice and lifted himself into the air.

"They've got to get these doors fixed. Such an unfortunate mess," Galen said with feigned disgust as they squeezed through the gap.

Matt grinned and followed him into the dimly lit tunnel winding down into Gremonte. It was warmer inside without the chilling wind.

"Do you know what Lucian wants?" Matt asked as they walked down the declining tunnel.

"No, but he seemed excited."

The walls of the tunnel disappeared and the tunnel opened up onto the city. Simple stone buildings were arranged neatly throughout the enormous underground cavern, lanterns and torches fastened to every wall. Two guards lounged on a stone partition at the edge of the tunnel and waved cheerfully at Matt and Galen.

The city was considerably livelier than it had been a month earlier before the healing water had saved most of the citizens from death. Workers strode happily through the town, brooms and tools slung over their shoulders as they went about repairing buildings and cleaning the cobblestones. Laughing children waved at their mothers and fathers as they ran through the streets and along the top of the short walls that curved through the city.

"Lucian's on the top floor," Galen said as they approached the library.

The top level of the library was filled with bookshelves and comfortable armchairs and rugs. Lucian, a tall man with gray-peppered hair and wise gray eyes, sat in one of the chairs. His chin was covered in heavy stubble and he held his long staff in one hand. Another man, looking very travel-weary, sat in the chair beside him, his bald head resting against the back of the chair.

Lucian looked up as he heard them approach and smiled. "Hello, my friends."

The man beside him perked up and turned to face Matt and Galen as well.

"Beagan, you remember Matt?"

Matt recognized the man at once. On their journey to find Oberdine, they had traveled to Dornhelm in search of Dorn the Adventurer's clues. There, they had met Beagan, an old friend of Lucian's.

Beagan smiled and heartily shook Matt's hand. "Of course I do! How are you? Lucian tells me you found the answer to Dorn's riddles."

Matt grinned. "It took us some time, but we did. What are you doing in Gremonte, Beagan?"

"He has kindly returned our horses," Lucian answered for him.

"When they came to me a few weeks ago, they were quite spooked. Lucian tells me they ran from a herd of garans. I'm amazed they made it back to Dornhelm," Beagan added.

Silence settled over the room. Matt shifted from foot to foot.

"Galen said you wanted to see me, Lucian," he said finally.

Beagan got to his feet. "I think I'll have a bit of rest, Lucian. I have gotten a decent sleep in days."

Lucian nodded to him and Beagan disappeared down the stairs.

"Sit down, Matt," Lucian said, proffering Beagan's vacated seat.

Matt fell into the comfortable armchair, Galen pulled up a chair on the other side, and they both looked at Lucian.

"Beagan has just given me some very interesting information," Lucian began. "He said that a traveler stopped at his inn and spoke of rumors from the south. There have been sightings of flying beasts in the Southern Province."

"Flying beasts?" Matt said incredulously. "Like aloraths?"

Lucian nodded. "My thoughts exactly. I believe that there may be an alorath colony in the Southern Province."

This time it was Galen who spoke. "Alorath colony? Why have we never heard of this before?"

"There has always been talk of strange creatures throughout Mundaria, but these rumors from the Southern Province are recent and numerous."

"Why does it matter to us that there might be an alorath colony?" Matt asked, even though he was excited about the idea.

Lucian's eyes twinkled. "It could be very beneficial for us, Matthias. If we befriend the aloraths, they could prove to be powerful allies in the future. Perhaps they could aid us in defeating Malik. And the best way, I believe, to encourage friendship with the aloraths would be to send another alorath."

"Sam?"

"Yes. I think that Samsire should search for the colony."

Matt opened his mouth to speak but shut it almost immediately. As much as the idea of other aloraths excited him, the idea of Samsire leaving did not. Who knew how long it would take him to find them?

"Does he have to go now?" Matt said, trying to keep his distaste for the idea out of his voice.

"It would be very advantageous for us if we discovered the colony before Malik does," Lucian answered.

Matt stared at his feet for a moment. Lucian was right, of course, but Sam was Matt's first and closest friend.

"Fine," Matt said at last. "I'll tell him later."

"Good," Lucian said with a warm smile. "Thank you. Now we must discuss our next move."

"Right," Matt said, shifting into a more comfortable position. He sensed a long conversation was coming.

"Lord Balor's proclamation banning you or any of your allies from Amaldan Forest still holds, so your desire to heal the darkening forest cannot be achieved at the present time."

"That elf is an idiot," Galen muttered.

Matt resisted a grin. Galen had been born in Amaldan to an elf mother and a human father whom he never knew. Most elves' disliked merglings, and they had not hidden their feelings about Galen as he was growing up there. He was now distrustful of most elves.

"Since Amaldan is not an option, and we have no leads on the location of the Wind Stone, do you still wish to search for your parents?" Lucian continued.

Matt did not hesitate. "Yes. I want to know who they are, even if they aren't alive."

"Very well. But, unfortunately, there is one other thing we must discuss, Matthias."

Lucian sighed and the twinkle disappeared. Matt's stomach twisted into a knot. He could tell that Lucian was dreading whatever he was about to say.

"I have been contacted by the wizard council of Karespurn. They have somehow discovered you. I tried to dissuade them, but they would not be convinced otherwise. They have ordered that you be presented before them. They demand to see you."

"What?" Matt was outraged.

"There is nothing that I can do. Technically, I am still under their command. Even if I was not, the council would have its spies track you down and it would be a much less pleasant meeting. There is nothing we can do but comply with their wishes."

Matt clenched his teeth. He knew that he was the One of the Prophecy of the Elements whether he liked it or not. And with that title, came the responsibility of choosing his path, the path that would determine the fate of the rest of the world. Salvation or destruction. Balor and the elves of Amaldan had already assumed that he would fail. It was likely that the wizard council of Karespurn had assumed the same.

"Don't fret, Matt," Lucian encouraged. "I will not let them hinder your quest, nor will I allow them to exploit your power. We will travel to Karespurn merely to comply with their desire to meet you, not to submit to them."

Matt nodded resolutely. "All right, then. I'll go."

"Thank you, Matt," Lucian said with a smile. "In two days' time we shall leave for Karespurn."

Matt nodded, his heart sinking deeper. Glumly, he pushed open the door to the library and stepped outside. He stood there for a long moment, debating where to go and then found himself walking down the narrow path to the underground river.

"Matt!" somebody shouted.

Emmon and Arden were running toward him, with Natalia stumbling close behind. They all looked excited, exactly the opposite of the way he felt. Arden ran ahead of Emmon and Natalia, grinning.

"Where have you been, Matt? You've been missing out on all the fun!"

Before he could answer, she had grabbed his arm and was pulling him along with her.

"Arden," Matt laughed despite himself. "What's going on?"

"We've got things to explore, that's what," Emmon said. "Natalia discovered this maze of caves at the mouth of the river. You wouldn't believe how deep they go."

"I didn't exactly discover them," Natalia piped in quietly, her face flushed with embarrassment. "I was looking back through the city records, and I found a passage in one of the founder's books about a group of tunnels that they used to live in but had since abandoned. I never thought we'd be able to find them!"

They hurried down to the river where Hal was waiting for them impatiently. After weaving between boulders along the river bank, they soon came to a small dark entrance tucked into the hillside.

"Let's go in," Hal said with a hint of bravado. "Let's see how deep they go."

Emmon and Arden nodded and Natalia peered in anxiously.

"Some light then, Matt?" Emmon suggested.

Grinning, Matt picked up a stone off the ground and held it out in front of him. He concentrated for a moment until he could feel the magic coursing through him and the stone began to glow. He held it aloft and stepped inside the cave. It was cold and damp, and a chill went down his spine as he wondered what they might find in the maze of caves.

"Let's try this way," Emmon suggested, pointing to the right.

They ducked down the passage, pointing out shiny stripes of metal, silver perhaps, snaking through the rock walls.

Arden suddenly froze. "What was that?"

Matt held up his light stone so he could see her face. "What?"

"I heard something," she whispered, looking around. "And I thought I saw something move, too."

Natalia grabbed Emmon's arm and Hal took a bold step forward as they all fell silent, straining to hear.

Arden shook her head. "I must have imag-"

Her voice was drowned out by Natalia's scream and Hal's shout as something shot out of the darkness at them. Matt staggered backward, struggling to hold the light stone up. In the bright glow, he caught a glimpse of a small creature squirming on the cave floor. It was the size of a very undersized squirrel, with thick black fur, a long nose, and a straight, wiry tail. It stared up at Matt with wide brown eyes and then jumped straight into the air, like it had springs in its feet.

Arden yelped as the strange creature landed on her head.

"Hold still Arden," Matt said quietly as he moved his hand toward her head.

But the creature scurried down her neck and onto her shoulder, cowering behind her head. Arden stood motionless as she slowly turned her head to look at the furry creature.

"Wait!" she whispered urgently. "It's shaking! It's doesn't mean any harm. It's terrified!"

"Arden, we don't know what it is. How do we know it won't try to hurt you," Emmon protested.

"Shh!" Arden said, slowly moving her arm.

With slow movements, she reached up to her shoulder, paused, and then slowly closed her fingers around the little creature. Cautiously, she lifted it out in front of her and held it in the air.

"It's sort of...cute," Natalia said.

Arden laughed as the creature squirmed in her hands. "It's all right, little guy, we're not going to hurt you." She turned to Matt. "Look, he's harmless."

Matt dropped the arm he had lifted to make a shield around Arden. His heart was still hammering, but he smiled when Natalia and Arden laughed at the creature wriggling in Arden's grip. Maybe it was harmless.

"Natalia, have you ever seen one of these things before?" Emmon asked.

Natalia shook her head.

"Let's go see if Galen or Lucian know what it is. Just...don't let that thing bite you," Matt said.

Matt kept a close watch on Arden as he led the way back to the front of the cave. He resisted the urge to grab the creature away from her as she cuddled it between her hands. At that moment, he realized that the creature's fur had suddenly changed from black to white.

"Did you see that?" Emmon exclaimed. "It changed color!"

Arden held the creature further away from her body. "Um...let's get to Lucian quickly, why don't we?"

They hurried down the path and onto the street winding back to the library, moving as fast as they could. Just as they neared the library, a squat little man with a long, brown beard and a tiny wisp of hair on his otherwise bald head walked up.

"Hello, young friends," Alem started to say, but then stopped. "What in Dorn's name are you holding? Do you have a skunk there?"

"We were hoping someone could tell us what it is," Arden said, much less keen on holding the creature than she had been. "Alem, do you know what this is?"

Alem shuffled closer, peering at the creature with interest. His round face lit up in amazement.

"I haven't seen one in decades, not since I was a small child. I thought they were extinct! Wherever did you find him?"

"It...he found us, actually," Emmon said. "Jumped on us is more like it. There's a maze of caves down by the river..."

Alem was barely listening as he reached out to take the creature from Arden. As it squirmed, its fur changed from white to brown. Alem laughed, a sound rarely heard from the dwarf.

"It's a morphcat," Alem said in a wondering voice.

"What's a morphcat?" Hal demanded, staring at it warily.

"A very interesting creature, a morphcat," Lucian declared, striding out of the library door. "You would most likely exhaust yourself trying to keep up with. They move constantly."

Lucian smiled when he saw the tiny animal. "Astonishing. I believed morphcats to be extinct."

"They are," Alem said, rather absently.

"Of course," Lucian said looking up at Matt. "You do seem to have an uncanny ability to attract magical creatures, Matthias, even those that are thought to be extinct."

"Actually," Matt replied, "I think it's Arden who he likes."

As if on cue, the morphcat leapt out of Alem's hands and landed nimbly on Arden's shoulder.

"Morphcats are supposed to be able to jump to enormous heights," Natalia said. "I've read about them. Changing color is a magical ability that allows them to blend into their surroundings. But...they were thought to have died out decades ago. And the tunnels where we found him were thoroughly searched before they were abandoned. I wonder where he came from."

"Yes," Alem agreed, watching the morphcat climb onto Arden's head. "The Gremonte dwarves confirmed long ago that there were no more morphcats in Gremonte. Or anywhere else, for that matter. This morphcat does look different than any I've seen before. Those creatures had shorter snouts and tails. So this morphcat…well, it may not be from Gremonte."

"You mean it found a way to get in here?" Matt asked. "Why would it come here?"

"I think we have to assume that it came from one of the few locations where they lived before they became extinct," Lucian said.

Matt looked from Lucian to the morphcat, who was now jumping from Arden's head to Natalia's shoulder. If there were so few of them left, if there were any others, why would this magical creature suddenly show up in Gremonte?

"In any case, he is harmless," Lucian said and then turned to Matt. "It never ceases to amaze me the way you manage to find some sort of trouble, even in the last days before we leave, Matthias."

"Leave?" Arden demanded, peeling the creature off of her head. "What do you mean?"

They all stared at Matt and he reluctantly explained what Lucian had told him earlier.

"When do you go?" Emmon asked after Matt had finished.

"Two days."

Arden looked at him morosely.

"At least it'll get you out of this claustrophobic cave," Emmon said.

"Now, don't you insult Gremonte, young friend. It was once a great dwarf city, you know," Alem said. "This city is a marvel. I'd like to see the elves attempt to build something like this."

They all exchanged knowing grins, while the little dwarf shook his head, muttering about disrespect while he huffed back into the library.

CHAPTER TWO

Matt sighed as he rolled up his small stack of tunics and shoved them into his bag alongside the food Lucian had given him to pack. He was beginning to hate packing for these long journeys. Carefully, he placed his knives inside his pack, attached his bow to the side of it, and fastened Doubtslayer around his waist. Hesitating slightly, he reached for the small, black pouch lying on the bed. Enclosed were two of the three Stones of the Elements, the Fire Stone and the Water Stone.

He immediately felt the surge of power from the Stones as he placed the pouch around his neck. He had not worn it for some time and was unaccustomed to the constant swell of magic they transmitted to his body. He could feel the wild yet comforting heat of the Fire Stone and the gently coolness of the Water Stone, which Lucian constantly warned him was just as wild and dangerous as the Fire Stone.

After fastening his cloak, Matt shouldered his pack, looked around his room one last time, and shut the door behind him. Emmon, Arden, and Natalia were standing in the hall, waiting to walk down with Matt.

"Hurry up, Hal," Emmon said irritably. "Or we're going without you."

He banged on the older boy's door once more and then shook his head.

"What's taking him so long?" Natalia asked.

"He's probably been combing his hair for the past twenty minutes," Arden said. "Who does he think we're going to see? His precious Cadia?"

At that moment, the tall red-haired boy opened his door, his hair very neatly combed and his shirt buttoned to his throat, a stark contrast to the rest of them in their work clothes and Matt in his worn traveling clothes.

"What took you so long?" Matt asked.

Hal shot Matt a mutinous glare. "Well, are we going or not?"

Matt led them down the stairs to the gathering room where Galen was standing by the door, impatiently tapping his foot against the floor.

"Lucian and Alem are already up at the gates. Why the delay?"

Matt nodded his head in Hal's direction and Galen raised an eyebrow. A mischievous grin spread across his face.

"My, don't you look dapper, Hal," Galen said as they walked down the street.

Hal pretended not to hear him and began to fuss with his top button, which only encouraged Galen.

"I had no idea that you were so attracted to aloraths, but your dashing appearance has proven me wrong."

Matt, Emmon, Arden, and Natalia tried to stifle their laughter as Hal's face grew red in anger. He dived at Galen, who easily sidestepped him and chuckled softly. Hal eventually gave up trying to get to the mergling, but Matt noticed that by the time they had reached the path up to the gates, Hal had ruffled up his hair and undone the top button of his shirt.

As if he understood what they were laughing about, the morphcat jumped from Arden's shoulder, where it had taken up residence over the past two days, onto Hal's head. Hal swatted wildly at the morphcat as it gleefully made chaos of his hair.

"Stop it, Murph!" Arden said, laughing.

"Murph?" Matt asked.

Arden grinned. "Well, he has to have a name, doesn't he?"

The morphcat seemed to like it, too, bounding back to Arden's shoulder and curling its furry body into a ball against her neck. Matt still wondered where it had come from and why it had come here. He could not shake a feeling that there was something strange about the morphcat's appearance, but he had no idea what it could be.

They met Lucian and Alem at the stables. Lucian's horse, Innar, and Matt's horse, Striker, stood beside them, already saddled.

"Good morning, Matthias," Lucian said quietly.

Matt only nodded, afraid his voice would reveal his unhappiness. He stroked Striker's black mane and fastened his pack to the saddle. Lucian did the same, fitting his staff into a strap along the side of the saddle for easy access. The horses' hooves clopped loudly against the stone path and echoed off the rock walls as they led them up the sloping tunnel. When they reached the doors, still hanging awkwardly on their hinges, Lucian moved his staff and they eased apart with a groan.

Matt shivered at the cold wind as he stepped into the open air He scanned the sky, searching for Sam, and soon spotted him in the distance, flying toward them. Within minutes, they could hear the steady flapping of his wings. The alorath landed loudly and turned his enormous head to Matt and his friends.

"I wasn't expecting such a grand farewell," he rumbled, grinning toothily.

"You have done much for us, Samsire, and you are about to do much more. The least we can do is to give you a proper goodbye," Lucian told him.

Matt felt a knot forming in his stomach. Lucian made it sound like Sam was leaving forever.

"I'm doing it for all of us, Lucian," Sam responded, swishing his tail through the tall grass and nudging Matt with his head.

A tense silence settled on them until Murph suddenly shot straight up as if to leap onto Samsire, but then seemed to think better of it, turned white, changed directions in midair, and lunged back to Arden's neck, trembling violently.

Samsire snorted. "That's a peculiar little creature you have there, Arden."

Murph and Sam had met the day before when Sam had mistaken Murph for a hairball. When Sam realized that Murph was actually an animal he had snorted loudly, accidentally blowing Murph off Arden's shoulder into the grass.

Arden grinned now. "You're just jealous, Sam."

Matt noticed Sam held his breath as he leaned in to nudge Arden with his snout.

"Well, enough of this lollygagging," Alem said, stepping up to Samsire and placed a short, wide hand on his foreleg. "I, for one, shall miss you, Samsire. It seems strange that it has been only eight months ago since you were a feisty little creature terrorizing my home."

"Much has happened since, Alem," Sam said in his low voice. "Though I must admit, your books were some of the most delicious things I have ever eaten."

This comment earned the alorath a fuming stare from the dwarf, who often shifted moods in the blink of an eye. Arden pulled Alem out of the way and flung her arms around Sam's lowered face, whispering quietly to him for a moment. Natalia and Emmon said their goodbyes in a similar fashion. Hal nodded his head and gave a swift pat to Sam's leg. Galen spoke to Sam for several minutes before stroking his nose and stepping back.

Lucian laid a hand on Matt's shoulder and guided him toward Sam. The alorath looked down at them fondly.

"Goodbye, my friend," Lucian said. "I hope your travels are laden with good fortune."

"And yours, Lucian," Samsire answered. "And try to keep this one out of trouble."

A smile crept onto Matt's face. Samsire grinned at him and gave him a playful nudge with his nose.

"Undeniably impossible," Lucian replied. "Matthias is never out of trouble."

"Like you're not involved in the trouble with me most of the time, Sam," Matt retorted.

The alorath nudged Matt more forcefully this time, knocking him off his feet. Lucian pulled Matt up, and they both faced the alorath again. Sam's grin had disappeared.

"I'm going to miss doing that."

"Goodbye, Sam," Matt whispered.

He reached up one last time and rubbed the alorath's nose.

"I'll be back, Matt."

And with those final words, Samsire pumped his wings, rose into the air, and disappeared into the distance. With a heavy heart, Matt watched until his friend was nothing more than a shadowy speck on the horizon.

"It is time, Matthias," Lucian said at last.

Matt nodded. Galen smiled at Matt and put his shoulder around his shoulder.

In a low voice he said, "Be careful, Matt. The council is a treacherous bunch. Don't let them fool you."

"You've met them?"

"Yes, when Lucian and I first started traveling together. They didn't much care for me and they will be wary of you, too." Matt followed Galen's gaze to the pouch that hung from his neck. "They fear you, Matt."

"It seems like everyone does these days," Matt replied.

"Not everyone," Emmon said, smiling as he bear-hugged his friend.

"Take care of yourself, Matt," Arden whispered as she leaned in for a hug.

"Do try to stay out of trouble, Matt," the dwarf said gruffly.

"You too, Alem," Matt replied.

Alem was silent for a moment and then he mumbled, "Three goodbyes in one day…it's too much to ask of one dwarf." He took Matt's hand and patted it. "Goodbye, my friend."

Matt took a final look at his friends and turned to Lucian. They mounted their horses, and with a wave, slowly trotted out into the fields. The cold breeze seeped through Matt's clothes and he shivered, pulling his cloak tighter around him.

"Winter will come early this year," Lucian said quietly, glancing at the gray sky.

Matt nodded, but his thoughts were elsewhere. This was how it had all begun, just he and Lucian. It seemed so long ago that Lucian, then only a mysterious stranger, had rescued him from a strange tavern brawl. But now, eight months later, here they were. Matt's past was behind him. No longer did he have to deal with his abusive, angry, counterfeit parents; no longer did he have to work the fields. No, now all he had to do was to find a way to defeat the most evil being ever to walk the earth.

Lucian seemed to sense his thoughts and said, "Do not dwell on the past or future, Matthias. Focus on the task at hand."

"I know," Matt sighed. "It's just that…so much has changed."

Lucian studied him with his wise, gray gaze. "I think it has changed for the better. It is strange to think, though, that you have gone from a helpless, ordinary boy to being summoned by the wizard council of Karespurn."

Matt smiled. "I'm still a little helpless."

Lucian looked at Matt knowingly, a twinkle in his eye.

"How far is Karespurn?"

"About ten days if we ride at this pace and there are few settlements along the way, so there is little chance that we will have a warm place to rest during the journey."

Matt nodded grimly and urged Striker forward. It would be a long ride.

CHAPTER THREE

Matt pulled a blanket out of his pack as he and Lucian slid off their horses to stop for the evening. The sun had already disappeared and the air was very cold. Lucian gathered some branches and set them up to make a fire. With a nod from Lucian, Matt reaching into the pouch resting on his chest and withdrew the Fire Stone. He stared at the warm, semi-transparent, black stone, watching the flickering red and orange streaks at its center.

Taking deep breath, Matt shut his eyes and focused on his own magic. He allowed it to fill his body and then gently extended it down his arm and fingers to the Fire Stone. The wild dancing magic of the Fire Stone immediately joined with his, warming his body. Careful not to lose control, Matt allowed the stone's magic to intensify his own.

He opened his eyes and focused on the pile of wood, willing the magic toward it. A small jet of flame appeared on his palm and he held it out to the wood. He maintained control over the flame until it grew into a blazing fire. Satisfied, he released the power and returned the Fire Stone to the pouch.

"Excellent," Lucian praised him. "You have not practiced for a while, but still, you demonsttrated exemplary control over the Stone's power."

Matt felt his cheeks grow hot. The wizard did not often hand out praise. Lucian smiled. Raumer, Lucian's messenger hawk, sensed that they were both pleased and bounced merrily on Lucian's shoulder as he made a stew.

After their meal, they sat in silence, staring into the fire.

"Is there anything I should know about Karespurn and the council?" Matt asked at last.

"Yes, many things. Karespurn is the largest city in Mundaria and it is also the largest military stronghold. As you may know, it is the capital of the Middle Realm and its ruler is the military commander.

"All of the other cities in the Middle Realm are led by retired military officers. But Karespurn is led by Commander Conlan, a very strong leader who has seen and dealt with much strife. He was a soldier for a long time and he is very wise, but sometimes I fear he listens too closely to the wizard council's advice."

"Will you explain the council to me?" Matt said eagerly.

"Of course. It is important that you know as much as you can about them before you face them. The council was created after Cosgrove stabbed Malik in the chest with his sword and Malik was presumed to be dead. The aim of the council was to prevent abuse of magic and once it became clear that Malik was still alive, the council also took on the responsibility of stopping him.

"Unfortunately, the wizards on the council are an insecure bunch and are easily threatened by new talent unless they can mold it to their will. When Galen and I were first traveling together, we were in Karespurn and decided to meet with the council. They were very wary of Galen and eager to have him watched because they feared his strength and independence. They do not understand merglings and they wanted to control his power.

"The council can be very corrupt. Do you remember when I told you that I had a falling out with the council? I left to search for signs of the one of the Prophecy of the Elements, and that is when I found you. Well, I have had little communication with them since until they contacted me about you a few days ago.

"You must be very careful, Matthias. They fear and desire your power."

"Then why have you agreed to take me to them?"

Lucian sighed. "We have no other choice. They will get to you no matter what. This way it is our decision to go there, not theirs."

Matt nodded determinedly. "I won't let them take advantage of me."

"That is exactly the spirit you must have! You must stay very alert. Do you remember how to mask your aura and activate the sight?"

Matt nodded. Masking his magical aura was completely natural to him now, and he was skilled at detecting unmasked magical auras.

"Good. Practice both every morning as a precaution. Now let us rest. We have a long journey ahead of us."

Matt laid down on his bedroll, pulled his blankets close, and fell asleep instantly.

The following days passed slowly as they braved the cold, windy plains, and they spoke little. On the fourth day of their travels, they received relief from the wind in the form of a small shelter of trees on the edge of the forest outside of Borden, but the reprieve was short-lived. Every evening, Matt would use the Fire Stone to create a fire, and they would fall asleep beside it, wrapped tightly in their blankets.

On the morning of the ninth day, Matt woke early, his fingers once again stiff with cold. Clumsily, he reached into the pouch around his neck and withdrew the Fire Stone. He sighed as the stone's surface warmed his icy hands. Matt glanced first at Lucian, who was still sleeping, and then at the sky where the clouds were darker and more threatening than before.

Feeling slightly warmer, he decided to perform the sight invocation which he had done for the past eight mornings, as Lucian has suggested. He no longer needed to use the word to channel his magical energy into an invocation. He glanced down at himself to make sure that his aura was masked and then, searching for something to distract himself from the cold while he waited for Lucian to wake up, he rifled through the contents of his pack and his pockets.

His fingers closed around something long and soft. Sam's feather. Sam had given it to him not long after Matt had found him. Matt withdrew it from his pocket and dropped it into his other hand. He looked down at it with a smile, expecting to see the shimmering blue and green along the spine with the silvery letters that spelled out *Samsire*, but his breath caught in his throat. The surface of the feather was a dull gray around the silver writing - the normal blue-green sheen was gone. Samsire was far away now, so the feather was dull and dark. Just like Sam's absence made Matt feel.

When Lucian woke, they ate stale bread for breakfast. Lucian quickly packed away his things, but Matt ate his breakfast absently, his mind drifting from Sam to his friends back in Gremonte.

"Lucian," he said. "I've been thinking about that morphcat showing up in Gremonte."

"It doubt it means anything, Matthias," Lucian assured him. "As hard as it may be to believe, some things are just coincidences."

Matt nodded. "All right, but if a creature like Murph exists, doesn't that mean that there are other magical creatures out there, too?"

Lucian paused. "Over the centuries, there have been many species of magical creatures, but few of those species still remain. Most are extinct. You see, over the years those creatures were hunted. Back when Malik rose to power, he and his men set about exterminating any animal that possessed magical qualities because Malik considered them a threat to his reign. Since then, their populations have slowly dwindled into extinction or nearly so."

Lucian straightened. "If Samsire were to be successful in locating any remaining creatures from the magical realm, it would be very helpful to us. But now, it is important for us to keep moving."

As Matt climbed to his feet and fastened on Striker's saddle, he kept thinking about Murph. How strange it was to come across two magical creatures that were both thought to be extinct, first Sam and then Murph.

A frown etched into Lucian's brow as he turned his eyes to the west.

"We must travel quickly," he declared. "Those are not friendly clouds."

They urged the horses into a slow canter, hoping to outrun the storm, but by late afternoon, the rolling dark clouds were hovering ominously over them, and the wind had grown much colder. They pulled their hoods tightly across their faces. In the distance they could see a small house and barn. They were still a good distance away from the farm when the sky opened up.

"It's snowing, Lucian!" Matt cried as thick white flakes covered their clothing within seconds.

Lucian smiled at Matt's excitement, but a surge of blowing snow caused them both to lower their heads and ride more quickly toward the farm.

"Stay here," Lucian told Matt as he dismounted in front of the house and brushed the snow off his cloak.

Matt waited astride Striker as Lucian trudged to the door and knocked loudly. A small, agitated man answered the door, his thin gray hair combed neatly along the sides of his head. Lucian spoke to him quietly, gesturing at Matt. The man hesitated and then nodded, pointing to the barn. Lucian handed him a few coins and the man hurriedly closed the door.

"The kind farmer has allowed us to stay in his barn for the night as long as we do not disturb his animals," Lucian said as he led Innar to the barn.

It was much warmer inside the barn and there were several empty stalls where they could sleep. The animals eyed Matt and

Lucian sleepily as they led the horses into stalls, but Matt ignored them as he dropped into a stack of hay and fell asleep.

* * *

Galen leaned casually against the pillar, half listening as Chief Golson and his advisors rambled on about the city's defenses. His thoughts drifted elsewhere, far from the stuffy protocol of the chief's hall.

"What do you think, Galen?" Golson asked him.

Galen pressed off the pillar, straightening and clasping his hands together in feigned interest.

"Oh, I quite agree," he said easily.

"Good, it's settled. We'll repair the doors and increase our guard at the main entrance," Golson said decisively. "That should be all. Thank you, gentlemen."

Galen nodded his farewell and bolted to the door. With Lucian gone, he had been asked to sit in on Gremonte's town meetings. He would normally have declined the invitation, but Lucian had asked him to go in his place.

He breathed in deeply, but the air in the massive cavern was stale. He envied Matt's freedom until he remembered that he was soon to face the council. He stretched his side. Soreness still rippled through his muscles, but he was long past being an invalid. It was time to get back to work spying on Malik. He would leave soon, but since he was still in Gremonte for the time being, he might as well do what he could here.

He veered left, toward the path leading down to the river. Emmon and Arden had described to him where they had discovered Murph the morphcat, and he had an urgent desire to see the cave for himself. He had been around magic long enough to know that magical creatures were rare and that they didn't usually show up without a reason.

Galen reached the mouth of the river, jogging down toward the large boulder Arden had described. He peered inside the cave. After a moment, he pulled his light stone out of his pocket, conscious of the knife he had strapped to his boot. Better to be prepared. Holding the stone aloft, he stepped into the cave, letting his mind focus on the sounds around him.

"Where did you come from, little morphcat?" he muttered to himself, stepping deeper into the cave.

The cave was silent except for water dripping from the stalactites. He relaxed the hand that had been inching closer and closer to his boot. There was nothing here. He continued through the tunnel, sidestepping puddles and rocks. Something compelled him to keep moving, an instinct that often compelled him to dig a little deeper to uncover the truth.

Something clattered deeper in the tunnel. Galen froze, holding his light stone further out in front of him and he pulled the knife from his boot. Another clattering sound came from the depths of the cave.

"Who's there?" he called, in case it was a citizen of Gremonte exploring the caves, though he knew differently.

The seconds passed, but he did not relax. He knew he was not alone. He stepped back, feeling for the stone floor beneath his boot as he moved back toward the entrance of the cave.

A scream erupted in the darkness and Galen jumped backward just as something dark sprung out of the shadows, ramming into him and sending him sprawling backward. As the light stone clattered out of his hand, he caught a glimpse of the blank white eyes and spindly black limbs of a garan. Galen scrambled backward on his elbows and the creature screamed again, lunging through the air. Its sharp claws were extended toward him, but Galen managed to kick out his foot just in time, catching the garan in the stomach before its deadly claws could reach him.

The creature shrieked as it flew backward and Galen lunged forward with his knife, sinking the blade into the creature's shoulder. It shrieked again, bouncing backward and out of Galen's reach. Galen jumped to his feet, ready with his knife, but the garan did not move. Instead, it looked past Galen, and after a long moment, gave one last shriek and sprinted back into the depths of the cave.

For a moment, Galen could only stare after the creature in bewilderment. But then he felt the cold creeping in behind him, and with a pounding heart, he scooped the light stone off the ground and whirled around. A mass of black mist hovered just behind him, as large as man and as spectral as a ghost. A shadow.

Galen barely had time to react as the shadow flew toward him with frightening speed. He threw up his hands, summoning the magic within him, and he managed to conjure a weak shield just as the shadow reached him. He could almost imagine the thing screaming as it collided with the shield, spiraling backward in a sheet of hazy mist.

Quickly, it reformed and streaked back at him.
This time Galen was ready.

Focusing all of his energy, Galen held the light stone aloft and with a yell thrust his magic forward. A shockwave of light and magical energy shot off in all directions. The shadow writhed as the attack sliced through it, the strands of magic ripping it apart until the black mist congealed into an indiscernible cloud and then disappeared.

Breathing heavily, Galen slowly lowered his hands. The cave was once again silent. Ears alert, Galen knelt down and picked up his knife, stained with the garan's blood. A garan alone was bad news, but the presence of the shadow, one of Malik's messengers, was the worst kind of omen. Few had lived to tell of an encounter.

"I hate it when my hunches are right," he muttered to himself.

Glancing one last time over his shoulder, he made his way back toward the entrance of the cave. Another garan, he could handle, but the shadow was something else.

Galen reached the edge of the cave, rolling his shoulders as he tried to shake off the ache from hitting the ground and the adrenaline from the encounter.

"Galen!" a voice shouted.

Arden was running down the path by the river, Emmon, Hal, and Natalia close behind her. They looked terrified.

"What's going on?" Emmon exclaimed. "We heard screaming. Are you all right, Galen?"

Galen held up his knife, black with the garan's blood. "I think we should warn the guards that a garan is running wild in the cavern."

They stared at the knife and Arden managed to choke, "What happened?"

Galen smiled at her as Murph peered around her neck, his fur green like her top.

"I think, Arden, that there's more to our new little friend than meets the eye."

CHAPTER FOUR

The final day to Karespurn was slightly warmer. The sun shone brightly, turning the foot of snow into slush beneath the horses' hooves. Matt and Lucian were no longer shivering under their cloaks, and the journey was much more pleasant. Karespurn was first visible in the early afternoon, large walls and a towering castle peeking over the horizon. The closer they drew to the city, the faster they rode, rejuvenated by its proximity. By late afternoon, they had reached the walls of the city.

Matt marveled at the height of the massive stone wall surrounding it. Gates were wedged into the thick wall at several points, all heavily guarded from above by soldiers armed with bows and crossbows, and from below by sword-bearing soldiers around the gates.

"I am Lucian, the Wizard of Light," Lucian said when they reached the largest gate. "I am here to present my young companion to the wizard council."

The guards studied him carefully for a moment and then gestured for their companions to open the gate. The gate groaned open slowly and Lucian nodded at the guards before urging Innar forward. Matt and Striker followed closely, and the gate closed as soon as Striker's tail cleared the opening. They rode along a narrow dirt street weaving between many rows of small, ramshackle huts. People wandered aimlessly about, their eyes dazed with hunger as they stared at Matt and Lucian, their spindly limbs covered in tattered clothing. Matt glanced at Lucian, unable to hide his troubled feelings.

"The poorest live closest to the gates," Lucian murmured quietly. "The dues that they must pay the council are so high they cannot buy bread for their families. They are forced into servitude to wealthy merchants or rich families. Often they must sell their children into servitude, as well."

"That's terrible," Matt said, watching a small child stumble as she tried to lift a bucket of dirty water.

Unable to bear it any longer, Matt reached into his pack fastened to the back of his saddle and withdrew a half of a loaf of bread wrapped in a cloth. He called quietly to the little girl. She perked up immediately, dropped the bucket, ran to him, and snatched the bread from his hand. She looked up at him, smiled sweetly, and then started to yell incomprehensible words. All around her people began to flock toward Matt, joining in the cry.

Lucian turned around, saw what was happening, and yelled above the din, "Ride, Matt! Quickly!"

Matt kicked Striker ferociously, and the horse lunged after Innar, closing the space between the two horses before it was filled with people. Lucian and Matt raced forward, the crowd still close on their heels. They weaved through the streets, increasing their pace, but the stream of people followed. Eventually, the horses cantered up a small incline at the end of the dirt road. As they reached the top of the hill, their pursuers suddenly stopped and retreated back down the path without a sound.

"What was that all about?" Matt asked Lucian incredulously.

Lucian shook his head bitterly. "I should have warned you. I made the same mistake once myself."

"Mistake? Giving them food is a mistake?"

"It seems wrong, doesn't it?" Lucian said. "But once you do, the people recognize that you have strong compassion, which is considered to be a weakness. You are permanently marked as one they can harass for food. They will follow you whenever you enter their territory. Travelers often call them the Karespurn Horde.

"But if you were starving, wouldn't you do the same? It is the fault of the wizard council. Their laws prevent the poor from gaining employment because they are labeled thieves. As long as they remain in Karespurn, the poor will remain poor for their entire life."

"Why didn't they follow us?"

"Because we have crossed into the commerce area populated by wealthier merchants," Lucian replied.

Matt looked around and realized that the buildings around them now were made of stone. There was a stark comparison between the life of the poor and of those in this part of the city. Vendors hawked their wares from shop windows, wooden stalls, or overflowing wagons placed alongside the street. There seemed to be a large number of taverns and alehouses.

"Are we stopping in the city?" Matt asked Lucian as they delved deeper into the maze of buildings.

"No," the wizard replied. "We will go immediately to the castle where the council sits."

Matt look ahead and saw the most magnificent structure he had ever seen towering before them. The castle was constructed of gray stone and had three soaring towers. There were large, walled gaps between them, which Matt guessed to be courtyards. The castle split off into three different wings, one in the center and one on each side. Ramparts, patrolled by dozens of watchful soldiers, surrounded the castle. The doors were made of thick, weather-hardened wood and reached nearly ten feet high. They were covered by a grate of heavy iron bars.

Matt followed Lucian along the street up to the castle. The path was lined by soldiers on either side, standing at sharp attention but not looking directly at Matt and Lucian. Matt shifted uneasily in the silence of the pathway, listening to the noises of the city behind them. Lucian rode until the stone pathway split and then he dismounted, signaling for Matt to do the same. Matt did so, patting Striker encouragingly, as the horse had begun to whinny nervously in the strange silence. They led the horses along the left-hand path until it ended at a stone courtyard in front of the castle doors. A soldier approached them.

"What business do you have here?" he asked briskly.

"I am Lucian, the Wizard of Light, here to present my young friend, Matthias, to the council," Lucian said calmly.

The soldier glanced at Matt. "Stay here."

The soldier unlocked a side door and disappeared, leaving Matt and Lucian to wait with the solemn-faced soldiers. Matt could feel his nervousness grow with each minute that passed. Finally, the soldier came through the door followed by a sour-faced man. Lucian nodded at him.

"I have informed the council of your arrival," the man said, examining Matt and Lucian. "They will meet with you tomorrow. You will be given rooms in the castle so that you may…ah…freshen up."

Matt glanced down at their soiled, worn clothing and dirty hands and faces.

Lucian's eyes glinted dangerously. "Very well. What of our horses?"

"I will have them taken to the castle stables. Follow this soldier here to your quarters."

Matt unfastened his pack from Striker's saddle and patted the horse on the neck. Lucian did the same, holding tightly to his staff.

They were led down a long, wide hallway with many doors on each side and then up a marble staircase. Finally, the soldier stopped at the last door on the left.

"This room and the one across the hall will be yours. Dinner will be brought to you so please remain in your rooms. You will be called forth tomorrow when the council wishes to speak with you."

He waited to leave until Matt and Lucian had each entered their room. As the man walked away, Lucian nodded encouragingly at Matt before closing his door. Matt smiled weakly and looked around the room. The walls were white and bare. There was a long, narrow bed in the corner with a large trunk at the foot, and a small table with chairs in the middle of the room. Sighing, he dropped his pack on the floor and shut the door. Already, he did not like Karespurn.

* * *

Someone was shaking Matt awake. He blinked his eyes open, forgetting for a moment where he was. Lucian was staring down at him, holding his glowing staff aloft in the darkness. Matt was awake instantly and slipped his feet into his boots.

"Lucian, what's wrong?"

"Shh," Lucian said quietly. "Hurry. Get up. We do not have much time."

Matt stood up, checking to make sure that the Stones were around his neck and looked at Lucian expectantly. They had just arrived in Karespurn hours ago. Could they be leaving already?

"Forgive me for not telling you earlier, Matthias," Lucian said. "There is another reason I consented to come to Karespurn. Come, follow me, but be very quiet."

Matt was bursting with questions, but he knew eventually Lucian would explain. Matt followed him to the door and Lucian stepped silently into the hallway. After a moment, he held his hand up to his staff and extinguished the light.

"It's best not to use magic if we can help it," he whispered to Matt. "The council monitors all magical activity."

"Lucian, what-"

Lucian held up a hand to stop him. "We are going into the wizards' record room. I believe that they may have some information about the Wind Stone."

"The Wind Stone?" Matt breathed back.

"I did not want you to think of anything else but your meeting with the council," Lucian muttered as they snuck down the hall. "I do not like the way we have been welcomed here, though, so we must do this while we can. If we do not act now we may lose our opportunity. Here, this way."

Lucian pointed down the side hallway and Matt moved as quietly as he could behind him. He was exhilarated at the thought of seeing the council's records, of learning some of their well-protected secrets. In a way, he was thankful Lucian had not told him before, because Lucian was right, it would have been all that Matt could think about.

Lucian moved quickly down the hallway, stopping suddenly at a door to the left.

"If I recall correctly, this is the record room," he whispered as he tried the handle. "Locked, as I expected. Stand back, Matthias. We will have to move quickly since I am forced to use magic."

Lucian took the handle in his hand and Matt felt the air crackle with magical electricity as the lock clicked open. Lucian ushered Matt inside, closing the door behind them.

"No doubt they have enchanted the door to notify them of a break in," Lucian said, relighting the tip of his staff. "We do not have much time. Quickly, go through that stack there."

The room was filled with tables with stacks of carefully organized papers on them. Matt lunged for the first stack, hastily flipping through the papers. Lucian glanced toward the door and shook his head.

"They will know that somebody is here, already. Use a revealing invocation."

Matt hesitated for a moment, his mind scrambling to remember the invocation. He had not used it since they were in Hightop, searching for an incriminating letter. But now wasn't the time to forget. Matt stuck his hand out toward the piles, thought about the Wind Stone and concentrated. A moment later, papers began to fly into the air, flapping wildly in all directions. Matt kept his hand extended, focused all of his magical power, until finally, everything lay still, and a small stack of glowing papers sat in front of him.

"Lucian!" Matt hissed.

Lucian ran to him, peering over his shoulder to read. There were notes written all over them. One read: *High traces of magic from the South.* Another: *Reports of disturbances near Aresburg. The creatures are moving.*

"Creatures?" Matt whispered.

But before he could ask Lucian, something else caught his eye at the bottom of the page. *Wind Stone remains undiscovered.* Small passages of text surrounded a map of the Southern Province of Mundaria.

Someone was moving quickly down the hall outside the room. Matt and Lucian jumped, whirling around to face the door. Matt's heart pounded as he waited for the door to open, but it did not.

"We have to get out of here!" he hissed at Lucian. But the room was a mess. "They'll know that we were here!"

"I will handle it, leave, Matthias," Lucian ordered him.

Matt dropped the papers and made toward the door, but did not leave. He was not going to leave Lucian here, even if it meant getting caught. He would rather be imprisoned by the council with Lucian, than be forced to face them without Lucian's support. Matt listened anxiously for other sounds as Lucian raised his staff and his other hand. In a flurry, the papers flew through the air, this time rearranging themselves into orderly piles until it looked like the room had never been touched.

Lucian paused for a moment to listen at the door and then pulled it open. Matt followed him down the hallway. He had rarely seen Lucian move with such urgency. He occurred to him that the council was one of the few things that Lucian feared, and that thought alone sent a shiver of fear down Matt's spine.

They heard voices behind them as they sprinted down the hallway. Matt ducked around the corner as Lucian grabbed him by the arm.

"It is imperative that they not see you!" he said urgently, pushing Matt in front of him. "Go!"

Matt ran down the hallway and flung himself inside his room. As he closed his door he saw Lucian disappear into the room across the hall. Matt did not pause before kicking off his boots and lunging into bed. His heart was pounding, but he forced himself to lie still, just in case the guards came into the room.

"It all looks quiet here," a voice from the hallway said.

"Fine, then," another said. "It must have been a mistake."

As the voices faded, Matt rolled over, staring at the closed door. His heart was thumping and his thoughts were racing. He wanted to talk to Lucian about whatever it was they had just found, but he knew he could not risk it. It would have to wait until morning. And who knew what the morning would bring?

* * *

Five hours later, Matt sat in Lucian's room dressed in clean clothes, wearing the Stones around his neck and Doubtslayer at his hip. Lucian had suggested that he look as strong as possible.

"Your aura is masked, I see," Lucian said quietly as he twisted his staff in his hands.

Matt nodded, his mouth too dry to speak. He wanted desperately to discuss what had happened the night before, but Lucian had silenced him when he had brought it up. Now was not the time, it was not safe to speak openly here. All of this waiting was making Matt even more nervous.

"You remember everything I've told you, Matthias?" Lucian said in a low voice. "They will test you and try to manipulate you. Do not let them exploit their position or their power. The wizards of the council are devious."

Matt licked his lips and said with a slight smile, "Don't worry, Lucian. I won't let that bunch of cranky old men manipulate me."

Lucian smiled. "Good. I am hoping you won't cause as much trouble as Galen did. I don't think the council chamber has been the same since he appeared before them."

Matt grinned. It was typical of Galen to create a ruckus. It made Matt feel better just imaging it.

"What did-" Matt began to ask, but was interrupted by a knock at the door.

Lucian patted him on the shoulder and walked to the door. Matt took a deep breath and followed.

"You are both wanted by the council, sir."

The soldier led them down the stairs and through a door into a large, pentagonal hall. The ceilings were high and curved, and the pale winter sun seeped through the many skylights. Soldiers guarded three large sets of doors situated around the room and dozens of chairs lined the walls.

"The doors on the left lead to Commander Conlan's hall and the doors on the right lead to the council's chamber," the soldier explained. "You will be meeting the council now."

Lucian and Matt started toward the door. Matt tried to ignore the jittery feeling in his belly and his limbs.

The soldier stopped them. "Wait. You first, wizard. Alone."

"What? I have been instructed to bring this boy before the council," Lucian argued.

"No," the guard replied. "He is to wait. The council wishes to speak to you privately first."

Matt's heart sank. Now it was likely that he would have to face the council alone, as well. The soldier grabbed Matt's shoulder, and Matt let him guide him to a chair along the wall. Lucian disappeared into the chamber and the doors clanged shut behind him.

CHAPTER FIVE

Lucian entered the chamber, secretly seething. The council was already attempting to destroy Matt's defenses. Grimly, he looked around the chamber, a long room with a high ceiling decorated with patterns of red and yellow stars. Narrow at first, the room fanned out into a large semi-circle where eleven men sat in large, high-backed chairs. Most of them had long white beards and each held a staff in his hand. The Council of Wizards.

Lucian walked across the cold marble floor until he stood in the center of the circle, facing the chief wizard. He bowed his head respectfully, holding his staff before him.

"I have come as requested, Honorable High Wizard Rainart, head of the council of Karespurn."

"Welcome, Lucian," Rainart replied, twisting his beard around his finger. "I trust you see that, unfortunately, we could not be a council with only ten members, so we filled your seat."

"So I noticed," Lucian said, his voice flat. "I was told that you wish to speak with me privately."

Rainart smiled slightly. "It seems that your years of traveling have made you rude and impatient."

Lucian struggled to mask his anger. "My apologies, Rainart."

"But, I suppose, you are right. We must talk," Rainart gestured around the circle with his staff. "The council is intrigued by your claim that you have discovered the One of the Prophecy of the Elements. We also believe it is dangerous for you to trust this boy. He could be an instrument of the Commander of Shadows."

"Well, in that case," Lucian said mildly, giving them an innocent smile. "It would be wise for you to tell me anything you know about the Commander so that I am prepared to deal with him and his tricks."

As expected, the wizards exchanged furtive glances.

"Why should we?" one wizard asked. "You have done little for us, Lucian, choosing instead to cavort across Mundaria with that undisciplined mergling. We have not forgotten what a menace he is."

Lucian glared. He remembered this wizard well, Ogden of the Eastern Edge, formerly a wizard of Marlope.

"Peace, Ogden," declared Shaw, a younger wizard with a brown beard. "If Lucian has, indeed, found the One of the Prophecy, he has done much for us and for Mundaria. Or have you forgotten our purpose, Ogden? You do wish to see the Commander of Shadows' demise, do you not?"

Lucian allowed a small smile to creep onto his face as Ogden sputtered in indignation. Shaw was one of the few decent wizards on the council.

"How dare you question my motives!" Ogden cried.

"I was merely suggesting that Lucian deserves to know what we know. After all, he was a wizard of the council. Do I not speak the truth, Rainart?" Shaw challenged.

Rainart chuckled quietly, but his eyes glinted dangerously. "Yes, Shaw, yes. Very well, Lucian. You will be told. Merle, report what your spies have learned."

A dark-haired wizard leaned forward in his chair and cleared his throat. "I have spies planted deep in Marlope. Through much work and many magical disguises, I have managed to penetrate Malik's stronghold." Merle paused dramatically. "We have uncovered the answer to a question that has long haunted us all; how Malik still lives more than a hundred years after he was presumed dead."

Despite himself, Lucian felt his heart skip a beat. Long had he searched for the answer, but never had he been able to solve the mystery. Merle waited, savoring the moment. Finally, Lucian cleared his throat and the black-haired wizard relented.

"According to my sources, Malik has employed a sorceress of sorts. She is called Vivona."

"Vivona?" Lucia said in surprise, earning a puzzled glare form Rainart.

"You know of her?"

Lucian inwardly cursed himself. It would be better, as he had instructed Matt, for the council not to know that Matt had spent the first fifteen years of his life under Kerwin's thumb, believing all the while that Kerwin and Vivona were his parents.

"I have heard of her, Rainart," Lucian said smoothly. "Please go on."

With a nod from Rainart, Merle continued. "This Vivona has been brewing a potion, a sort of antidote to aging, that has been extending both Malik's and Kerwin's lives for many years.

Unfortunately, none of us are trained in the ways of Dark magic so we do not know how the potion is made."

Lucian merely nodded, but silently he wondered how many of the council actually did know Dark magic. All the same, he felt a small sense of satisfaction that he had finally learned the reason for Malik's long life.

"But," Shaw cut in, "this potion now seems to be weakening Malik. He takes it often, under careful supervision. He is strangely strong and weak at the same time. He still retains control over the elements, though the Stones of the Elements are separate and...lost.

"But something is preventing Malik from using his power to its full potential. Whether it is the potion or something involving the Stones...we do not know. We know he desires and searches for the Stones of the Elements so we can only assume that he needs them to gain full use of his power."

"But Malik's power is vast," Rainart cut in. "And he has returned as the Commander of Shadows. He has also passed some of his skills to his captains as they now also communicate constantly with shadows. As you know, we are unable to track the shadows."

"But you know that Malik is in Marlope?" Lucian asked.

Surprisingly, it was Ogden who answered. "No, we do not. Our spies have not communicated with us for a month."

Lucian nodded slowly. It seemed one answer only led to another question. There was still much work to be done.

"And now Lucian, since we have told you what we know, it is time for you to return the favor," Rainart said with an accusatory tone. "What of this boy who you claim is the One of the ancient Prophecy of the Elements, the one who will be an equal to Malik? I speak for the rest of the council when I say that I greatly desire to meet him. What is his name...Matthias? Yes, bring forth young Matthias."

There was no more avoiding it. Matt would have to face the council, but Lucian was determined that he was not going to do it alone.

* * *

Matt sat in the silence that followed Lucian's departure into the council chamber. The soldier who had brought them to the hall had disappeared, leaving Matt to ponder what was to come. He nervously gripped Doubtslayer's pommel, wondering why the council wanted to speak to Lucian alone first.

Were they trying to isolate Lucian from him so the wizard could not aide him? Matt gripped his sword more determinedly, wishing he had a staff like Lucian's. But he had the two Stones of the Elements, and if he needed to, he could follow Galen's lead and make sure the council chamber was never the same after his visit.

A sound caused Matt to jerk his head around, but the chamber doors were still closed. The doors leading to the hall of Commander Conlan, leader of Karespurn and the Middle Realm, had opened and three soldiers exited the doors, followed by a tall, muscular man with graying hair. He wore a red cloak with a long knife hanging at his hip. The soldiers walked purposefully past Matt toward the doors at the end of the hall. The tall man glanced curiously at Matt and then stopped in front of him.

The soldiers were just as surprised as Matt.

"Commander Conlan, sir!" one of them called.

He waved them off. "Go. I did not get this job for being defenseless."

The soldiers nodded, and they moved to the end of the hall, watching anxiously from a distance. Commander Conlan turned back to Matt and smiled. Matt looked at him warily, remembering that Lucian had said Conlan was a good man, but was sometimes too subservient to the council.

"You are young, yet you carry a sword with confidence," the commander said, and then his eyebrows rose as he glanced at Matt's sword. "And an interesting one at that. May I see it?"

Matt nodded silently and unbuckled his belt, offering it to Commander Conlan. He examined the strange scabbard and his eyes lit up when he drew the sword. He ran a hand along the blade, examining it closely.

"A good weapon for disarming, I am guessing" he said.

Matt nodded. "Yes, sir."

Commander Conlan returned Doubtslayer to its scabbard and handed it back to Matt. "What is your name, lad?"

"Matthias, sir. Matt for short."

"I am guessing you have traveled a great distance. Why have you come to Karespurn, Mathias?"

Matt did not answer at first, unsure of how much to say. "I am here to be presented to the wizard council, sir."

"The wizard council?" Conlan said, surprised.

He frowned, obviously disturbed by this and sat in the chair beside Matt.

"Are you here alone?" the commander asked quietly.

"No," Matt answered. "I am here with my friend, Lucian, the Wizard of Light."

"Ah, Lucian. A good wizard if there ever was one. It is my privilege to have met him many times. And he brought you here to the council?"

"The council requested that he bring me here. He is in there speaking with them, right now."

Conlan nodded, and then after a moment's thought, he added. "You should be careful. The wizards of the council are slippery fellows. They are likely to attempt to trick you at every turn. A wary mind always fares best with them. If you have been personally requested by the council, there must be something special about you. I feel certain that you will be able to handle them."

Matt's mouth grew dry again and he nodded. Conlan seemed to sense his unease.

"Where did you get that sword, Matthias?" he asked.

"A friend, a great swordsman, gave it to me. He taught me everything I know about swordsmanship."

"You are going to need more than a sword when you enter that room," Conlan said with a smile, gesturing to the council chamber.

Matt nodded. He could tell that Commander Conlan was curious about Matt's presence. Conlan seemed trustworthy enough, and Matt was surprised by his opinion of the council, but before he could respond, the doors to the chamber opened and a soldier emerged. He bowed slightly to Commander Conlan.

The soldier turned to Matt. "The council will see you now."

Matt stood up and walked slowly to the door. He was ready to face the council.

As he walked through the doors, he heard Commander Conlan say softly, "Good luck, Matthias."

CHAPTER SIX

Matt stopped when he reached the circular portion of the room, feeling the appraising stares of the eleven seated wizards. Matt was very relieved that Lucian was still standing in the center of the room. He would not be alone. Lucian caught his eye and motioned very slightly with his head for Matt to join him.

"Are you going to introduce us, Lucian?" the chief wizard asked, his dark eyes inscrutable.

"Very well," Lucian said. "Wizards of the council, Rainart, head of the council of Karespurn, I present to you Matthias of the Western Reaches."

Matt felt a jolt of nervous energy and stepped forward to face the council.

Rainart threw back his head, laughing heartily.

"You, a title-less, little boy, are the One of the Prophecy of the Elements? I think not," Rainart chortled.

The majority of the council joined Rainart's laughter, but Matt stared back at them defiantly.

"I am not a little boy," Matt said quietly, the rage beginning to build within him.

The council fell silent. A short, gray-haired wizard leaned forward in his chair, sneering at Matt.

"Then prove yourself, little man."

"Ogden, of the Eastern Edge," Lucian said whispered to Matt.

Matt was silent for a moment. They were goading him. They wanted to make him feel inferior. Matt did not care if they believe he was the One or not, perhaps it would be better if they did not, but he could not stand by and do nothing. Lucian shifted uneasily beside him.

"Fine," Matt said decisively. "What do you want me to do?"

Rainart smiled coldly. "Tell us, Matthias, what is the difference between elemental and non-elemental magic?"

Matt's heart began to race. So now they were going to test him to see how much he knew, to see if he was a threat. But this was the very first thing Lucian had taught Matt.

"Elemental magic is the magic of fire, water, air, and earth. Non-elemental magic does not depend on the elements to function," Matt answered without hesitation.

Rainart nodded and looked around the council, requesting more questions.

A dark-haired wizard took up the challenge. "How do you perform non-elemental magic?"

"Using invocations, otherwise known as spells. There are different ways to perform each invocation and focus words are used to channel power," Matt answered quickly.

"Are non-elemental magic and elemental magic the only types of magic?" another wizard cut in.

Matt opened his mouth to answer, but stopped. Lucian had taught him about Light and Dark magic, but he was unsure whether the council knew that Lucian had mastered the art of Light magic. He glanced sideways at Lucian who nodded almost imperceptibly.

"No. There is also Light magic and Dark magic."

The questioning continued. The council quizzed him about his general knowledge and also about specific invocations. Matt answered each question carefully, attempting to avoid any mention of the Stone of the Elements and elemental magic.

At last, Rainart chuckled. "You have obviously taught the boy many things, Lucian. But I am not convinced. Any young wizard can learn these things. What about elemental magic?"

"What about it?" Matt asked uneasily.

"How do you use it?" the wizard called Ogden asked.

Matt felt a cold grip around his heart. They were trying to make him reveal his abilities with the Stones. He clenched his jaw in determination. If that was the game they were going to play, Matt would do the same.

"Well," he said hesitantly, trying to give the impression of deep thought. "You would need to be an elf or have one of the Stones of the Elements, depending on what type of elemental magic you want to use."

Matt watched as Rainart and the other wizard tensed.

"And how would you use the Stones?" Rainart challenged, choosing his words carefully.

"Why do you want to know?" Matt retorted, the words flying out of his mouth before he could stop them.

Lucian grunted softly beside him and several members of the council leapt to their feet, their eyes locked on Matt and their staffs extended.

"Sit," Rainart commanded his fellow wizards and then turned to face Matt, his eyes glinting with anger. "Do not play with us, boy. We know full well that you have possession of the Fire Stone and the Water Stone. We are not to be trifled with."

Matt tensed as he realized that any one of the eleven wizards could easily blast him through the doors and imprison him if they wanted to.

"Show us the Stones."

Matt felt Lucian freeze beside him. The council could take the Stones and all would be lost. They did not understand what Matt was just beginning to fully understand himself; he really was the One of the Prophecy.

"No," Matt said, his voice scarcely above a whisper.

Lucian placed a hand on his shoulder in support. But Matt was too intent upon watching Rainart's reaction to notice. If Rainart was angry, he did not show it, merely nodding as if accepting a challenge.

"Leave us, Lucian," he said after a moment.

Matt looked up at Lucian as the wizard stepped forward in protest. "Why should I leave, Rainart? Is this not my concern, as well? Matthias, after all, is my student."

"When you left the council, you lost your say here," Rainart said coldly. "Leave or I shall have you escorted out."

Rainart motioned with his fingers and a soldier moved out of the shadows on either side of the hall.

"Go, Lucian," Matt breathed.

Lucian glanced at him. "Very well. Remember, I am very interested in the outcome of this meeting, Rainart."

With a last glance at Matt, Lucian strode down the hall past the soldiers and pushed open the heavy doors. Matt turned back to face Rainart, who wore a smug smile on his face.

"Lucian seems to enjoy the company of impudent youths. The last one he brought us, that mergling, was a dangerous creature."

"Galen is not a creature," Matt growled, unable to ignore the anger rising in his chest.

"Oh, so you know him," Rainart said indifferently. "He practically destroyed my chair. It's never been the same again."

The wizard pointed to his stone chair, visible dented and crooked.

"What do you want with me?" Matt demanded.

Rainart did not answer, but snapped his fingers. One of the soldiers momentarily disappeared through a small side door and then reappeared a moment later bearing a platter with a water pitcher and goblet. Rainart took it and poured himself a glass of and then waved away the soldier. He slowly took a sip and smiled contentedly.

"You know very well what we want. Proof. Show us the Stones."

"No," Matt said defiantly, his voice getting louder. "What use would they be to you? Whether you like it or not, I am the One of the Prophecy. Only I can wield the Stones. They will be useless to you, and Malik will only find a way to take them from away from you."

Rainart merely smiled. "Very well then. Guards!"

The soldiers moved in on Matt before he could turn around. They grabbed his arms and, despite his struggles, forced him to his knees before the council.

"Rainart!" a younger, brown-haired wizard cried, getting to his feet. "This is not right! There are better ways to handle this. You must see reason."

"If you wish to keep your seat on this council, Shaw, you will be silent," Rainart retorted sharply.

Shaw hesitated for a moment and then sat down, staring at his hands. Matt's heart plummeted. He was trapped. The anger grew louder and stronger, coursing through his veins.

"The Stones, boy," Rainart prompted.

Matt tried to look up, but the soldier's grip allowed him only to see the crooked legs of the wizard's stone chair.

"No? What a pity. Take them from him," he said to the guards."

One of them reached for the pouch, but Lucian had taught Matt an invocation that prevented anyone but him from lifting the pouch from his neck. Matt focused fiercely on the invocation. Frustrated, the soldier finally drew out a knife to cut the string that held it around Matt's neck. Adrenaline coursed through Matt and his fingers began to tingle.

He focused on the magical energy until a jolt of energy threw the soldier backward. Matt wrenched away from the second soldier, but quickly realized he had nowhere to go. In an instant, both soldiers regained their footing and pinned him violently to the stone floor.

The side of Matt's face was pressed hard against the cold granite. His eyes settled on the crooked legs of Rainart's chair. Galen had done that. Galen, his friend, who Rainart had called a creature. Matt moved his gaze, searching for the pouch. He couldn't feel it against his chest and he needed contact with the Stones. He quickly realized that it was beneath him, still around his neck, but not in contact with his skin. His arms were trapped behind him.

Fueled by rage, he struggled fiercely, pulling his arms free and grabbing the pouch in his right hand. Before the soldiers could stop him, he extended his left hand toward Rainart. A flame erupted from Matt's palm and arched through the air, landing at the base of Rainart's robes. Rainart panicked, moving the fabric into the flame and setting them ablaze.

The wizards began to yell and point but did nothing to help Rainart. Finally, in response to Rainart's screams, one of them grabbed the water pitcher and dumped it on his robes. When the council had calmed down, the soldiers holding Matt pulled him to his feet. Rainart turned to face him.

To Matt's great surprise, he chuckled.

"Interesting. So you do know how to use the Stones. We must watch you closely, I see." He paused, his eyes gleaming. "And I also see now that it is imperative that the third Stone not be found. You are dangerous. Take him to his room and lock him in."

This time, Matt did not protest, but allowed himself to be escorted to the doors. The soldiers pulled him out of the chamber into the hallway, and Matt was careful not to look back, knowing that Rainart was watching him closely.

As they crossed the pentagonal hall, the door to Commander Conlan's hall swung open and three, soldiers emerged, followed by Commander Conlan. Matt stopped moving, forcing the soldiers to drag him by his arms to move forward.

"What's going on here?" Commander Conlan said loudly as he caught sight of Matt.

Matt saw his opportunity and cried, "It's the council, sir! They-"

Matt was cut off as one of the soldiers roughly clapped a hand around his mouth and nose. He struggled to breathe.

"Let him go! I order you to-" Commander Conlan said but then stopped. Matt tried to yell through the soldier's hand but Conlan shook his head. "You are the wizards' soldiers. You won't listen to me anyway, will you?"

"That's right," one soldier said smugly.

This seemed to inflame Commander Conlan. His muscular arm shot out and he grabbed one of the soldiers by the collar. "You listened to me, soldier. The wizard council may have its own guard, but I am still the Commander of Karespurn and the Commander of the entire Middle Realm. Whether they like it or not, the council is under my jurisdiction."

He let go of the surprised soldier. "What are your orders?"

The soldier hesitated, but then answered, "To take the boy and lock him in his room."

"That does not seem to mention treating him in such a rough manner. Let go of him."

The warning in Commander Conlan's voice refused to be disobeyed. The guards let go of Matt's face and arms, and he dropped to the floor, gasping for breath.

"Are you all right, Matthias?" Conlan asked.

Matt nodded, massaging his arms as he stood up. "Thank you, sir."

The commander laid his hands on Matt's shoulders, leaned close and, very quietly so the soldiers could not hear, said, "Listen to me, boy. I do not know anything about you or why you're here, so I must listen to the council, as must you. Do as they say and go to your room, but heed my words – be ready for anything."

"I will," Matt replied. "Thank you, sir."

Commander Conlan nodded and walked away, his soldiers following close behind. As soon as the Commander left, the wizards' guard grabbed Matt's arms again and pushed him forward, though with noticeably less force. Matt allowed them to lead him through the door and into the hall that led to the bed chambers.

Commander Conlan's words still rang in Matt's ears, but as they climbed the stairs, fear crept into his thoughts. What would the council do with him once he was locked away? He stared down the hallway of doors. Maybe he could find Lucian before he was forced into his room.

As if he had heard Matt's thoughts, the door to Lucian's room opened and the wizard emerged. Matt stared at him desperately as they approached each other, but the wizard merely smiled and nodded at him as they passed each other. Did Lucian not see that Matt was being dragged down the hall? Matt watched Lucian's departing back as one of the soldiers opened the door to Matt's room.

"Lucian!"

Lucian stopped, turned to look at Matt, and smiled again before continuing down the stairs. The soldiers pushed Matt into the room, the lock clicked, and he was alone.

CHAPTER SEVEN

Lucian's thoughts were racing as he entered the main hall. The council had obviously ordered Matt to be taken to his room, either because they were delighted by what they had learned or because he had angered them greatly. Knowing Matt, it was likely the latter. But Lucian could not allow him to be held indefinitely by the council. Not only would they greatly hinder Matt's quest and prevent all chance of defeating Malik, but Matt would suffer, as well. Lucian sat down in a chair outside of the doors to the council chamber and put his head in his hands. Nearly all of Karespurn was under the wizard council's control. There was little he could do.

The doors opened and a soldier emerged. "The council wishes to see you again, sir."

"I thought they might," Lucian said as he stood up and followed the soldier back into the chamber.

The eleven wizards of the council were all looking slightly frazzled. Lucian nodded at Rainart.

"You wished to see me?"

"Yes, Lucian," Rainart growled. "That boy you brought us is quite a bit of trouble. Dangerous even."

Rainart pointed to the bottom of his robes, and Lucian saw that a good deal of the fabric had been burned away and the edges were blackened and charred. He resisted the urge to smile at Matt's handiwork.

"I have noticed that he can be difficult, as well," Lucian said quietly.

"It is dangerous that he wields such enormous power. We will keep him here at Karespurn so that we can study him."

Lucian had expected this. Thinking quickly, he said, "Very well. I thought perhaps you might want to. I would ask that you bid him farewell for me. I have received word from a friend in Borden and I must leave immediately. You will tell the boy?"

A triumphant smile spread across Rainart's face. "It will be my pleasure."

"Thank you," Lucian said shortly. "I must go, then. It was a pleasure to see you all again."

He turned away from the council and walked briskly to the doors. When he entered the main hall, he stopped for a moment to deliberate his next steps. If he freed Matt, he would be seen riding away with him. They would need to leave separately. Matt could not stay here and Lucian needed to appear innocent of his escape. Suddenly, an idea struck him and he turned to the doors to Commander Conlan's hall.

"I must see Commander Conlan," Lucian urgently told the commander's guards.

The guards hesitated and then nodded, opening the doors to allow Lucian to pass. He entered the large hall. The walls lined with windows and intricate tapestries dangled from the ceiling. At the far end of the hall, a man was addressing Commander Conlan.

"We need to reinforce our western forces-" the man was saying, but paused as Commander Conlan motioned at him.

Conlan leaned forward in his chair as Lucian approached, obviously surprised by his presence. "Lucian, it is a pleasure to see you again, my friend. Many sunsets have passed. "

"Forgive me for intruding, commander, and forgive me for my rudeness," Lucian apologized. "But I have an urgent request to make of you."

"What is it?"

"I came here to present my young friend, Matthias, to the wizard council," Lucian began.

"So he told me," Conlan interrupted.

Though Lucian was surprised by this statement, he continued, "They have imprisoned him, but it is urgent that he be released! The fate of Mundaria depends on it! I beg you, sir, please order his freedom."

It was silent in the room for several moments.

"Will you do it?"

* * *

Matt angrily kicked the trunk at the base of his bed as he paced around the room. He was trapped. He had tried to open the door in a variety of ways by ramming it with his shoulder, blasting in with magic, and even trying to hack a hole in it with Doubtslayer, but it seemed that someone had placed a very powerful magical shield on the door so that it could only be unlocked with a key. Matt had also gone to the window, and although it opened easily, he realized that the castle was set on a hill that dropped off dramatically beneath his window.

Matt collapsed into one of the chairs. He had to find some way to get out of here. He thought back to what Commander Conlan had said. Be ready for anything. Matt snorted to himself. What sort of advice was that? That described his life – anything could happen and it seemed that it usually did.

Matt glanced around at his meager possessions scattered about the room. He stood up and began methodically loading his pack in case there was an opportunity to escape. He fastened his cloak around his neck, tightened his sword belt around his waist, and fell back onto the bed.

He shot back up immediately, though, as he heard footsteps in the hall and the jingle of keys. Matt listened as a key was inserted into his lock and the door swung open. He stood motionless as two soldiers entered the room.

"What do you want?" Matt asked, eyeing the open door.

"You are to come with us," one of the soldiers answered.

"What if I don't?" Matt responded defiantly and edged toward the door.

"I'm afraid that's not an option," the other soldier said, moving in on Matt and blocking his exit. "Those are our orders. You will come with us."

"I don't care about your orders!" Matt yelled, causing the soldiers to look nervously over their shoulders.

They converged on Matt before he could react, grabbing his arms and holding them behind his back despite his struggles. One of them grabbed Matt's pack off the floor and flung it onto his own shoulder. They led him out of the room, and to Matt's surprise, they locked the door behind them. They started to pull him down the hall, but Matt pulled back in protest.

One of them leaned toward Matt and whispered harshly in his ear, "You know, you really should care about our orders. They're from Commander Conlan, not from the council. I would follow along quietly, if I were you."

"Commander Conlan ordered you get me?" Matt breathed.

"Yes," the soldier whispered. "We will take you to a side road that leads to the castle stables. There you will find your horse ready to leave. You must move quickly and you must not stop for any reason. The wizard who came with you will meet you a few miles outside the walls of Karespurn. You must ride quickly."

The soldiers looked around cautiously as they reached the bottom of the stairs that led to an outside door. They opened it, shoved Matt through the door, and handed him his pack.

"Thank you," Matt whispered and the door closed.

Matt hoisted his pack and looked around. The hill continued to climb up on his right. In front of him was a winding dirt path that snaked down the slope. Matt quickly took off down the path, glancing around nervously, but no one was in the vicinity.

It was already late afternoon, and storm clouds were gathering overhead. He followed the path until he spotted a wooden structure and he hurried inside. He found Striker, already saddled and neighing anxiously, in the corner of the stables. Matt fastened his pack to the saddle and guided the horse to the door.

The road outside the stables led down to the city, in full view of the castle. Matt hesitated. Undoubtedly he would be seen if he cantered madly through the city streets. But if Conlan had released him without the council knowing, he would probably like for Matt to act like an escaped prisoner.

Staring determinedly at the road, Matt kicked Striker forward. The horse quickly gathered speed, his hooves clopping loudly on the cobblestone as they neared the entrance to the castle. Matt bent low against his neck, holding tightly to the reins. They passed the walls of the castle and the great gated door. Matt pulled Striker to the right as he cantered into the long street that led to the town gates. Matt glanced at the soldiers that lined the street and saw that they were moving toward him, yelling.

"Hey! Get him!"

Matt pulled Striker to the left, narrowly avoiding a soldier and kicked the horse's sides harder. Striker moved faster and faster, until they were running wildly through the city. Several people screamed as Striker bowled over baskets of food and nearly collided with a vendor's stall. Matt glanced over his shoulder and spotted a group of soldier sprinting after them, but then the soldiers suddenly fell back.

Matt breathed a sigh of relief, but was seized by a new fear as he was approached by crowds of ragged people on all sides. The Karespurn Horde. And it seemed to be growing bigger and bigger as it swirled around him. Matt looked toward the gates and his heart plummeted. The gates were closed. He was trapped.

But the Horde surged forward, taking Matt and Striker with them. The guards at the gate turned pale as they watched the throng making their way toward them. One of the soldiers ran to the gate, unlatched it, and darted along the wall out of the way.

Matt's fear became a yell of triumph and he laughed as he rode through the gate and away from Karespurn. He turned around, but no one was following him. He had done it! He slowed Striker to a comfortable gait and smiled when he thought about how unhappy the council would be when they discovered he was gone.

He hoped they would not suspect Commander Conlan of releasing him. Conlan seemed to be a good man. Unlike Rellin, the duke of the Western Reaches at Hightop, Conlan seemed to have the courage to do what he thought was right.

Matt turned his thoughts away from Karespurn to the land ahead of him. The soldier had said that Lucian would meet him a few miles outside of Karespurn, but where? With the thick layer of clouds, he wasn't even sure which direction he was traveling. He wished Sam was here. Sam always knew what direction they were traveling in. Matt continued to ride straight ahead, hoping that Lucian would find him.

CHAPTER EIGHT

Matt rode until the sky began to darken, and he was sure that he had ridden much farther than a few miles away from Karespurn. Yet, there was still no sign of Lucian. He patted Striker's neck anxiously and slid out of his saddle. He scanned the area around him, but saw nothing but endless fields of grass. He pulled his pack off the saddle and pulled out his bedroll, spreading it out on the ground. He rummaged around for food, but found that he only had a few pieces of stale bread and a small strip of dried meat. Maybe Lucian had supplies.

If he ever found Lucian.

He removed Striker's saddle and the horse lay down next to him just as Sam would have done. Matt felt another pang for the alorath, but tried to dismiss it. He shivered slightly and took the pouch from his neck, holding it in his hands. He had no wood, but maybe he could still make a fire. He extended his hand and a flame appeared on the dry grass. He expanded it until it was the size of a small campfire, but he knew he had to maintain careful control of it so that it did not spread through the dry grass.

He soon found that it took too much energy and he dismissed it tiredly. Several tiny, glowing sparks remained, and Matt reached into the power of the Water Stone, feeling its deceptively gentler power flow through him. A small stream of water dripped from his fingertips and extinguished the spark.

Eventually, he slipped on his gloves and pulled the blankets close as he nibbled on a piece of bread. He looked up at the sky, but the cloud cover was still so heavy that he could not see the moon and stars. It was very dark and he felt very alone.

And then he heard a snap behind him.

He twisted around, his hand on Doubtslayer. He stood up quickly and he peered into the darkness. His heart was beating rapidly.

"Hello?" he called.

There was no answer. At first he thought he had imagined the sound, but then he heard it again. Matt grabbed a stone and created a halo of light around it, scanning the area in front of him. He saw nothing at first, but then circled back. A movement caught his eye, and he stumbled backward as a dark figure moved toward him.

He yelled, reaching for Doubtslayer, but a firm hand gripped his arm. Matt brought his light stone near and saw the familiar calm gray eyes and stubbly chin.

"Lucian!" he breathed and the man chuckled.

"Hello, Matthias," Lucian said. "I thought it was you but I was not sure until you made the light stone. I apologize for startling you."

"I've been trying to find you for hours," Matt said, intense relief washing over him. "The soldiers said that you would meet me a few miles outside of Karespurn. Where were you?"

"It was too close to the city with the long, flat plains surrounding it. They could have spotted me and they would have realized that I was helping you to escape. I had told the council earlier in the day that I had an urgent appointment with a friend in Borden, and I wanted to keep that alibi intact. I believe that I can be of more use to you if the council does not know that I am helping you."

He sat down and pulled a large package of food from his pack. "Are you hungry?"

They feasted on a generous supply of food that Lucian had brought from Karespurn. Matt stuffed himself with fresh bread, meat and fruit, and then laid back on his pack contentedly. The tension of the day gradually melted away.

"What happened with the council?" Matt asked as Lucian packed away the food.

The wizard smiled. "I was going to ask you the same question. When I went back into the chamber, the council was very agitated, indeed."

Matt grinned. "I sort of set Rainart's robes on fire."

Lucian raised an eyebrow and Matt continued hastily.

"I know I shouldn't have gotten so angry and used the Stones, but…they were trying to take them away from me and it's so unfair – everything that they've done." Matt paused, thinking about the Horde of Karespurn and the things they'd said about Galen. "Can't Commander Conlan do anything about them?"

Lucian looked at him thoughtfully with his wise eyes and said, "He has official control over the council, but they are very secretive about their doings and could easily overpower Conlan with magic. He tries to undo what they have done. Take the poor, for example. Conlan has tried to create and enforce laws to aid the poor, but the council secretly spreads rumors of their thievery and the like because the council thinks of them as foul creatures, rather than people. People are often more likely to believe rumors that make them afraid, rather than believing the actual truth."

"Like Galen," Matt muttered.

"Yes. The council is afraid of Galen because he is different from them and because they do not understand his abilities. I believe they feel the same way about you. They put on a false mask of goodness, but in reality, they are afraid of true goodness. That is part of the reason they dislike me. I was able to master Light magic, the magical form of good, and they could not.

"Most of them do not seek goodness and honesty – that is not why they fight Malik - they fight him merely because they are afraid they will lose their own power. That is also why they claim that you are dangerous. You are a threat. In the same way, Lord Balor of Amaldan is threatened by you also, and that is why he has banned you from Amaldan. Conceit and the love of power are dangerous qualities. Especially when they are found together."

He lapsed into silence.

"Where will we go now?" Matt asked quietly.

"I sent Raumer to Galen, telling him to gather the others and meet us in Borden. I must return to the council soon and I cannot leave you without protection."

Matt's heart skipped a beat. The last time they had been in Borden, an old woman in the street had spoken to Matt of his parents. Maybe he could find her again and ask her what she meant.

"It is late, Matthias," Lucian said, breaking through Matt's thoughts. "And it is important that we are rested for our journey tomorrow."

Matt slept fitfully that night, dreaming of the council and of cruel laughter. By the time morning came, he felt as if he had just fallen asleep. Fortunately, the air was not as cold as it had been over the past week, so it was easier for him to roll out of his blankets and prepare Striker to leave.

They rode faster than they had for many days, the warm sun improving their travel.

"Lucian," Matt finally asked. "Did the council tell you anything about Malik?"

"Yes. They have answered many of my questions, but they have also created new questions in their stead."

Matt listened carefully as Lucian explained that Malik and Kerwin were still alive after all these years because of Vivona's potions. Matt thought of all the times he had gone to fetch strange plants for Vivona when he thought she was his mother. And of all the packages he had delivered to town for Kerwin to be sent to Marlope. The realization that he had been helping to extend the lives of Malik and Kerwin made Matt's stomach churn.

Lucian also explained that the council's spies had noticed that Malik was not fully using his powers and that he was communicating with his servants with shadows.

"It is important that I keep the council's trust, if possible," Lucian concluded. "As corrupt as they are, they have valuable resources and information which they still share with me."

Matt remembered Rainart's words, declaring that the third and final stone, the Wind Stone, should remain hidden. His heart began to race as he remembered what they had read the night before meeting with the council. In all of the excitement, he had nearly forgotten it.

"Do you understand what we found in the wizards' record room?" Matt asked. "What did it mean?"

Lucian's brow furrowed. "I am not sure. It appears that the council has discovered something in the south. Something magical and sinister. It was not what I was hoping for."

"Those papers talked about traces of magic. Do you think they've found the Wind Stone?"

"Found it?" Lucian said, absently. "I am not sure, Matthias. But I do not believe they know where it is."

"Then we have to hurry and find it!"

Lucian shook his head. "I think that Malik has guessed its location, but I think he is waiting, planning. He has now twice confronted us just as we found the Fire Stone and the Water Stone, and both times he lost. He will not want to risk losing again. I would guess he has something more lethal in mind this time."

Lucian saw Matt's despairing expression and chuckled. "Do not fear Matthias. We will find the Wind Stone when it is time. But the papers also mentioned something else. Creatures…"

Matt's heart leapt. "Creatures! Do you think it has anything to do with Sam? And the alorath colony?"

Lucian smiled slightly. "Perhaps that is not so far-fetched, Matthias. In fact, I would not be surprised if that is exactly what it was about."

The excitement that Matt felt at the thought of an alorath colony faded almost instantly. They did not really know anything new. Just when it seemed that they were on a new trail, it vanished. He glanced up at the sky, completely unsatisfied with Lucian's answer. He still felt hollow and without purpose. And he missed Sam.

"What do you think Sam is doing now? Do you think he's having any luck?" Matt asked.

"Sometimes, Matthias, I think you are a walking, breathing question. Honestly, is there a moment when you aren't asking a question?" He sighed. "I have no way of knowing what or how Samsire is doing. You might as well ask me to see into the future. I am beginning to see why the wizard council threw you out. It was pure exasperation."

Matt smiled as Lucian absent-mindedly rubbed his stubbly chin. He remembered how Lucian had once told him that he did not sit among the wizard council because he felt self-conscious about his inability to grow a beard.

He kicked Striker to catch up with Lucian. He would rather have the tetchy wizard any day over that deceitful council.

* * *

In a narrow pass, high in the peaks, a thick mist cloaked the mountaintops. The mist was unnatural, gray-tinged and deep, and stretching high and far like an ever-growing storm.

A man climbed slowly up the slope of the mountainside. He moved calmly and confidently, familiar with the terrain, and glanced up at the stars only occasionally to note his position. He heaved himself up over the edge of the ridge and slowly straightened as he gazed upon the misty sight before him.

He had expand its reach,grow. The thought filled the man's chest with prideful satisfaction. It would not be long now before the whole valley was consumed and the mountain pass would be blocked. The creatures of these mountains would have no choice but to move outward.

"Garan!" the man hissed, snapping his fingers.

The spindly creature bounded up the slope behind him, perching expectantly beside him as it waited for a command. The man considered the garan for a moment and then peered out into the mist. It was time to put it to the test.

"Go," he ordered, pointing toward the pass.

The garan did not hesitate and ran straight into the fog. The man watched as it disappeared into the dense gloom. He waited. As he stood, his mind drifted toward the beginning of all of this. How simple it had been to reach this point. It had not been so long ago that he had first sought out the Commander of Shadows and his men. He had been perfect for the job. Ambitious, ready to serve, and completely ordinary. Nobody would expect him to be working for the greatest magic-wielder of their time. He was just a humble citizen of Aresburg.

But now, he would be so much more than that. He could see himself now, rising through the ranks into the Commander's inner circle. Maybe even replacing the great Kerwin himself. With a simple gift of magic granted to him by the Commander, and careful planning, he had put himself on track to become someone important.

But only if this plan worked.

He scanned the mist, waiting for any indication that the planning he had put into this would actually yield something worthwhile. And then he heard it. The garan's scream pierced the night. A pack of crows erupted from the trees behind the man, flying in alarmed panic above the pass.

The man watched them carefully. A tendril of the dark mist twisted out from the floating mass and wrapped around one of the flying birds, yanking it downward into the depths of the cloud.

One by one the crows were pulled down. The man smiled grimly to himself. The crows, like the garan, was no more. The mist would destroy all who passed through it. Eventually all the creatures who lived on the other side of the pass would seek the lake and the meadows for nourishment, and they would need to pass through the mist to reach their destination.

Pride swelled in the man's chest. It was, after all, due to him that this scheme was succeeding. He snapped his fingers and held out his palms. A shadow separated from the mist, leaving behind falling wisps. The man considered his words carefully before addressing it.

"Make this report," he ordered. "The plan is working. Everything is on schedule. It will not be long before they are driven out. Proceed with the next step."

He paused and then clapped his hands together. The shadow spiraled into the air and soared swiftly toward the north, bearing the message. The man smiled to himself, and set off down the mountain toward Aresburg, leaving the dark shroud looming behind him.

CHAPTER NINE

Matt and Lucian rode through the streets of Borden, snaking their way through the crowds. The city was large like Karespurn, but it had a friendlier feel to it. Eventually, they found themselves at the foot of the enormous tower of Borden. Matt smiled, remembering the rotating observatory at the top of the tower where they had found the third of Dorn the Adventurer's clues. He wondered if the same shrewish woman still worked at the base of the tower. He glanced over at Lucian who was smiling, too.

Lucian led Innar down a narrow alleyway until they came to the same inn they had stayed at during their previous visit to Borden, tucked away in the shadow of the great tower. There was a small stable beside the inn where they left their horses.

The inn was small, but cozy, and the area around the bar was packed with large armchairs and tables. Lucian approached the innkeeper who was lazily flipping through a book, and asked for two rooms, dropping a few coins into his hands.

"Upstairs, first two rooms on the left. Nice to have you back, my friends," he said.

Lucian nodded his thanks and Matt wearily followed him up the stairs. "The evening meal should be soon. I will meet you downstairs in a few minutes, Matthias."

Matt dropped his pack on the floor by his bed and went to the window, overlooking the rooftops. He thought of the old woman he had seen on their last visit to Borden who had mentioned his parents. He wondered if she was still here and if she could answer some of his questions about the parents he never knew. Who were they, were they still alive, where were they? These questions had haunted Matt every day since he had learned that Kerwin and Vivona were not his parents. He often wondered why his parents had left him to be found by strangers. It was easy enough to understand why Kerwin and Vivona had taken him in – he had been free labor after the age of five.

He slipped on his remaining clean tunic for the evening meal in the tavern below. He met Lucian in the hall and they returned to the main room of the inn which was now occupied by a few locals. Matt's stomach was grumbling loudly. They had eaten sparsely and ridden hard the past few days, and he was looking forward to a proper meal.

"Galen and the others should not be here until the day after tomorrow at least, since Raumer had to reach them first," Lucian said as they ate.

"What will we be doing while we wait?" Matt asked.

"I assume you still wish to search for your parents," Lucian replied, and then added in a low voice, "And we must keep an eye out for any trails leading to the Wind Stone. It seems as though the Southern Province might hold some answers to our questions."

"Do you think we can find it?"

"Perhaps. I believe it is in a place of great magic so that the magical power of the stone can be concealed, just as the Water

Stone was hidden in the great underground city of Oberdine. Cosgrove and Pryor wanted the Stones to be as difficult as possible to detect and to reach.

"And the Wind Stone is arguably the most powerful of all three Stones. It is the magic of the air. Wind can change all things. It wears away the earth, it ripples the water of the ocean, and it fuels fire. It includes weather, storms, and cold. I do not think Cosgrove and Pryor would have wanted this Stone to be easily uncovered. They would want only those who are worthy of such power to be able to access it."

"Am I worthy, Lucian?" he said, his voice barely above a whisper. "Aside from being the One of the Prophecy, am I really worthy of this power?"

Matt was surprised that Lucian's normally calm eyes had grown angry. "I have told you countless times, Matthias, that you choose your own destiny, not the council, not Lord Balor, and not the prophecy. You make your choices because you believe them to be right. It is your duty to make your choices and then to follow them. When you accepted the Fire Stone, you chose to accept a responsibility. Now it is your duty to honor that decision."

Matt opened his mouth to argue that he did not choose, but Lucian stopped him. "You did choose, Matthias. Think back. Do you remember the reasons why you chose? Not because of inflated self-worth, but because you realized that this world needs to be ruled by goodness, compassion, and honesty, rather than evil. You were honest to yourself then, accepting that you *had* this responsibility. You chose for Mundaria and for its people. And that choice alone makes you worthy. Remember that, Matthias."

Lucian pushed back his chair, stood up, and disappeared up the stairs. Matt stared at the empty chair, stunned and angry at Lucian's words. He had never wanted this. Lucian had told him that he was the One of the Prophecy because he was a foundling with unseen powers. That it was a destiny that he could not ignore. It was not his fault that he had this responsibility.

He paused, trying to reason it through. Did he really have a choice here? Maybe Lucian was right. The Prophecy of the Elements had labeled him as the one to rise and control the elements, but Matt had chosen whether or not, and how, to do it. The Prophecy did not predict if he would use his powers for good or for evil. *He* had made those choices.

The prophecy had said that the one to rise would use the power of the Stones to either save or destroy the world by destroying or joining Malik. But Matt had chosen that he would stand for Mundaria and he planned to honor that decision, just as Lucian had said he should.

He would show the wizard council and Lord Balor that he was strong and that he would not give in. Setting his jaw, he stood up and followed Lucian up the stairs.

* * *

Lucian was sitting at one of the tables in the empty tavern when Matt came down the following morning. Matt grabbed a piece of toast from the plate on the bar and walked over to the wizard, just as he and Emmon had so many times during the time they had spent been here before.

"Good morning, Matthias," Lucian said.

Matt smiled through a crunchy bite of toast and sat down across from Lucian, pointing at a piece of paper Lucian was holding.

"What's that?"

Lucian smiled slightly. "A letter from Karespurn notifying me of your disappearance. It is likely that they suspect me of smuggling you out of the city."

"So?"

"As I've said before, the wizard of the council may be corrupt, but they will make valuable allies or dangerous enemies. I cannot afford to anger them. I must leave as soon as possible."

Matt nodded, feeling guilty for arguing with Lucian the night before. Lucian and his other friends had risked their lives many times already to help him with his task.

"In the meantime," Lucian continued, "I think we should try to locate your old woman."

With a rush of excitement, Matt swallowed his toast and followed Lucian out the door of the inn. They wandered through the streets and Matt tried desperately to remember where he had seen her. After a long, frustrating hour, he finally spotted a familiar-looking street.

"There!" he said. "She came right around that corner."

Matt could almost see her, hunched over her broom as she collided with him. Lucian was already inspecting the window of the nearest building.

"It appears that this is an artisan's shop of some sort," Lucian mused. "Perhaps she works in here."

Matt pushed open the door to the shop. It was dimly lit, and the shelves were covered with pottery and various containers. A small, bespectacled man wandered in from the back room.

"Can I help you?"

"Er…I was wondering if a certain woman might work here? I saw her many weeks ago outside your shop with a broom."

The man stared at him, and then finally said, "The only woman I know of is Ellyn."

"What does she look like?"

The man frowned. "Old, dark eyes with many wrinkles around them, walks hunched over."

Matt' heart leapt. It had to be the woman he had seen before.

"Is she here?" Matt asked eagerly.

The man shook his head slowly. "No. Sort of strange really. She worked here for a while, but left in a panic, mumbling about a letter from her daughter in…in…let's see…where was it? Ah! Aresburg! That's where she was going."

"Thank you," Matt said, turning to Lucian in disappointment.

They walked slowly back toward the inn, and Matt could feel Lucian's eyes studying him carefully.

"Aresburg," Lucian mused. "Hmm. Interesting. It all seems strangely connected, doesn't it? That is also the same region which the wizard's records referred to. It is no small trek from here. Aresburg is far to the south."

Matt's ear perked up. "Is it near where Sam is?"

Lucian nodded slowly, smiling. "Perhaps you and Sam shall be traveling together again soon, Matthias."

* * *

The following afternoon, they heard horses in the street outside the inn and they went out to greet their friends.

"Sorry it took us so long," Galen said as he dismounted. "We weren't excepting to be leaving quite so soon."

"We were surprised, as well," Lucian said.

Galen raised an eyebrow curiously at Matt. "I take it you'll tell me what happened in Karespurn?"

Matt smiled. "Well, I think the wizard council thinks the same thing about me as they do about you."

A smile crept onto Galen's face but before he could speak, Arden had appeared beside Matt and gave him a quick hug. Murph the morphcat peered around her neck with his huge eyes.

"You didn't get into any trouble without us, did you?" she asked, studying Matt's face.

"Knowing Matt, he probably set the castle on fire," Emmon said.

"Close. It was actually the wizard council," Lucian answered under his breath.

"What?" Hal exclaimed, obviously horrified. "That is blatant disrespect!"

Arden rolled her eyes, and she and Emmon grinned at Matt.

"Well, I tried not to be disrespectful, Hal, but they were going to lock me away," Matt said with his own grin and then turned to Emmon. "How was the ride? Where's Natalia? I thought she was coming with you."

Their smiles disappeared.

"Chief Golson wouldn't let her come," Arden explained.

"He claimed it was 'a dangerous, unnecessary trek for his daughter,'" Emmon added miserably. "She said to say hello, and Alem, too."

There was a rumble from the direction of Galen's stomach. "I don't know about anybody else, but I'm hungry enough to eat a horse!"

Hal's horse whinnied nervously and they all laughed. Galen patted the horse's flank encouragingly.

"Don't worry. You're a little too tough and furry for me."

For nearly a quarter of an hour, the only sounds at their table were moans of happiness as they shoveled food into their mouths. Finally, they all leaned back in their chairs with contented sighs.

"Finished?" Lucian said, his eyebrows high.

"Honestly, Lucian," Galen said with a grin. "What's the rush? It's not like we have anything important to do."

"Would anyone care to know what happened in Karespurn?" Lucian prompted.

Arden leaned forward in her chair. "Tell us, Lucian."

Lucian gave her a satisfied smile. "Very well, then. I shall."

He told them about his first meeting with the council and Galen listened intently.

"What about you, Matt?" Galen asked as soon as Lucian had finished. "What did they say to you?"

"They wanted to know if I could use the Stones," Matt said. He looked at Galen's kind, intelligent face and Rainart's words came back to Matt in a rush of anger. "They called you a creature."

Galen seemed unfazed by Matt's words and even smiled slightly. "I assume you defended my honor. What was that I heard about fire?"

Matt smiled sheepishly. "I did sort of accidentally set Rainart's robes on fire. They weren't very happy about it."

"Nice one, Matt," Emmon said with a grin. "You certainly know how to make an impression."

"And it was most certainly not an accident," Lucian grunted, his gray eyes twinkling. "Though…it was effective. The council ordered him to be locked away for later inspection."

"Inspection?" Arden exclaimed. "Do they think you're some sort of equipment?"

"Yes," Galen answered. "If their opinion of me is any indication of the way the council feels about anyone who stands up to them."

"What happened after that, Matt?" Hal asked.

"Lucian managed to convince Commander Conlan – he's the leader of the Middle Real-"

"I know who he is!" Hal cried excitedly, his knightly composure forgotten.

"Well, anyway, Conlan sent soldiers to let me out and I rode out of the city to meet Lucian."

"So now," Lucian said, "the council knows of Matt's abilities and they have declared that the Wind Stone should not be discovered. And now I must return to Karespurn."

"Why you? You can help Matt search for the Wind Stone and his parents. I will go to Karespurn. I'd like to pay those rotten wizards a visit," Galen said.

"No, Galen. It must be me. I must convince the council that I knew nothing of Matthias's escape. I told them that I would return, so I must do so. They have trusted me thus far, and they most certainly do not trust you. In fact, they would probably lock you up in their deepest dungeon. On sight."

"I'd like to see them try," Galen grinned, but he conceded.

"However, you are going to be doing more than just searching for Matt's parents. We did a little snooping around in the council's records room, and it appears that the wizard council has noted strong traces of magic in the region near Aresburg. We also saw notes stating that creatures were on the move."

"Creatures?" Emmon said questioningly.

As if on cue, Murph the morphcat jumped, suddenly and dramatically, onto Arden's head. She nearly fell out of her chair, and then he hopped onto the table. His fur was currently orange and brown. He sniffed around curiously. Galen smiled and reached out and pulled the morphcat toward him. Murph struggled in his grip as Galen held him up.

"In that case, it might interest you to know, that there is probably more to this little creature than we first thought. I went back into the cavern where he was found. I was attacked by a garan. And a shadow."

Lucian leaned forward. "A shadow? Malik only sends shadows as messengers or spies. Why would one show up in Gremonte? And how did a garan get inside Gremonte? You think that their presence has something to do with the morphcat?"

Galen shrugged. "Maybe. I think there's definitely something bigger going on here than just cute little Murph dropping in to say hello."

Lucian nodded slowly. "You must go to Aresburg and you must stay watchful at all times. You will not be safe – too many are now searching for Matthias and the Stones."

* * *

Matt was awakened the following morning by the sound of incessant murmuring. He sat up to see Hal picking crusted dirt from his boots, while complaining to a bleary-eyed, tousled-hair Emmon, who nodded sleepily and then lay back down without a sound. Reluctantly, Matt rolled off of his bed and reached for his own boots.

"I hate this time of year," Hal grunted. "First it snows and freezes you half to death, then the snow melts and your boots aren't clean until summer."

"I thought you used to work on a farm," Matt replied, stifling a yawn. "Seems like you'd be used to mud by now."

The older boy glared at him and walked out the door, shutting it loudly behind him. Emmon sat up with a start.

"Is he gone? Sheesh. I don't think I've ever heard anyone complain as much as Hal does. For someone who fancies himself a knight, you'd think he'd be more resilient."

Matt waited for Emmon, and then they made their way downstairs. It was early and the sky was still dark. Why did Lucian always insist on leaving at such ridiculous times? Matt was sure the scowl on Emmon's face meant he felt the same way. Lucian was waiting impatiently by the door of the inn with Galen, Arden and Hal.

"Good luck, Lucian," Galen said as Matt and Emmon joined them

"And to all of you, as well. Keep your eyes open for the council's men, as well as Malik's. Good-bye for now, my friends."

Without another word, the wizard disappeared into the chilly street. Matt and the others stood in sleepy silence for a moment until Galen clapped his hands.

"Right, then. Gather your things. We'll have some breakfast and we'll leave when the sky isn't the color of the inside of an inkpot."

At breakfast, Hal returned to the task of violently flicking the dried mud off of his boots. Galen shot him several warning glances as the loose dirt repeatedly hit his leg, but Hal did not waver from his task. Finally, Galen stood up, pushed Hal out of his chair, and walked from the room. Hal growled, but then in a very dignified manner, pulled himself back into the chair and continued to methodically flick away the dirt.

Matt glanced out the window. A faint, pale light was spreading along the horizon. The air was frigid when the teenagers carried their packs to the stables to ready the horses. Galen was waiting for them.

"You four look happy," he remarked. "Enjoying the warm weather?"

"Eat dirt, Galen," Hal muttered.

Galen raised an eyebrow. "Now that wasn't a very knightly thing to say. I thought you were a student of chivalry."

Hal grew very red in the face, but having lost many verbal duels with Galen before, he knew enough to remain silent.

"Get used to the cold," Galen said. "It may only be late fall, but winter has arrived. Fortunately, it's warmer to the south. But we will have to weave through the Crane Mountains on the way. There's a wide pass through the middle of the range that we should be able to make our way through pretty quickly if we hurry."

Matt felt his spirits lift. Soon, he would be one step closer to finding his parents and to seeing Sam again.

CHAPTER TEN

As he approached the gates of Karespurn at sunset on the third day of traveling, Lucian's hand automatically fell to his staff. He pulled Innar to a halt at the front gates. The guards glared at him and the back of his neck prickled.

"I am Lucian, Wizard of Light," Lucian declared.

"You are ordered to go straight to the council. If you resist, you will be escorted by force," the guard said tersely.

"Why would I resist?" Lucian said with a forced smile, knowing this was not a good sign.

He tried not to show his discomfort as he urged Innar through the iron gates. They clattered shut behind him and Lucian forced Innar into a brisk trot through the realm of the poor, though, strangely, none attempted to stop him. He felt pity pierce his heart as he looked around, but he knew that as long as the council ruled nothing could be done for the poor of Karespurn.

As soon as he reached the gate of the castle and dismounted, a soldier led Innar away and another guard escorted Lucian inside to the council chambers.

"We are most pleased that you have returned, Lucian," Rainart said, his voice icy.

"I came as quickly as I could once I received your letter," Lucian responded levelly. "It grieves me to hear that the boy has gone."

"Ah, but you already knew that, didn't you?" Ogden said, his voice threatening.

"How would I know?" Lucian asked, hoping that he sounded curious, not defensive.

"Did you not assist him in his escape?" Rainart pressed.

"Assist him? Preposterous! You know I was intent on learning all that the boy is capable of. Why would I wish to take him away from your careful eyes?"

Silence greeted his response as the council paused to consider what Lucian had said. Lucian waited anxiously, hoping that his ploy was working.

"It did seem to be difficult for the boy to escape," Shaw said, nodding slowly. "He was able to get through our shielded door, but then he was pursued by many soldiers. He was nearly taken by the Horde, as well."

"Yes," another wizard put in. "It is possible that Lucian did not assist the boy. Commander Conlan reports that his soldiers spotted Lucian riding away long before the boy managed to escape his room."

"Our soldiers report the same," Rainart agreed, but did not look convinced.

"I assure you," Lucian cut in, feelingly uncomfortable about lying, but aware of the importance of convincing the council of his innocence. "I had nothing to do with the boy's actions. In fact, I have been the victim of his disobedience myself. He is wild and untamed, much like my former charge, Galen."

"Ah, yes, the mergling. I see the likeness," Rainart muttered. "Very well, Lucian. For now we shall accept your innocence in this matter."

"And what of the boy?" Lucian asked hurriedly. "Would you like me to search for him?"

A twisted smile grew on Rainart's face.

"That is already being taken care of. We have dispatched our own men to find him. After several false leads, they seemed to have picked up his trail going northwest, toward Borden. They are two days behind him, but they are likely searching Borden for him now. I have no doubt that they will find him soon."

Lucian did not answer, his thoughts racing. Matt and the others were already traveling toward Aresburg, but they no longer had the shelter of a city to hide in, and if the council's men had found out that they were headed across the plains toward the southern mountains, they would be easily spotted from a distance.

"Good," Lucian said, his throat dry. "Since you are already searching for the boy, I would ask if there is any other task with which I may assist?"

Rainart glanced at his fellow wizards and several of them nodded. Rainart turned back to Lucian and eyed him carefully.

"We do have a favor to ask of you, Lucian. Given your familiarity with traveling it would be much easier for you to…ah…complete the assignment."

Lucian allowed a small smile onto his face. Yes, the wizards of the council were very sedentary indeed.

"What is it, then?"

Rainart smiled. "We request that you go to the heart of Malik's operations. To Marlope."

* * *

Four days after leaving Borden, Matt rode alongside Emmon as their small party passed through the endless, barren, muddy plains. It had rained for the past two days and the horses' hooves were heavy with mud. Fortunately, the ride was rarely boring since Hal seemed intent upon arguing with Galen or Arden as often as possible.

"You're wrong, Galen," Hal was saying. "Two-handed swordplay is always more effective."

"I disagree," Galen responded easily. "One-handed swordplay allows speed and versatility."

"Oh yeah?" Hal challenged. "Why don't we see about that, just you and me? Then you'll see I'm right."

Matt and Emmon exchanged glances. Hal had always been prideful and hot-headed, but he had been growing even more so every day since he had returned to Gremonte. Emmon nudged Matt as Galen pulled his horse to a stop.

"I suppose there's only one way to settle this," Galen said with a sigh and turned toward Hal.

"Do you think he's really going to fight him?" Matt whispered to Emmon

The elf's thoughtful green eyes examined the scene and shook his head. "Naw. Galen's up to something."

"In that case, we should probably back up," Matt suggested.

Hal reached for the sword fastened at his hip, and at the moment that he shifted his eyes, Galen reached over and gave Hal a mighty shove. Hal tumbled from his saddle and the mud swallowed him like a morsel of food. Matt, Emmon, and Arden burst into laughter as Hal tried to pull himself out of the gunk.

"Oh no, Hal," Arden said through giggles. "Mud!"

Hal lunged at her, but she artfully guided her horse out of the way. Murph bounced gleefully on her shoulder.

Feeling sorry for Hal, Matt dismounted and reached out a hand to help him up. Hal grabbed it, his eyes fixed defiantly on Matt, and then he yanked Matt with all his might, pulling him into the mud beside him.

"Hey!" Matt yelled, but Hal had a satisfied smile on his face.

"You're just asking for a fight, aren't you, Hal?" Emmon growled, jumping nimbly off his horse and landing lightly on the balls of his feet.

Hal turned around to run at Emmon, but Matt stood up, blocking his way. Hal pushed him aside and Matt fell heavily back in the mud again.

"Stop it," Galen said, his voice low and threatening.

The tone of Galen's voice made all of them hesitate. Matt pushed himself to his feet.

"What is it, Galen?"

"There's someone's out there. Someone is moving through the grass."

"Are you sure it wasn't an animal?"

"It wasn't an animal," Emmon said softly, and Matt saw that he already had his bow drawn and was scanning the grass. "It was too big. I saw it, too."

For a moment, they were all silent, looking for any sign of movement.

"Emmon!" Arden screamed, piercing the unsettled silence.

Matt whirled around to see a large man slam into Emmon, knocking his bow out of his hands. As Emmon struggled to twist out of the man's grip, another man jumped out near Galen and a third behind Arden. Galen yanked his sword from its scabbard. Hal was already fighting with a fourth man.

"Matt! Get out of here! They're here for you!"

CHAPTER ELEVEN

Matt stood there covered in mud, his mind racing. Galen was right, they had probably been sent by the council to find him. But Matt refused to leave his friends. Ignoring Galen's warning, he raced toward Striker and yanked Doubtslayer out of the scabbard hanging from his saddle. His muddy hands were slippery, but he held it determinedly and ran toward Arden. She held her two dagger-like knives before her, trying to fight off the sword ripping through the air toward her.

Together, they converged on the man. Matt swung hard at him, knocking him off-balance. The man fell and tried to scramble away, but Arden placed both her knives against his neck. The man laid still, his eyes fixed on Arden's hands. Arden looked at Matt, gesturing with her head toward the man and Matt replaced her knives with Doubtslayer against the man's neck.

Arden rushed over to Emmon who now had no weapon and was in a hand-to-hand battle with his opponent. Matt glanced around. The man fighting Hal had backed away and had lunged at Galen from behind.

"Galen! Look out!" Matt shouted.

In the brief instant that Matt's attention wavered, the man beneath Matt's sword kicked his foot hard into Matt's face. The man scrambled backward onto his feet as Matt tried to regain his balance. Within seconds the man had his sword in the air inches from Matt's head, but Matt blocked it, anger surging through him.

Suddenly, the man dropped his sword, and began to yell, frantically slapping at his own head as a furry object climbed over his head and shoulders. Murph chirped, as he ferociously attacked the man.

The man staggered backward and fell hard into the mud. Striker whinnied in alarm, rearing up on his back legs, his hoofs hitting the fallen man as he landed. The man screamed, holding his arms around his head as Striker jumped and landed on him again. Moaning, the man laid very still, staring fearfully at Striker, who put his snout inches above the man's face and snorted heavily. The man whimpered.

Murph jumped onto Matt's arm and climbed to Matt's shoulder, but Matt ignored him as he turned around to the others with his sword raised.

The man Emmon and Arden had been fighting was unconscious on the ground, but Emmon had bruises on his face, a bloody nose, and was limping as he went to retrieve his bow. Hal was on the ground and Galen was facing two opponents empty handed. In one brisk movement he reached down to his boot, withdrew a long knife, twisted it around the sword of Hal's opponent, and took it for his own. Galen kicked the man in the chest, sending him sprawling and advanced on the other man. Instead of standing to fight, the man ran.

Galen looked over his shoulder and yelled, "Emmon!"

In one swift movement, Emmon fitted an arrow into his weapon and sent it flying. It whistled through the air and burrowed into the fleeing man's thigh. He crumpled in agony. Galen, pulled a rope out of his pack, dragged him across the muddy grass, and dropped him next to his companion. He did the same with the other two men. Methodically, he tied them together while they moaned and cursed. When Galen was finished, they sat tied together in the grass, staring at him helplessly.

"We're just going to leave them here?" Matt asked.

Galen nodded grimly. "We can't risk that they'll follow us and I, for one, would prefer not to kill the council's men. It's likely they'll be found by other travelers if that makes you feel any better. We should leave."

They rode hard for the remaining hours of the day, until the Crane Mountains were casting a shadow over them. It was much colder that evening, and after making a small fire, Matt offered to heal Emmon's nose, which appeared to be broken, with the Water Stone.

By the time they laid down to sleep, Matt felt restless and strangely energized. He was still coated in mud and was uneasy about their encounter with the council's men. He wondered how many more were looking for him and how many would be sent by Malik.

Matt awoke the following morning after only a few hours of fitful sleep and immediately checked to make sure his aura was masked. Galen was already awake, saddling his horse while his intense gaze surveyed the mountains in front of them.

"I think we might catch the front end of a storm as we pass through the mountains. We should get moving so he can outpace it," he said.

They ate a quick, cold breakfast, and snowflakes began to whip around them as they mounted their horses. Soon, the snow surrounded them like a deafening curtain. By midday it had grown so thick that Matt could barely see Arden who rode only a few feet in front of him. They kept track of each other by talking, but sound was muffled.

After many hours, they were on the other side of the pass and the snowfall had ended. The sun broke through the clouds and Matt looked around at his friends all pink-faced and shivering, but grinning broadly.

They stopped in the plains south of the mountains, their clothing soaked, but their spirits high. It was considerably warmer south of the mountains and few clouds marred the blue sky. They rode through the plains for three more days until on the fourth day, the tenth since they had left Borden, they spotted a small, sprawling village at the base of another cluster of towering mountains.

"That is the village of Dirth," Galen told them. "We'll stop there tonight before we continue around the mountains to Aresburg."

As they rode through the tiny village, Matt was reminded of his home village of Sunfield. The buildings were small and ramshackle but the people had a healthy, wholesome look about them. Emmon pointed out an old sign above one building that read *Inn* where a steady stream of people went in and out. Dirth was obviously a frequented spot on the way to Aresburg. The teenagers led the horses to the stable behind the inn while Galen went inside to get them rooms.

That evening they ate a hot meal, while listening to the loud jabbering that filled the tavern. Matt enjoyed hearing the gossip of the villagers which once again reminded him so much of life in Sunfield. He was surprised to hear dark murmurings of strange beings moving about the region. Matt and Arden shared a meaningful look across the table, wondering what was happening here in the south.

At that moment, there was a piercing scream outside the inn. The room fell silent and then everyone rushed to the door, scrambling to get outside.

"Come quickly!" a woman screamed again, running down the path.

They ran out into the fields where the livestock grazed. The crowd of people was already gathered in a circle in one of the fields. In the center of a circle was a small girl crying as her mother tried to comfort her. Beside them, the grass was covered in extremely large golden feathers, like an enormous bird had landed there and left them behind.

"What happened?" one of the men demanded.

"A beast!" the woman said shrilly. "It swooped down from the sky and grabbed the cow!"

A chill snaked down Matt's spine. The men muttered nervously to each other and the girl cried harder.

"Can you tell us what you saw?" one of the bystanders asked her gently.

She shook her head. "Claws…feathers…and big yellow eyes."

One of the men growled under his breath. "Those foul creatures! They show their maws here again and it'll be the last thing they ever do."

Matt's thoughts immediately flew to Samsire. Could this have been an alorath? He turned toward one of the men.

"Have there been other sightings of flying beasts?"

"Aye. Been happening for years now. Never seen one myself, but plenty of folk around here have seen 'em. Seems to be happening much more often now. Take my advice, Don't venture into those mountains there, lad. It's a dangerous place," the man said and then lowered his voice. "People who go there come back talking of…evil magic….that is, if they come back at all."

Matt merely nodded, but shared a nervous glance with Arden. Maybe Sam was somewhere in those mountains. The crowd slowly began to disperse, but Matt lingered with Galen and the others, waiting until all of the locals had drifted back to the inn before he pocketed one of the golden feathers.

"The plot thickens," Galen muttered under his breath as they walked back toward the inn with grim smile on his face. "Let's get some rest before we have to face a whole pack of these mysterious beasts."

* * *

"Aresburg is a port city," Galen explained as they approached it the next day. "There's a very large canal that runs through it." He pointed to the orderly line of buildings near the shore. "It's the longest and widest canal in all of Mundaria and it empties into the sea. It's quite a sight."

By midmorning they had reached the edge of the city. Though it was completely surrounded by an enormous stone wall, there was no gate, only a large, open archway. Across the top of the arch were the words: *Life is an adventure. Live every day as if it is your last.*

"That sounds a little like Dorn the Adventurer," Matt muttered to Emmon. "*May your adventures lead you to good fortune.*"

"You're not far off. Those words there," Galen said, "are the words of Darrick Wanderer, the greatest adventurer of all time."

"Who's he?" Matt asked.

Galen stared at him in disbelief. "You've never heard of Darrick? I idolized him while I was growing up. He was one of the few men who had been permitted to enter Amaldan Forest at that time. I heard many stories about his adventures, though he disappeared when I was still young."

As they rode under the archway and into Aresburg, a man with a sword dangling at his belt approached them.

"Stop!" the man said.

"Yes?" Galen asked, smiling expectantly.

"Horses are not allowed further into the city," he said nervously. "You must shelter them in the public stables over yonder."

Once they settled the horses, they returned to the main street to search for a place to stay. The city was livelier and more cheerful than any city Matt had been to. Under the southern sun, people bought and sold goods, and bustled through the streets. There were large crowds, but despite the size of the city, everyone seemed to know each other. It was nearly as difficult to find an empty street as it was to find an inn.

They had been navigating the streets for over a half an hour when Matt heard a voice behind him.

"Hey! Hey, Matt!"

Matt glanced behind him at a tall, young man with sandy hair. Panic blossomed in his chest. He had been recognized. But Galen was already pushing through the crowd away from the man, pulling Matt with him.

"Matt! Wait!"

Matt hesitated – the voice sounded vaguely familiar – but he stayed close to Galen as they moved rapidly through the throng. The man jumped onto one of the barrels lining the street and stepped from one to the next to bypass the crowd. Matt tried to move faster, but to no avail. Within moments the man was upon them and before Matt could do anything, he had grabbed Matt's wrist and was pulling him toward him.

"Matt! I can't believe it!"

Matt stared at the man. He could feel Galen and the others beside him, ready to help, if necessary.

"Don't you remember me?" the man said with a friendly laugh. "From Sunfield? Gertrude's son?"

Gertrude. Gertrude, the village baker, had always been kind to Matt, watching over him while he lived with his cruel caretakers. Images went through his head. Running after a sandy-haired boy four or five years older than Matt. Sword-fighting with sticks. Sitting at Gertrude's table eating apple-cinnamon bread. Suddenly, Matt recognized him.

"Torrin?" he said in disbelief.

Matt hadn't seen Torrin a very long time, and the last Matt had heard, he was working at a boatyard in Condern. A wave of relief washed over Matt as Torrin grinned enthusiastically. Then he realized that Galen still had his hand on his sword.

"It's okay, Galen," Matt said hastily. "I know him."

Galen continued to glare at Torrin and did not move his hand.

"Yes, it's me!" Torrin laughed. "I haven't seen you in ages! How old are you now, sixteen?"

Matt nodded. "What are you doing in Aresburg? Gertrude said you were working in Condern."

"That was many months ago. Now, I'm working at the port here."

It suddenly felt like a long time since Matt had left Sunfield. He stood silently for a moment until Galen cleared his throat.

"Uh…right," Matt said quickly. "Torrin, this is Galen, Emmon, Arden, and Hal. They're friends of mine."

Torrin nodded at them and his eyes widened as he noticed both of the elves' pointed ears.

"Torrin," Galen cut in. "Do you think you can show us to an inn? We have traveled long and far."

"Sure," Torrin replied. "We can catch up on what you've been up to once we're there."

Torrin led them easily through the crowds, weaving into small alleyways and side streets until he finally stopped in front of a building in a quiet backstreet. He opened the door and led them inside. The tavern was already hopping with activity.

"I'll get us some rooms," Galen offered. "Why don't the rest of you have a seat?"

"So how've you been, Matt," Torrin said as they dropped their packs and sat around a large table. "What brings you to Aresburg?"

Matt hesitated. Emmon and Arden looked at him warily. "I've been...around. I've been traveling a lot."

"Why?"

Before Matt could decide how to answer, Galen sat down and took control of the conversation.

"So Torrin, what type of work do you do here?"

Torrin cheerfully explained that he helped with shipbuilding and cataloging cargo in the winter months and was part of the crew on a ship in the summer. Matt was still shocked that they had run into him. Torrin had changed so much since Matt had last seen him. He seemed to be about Galen's age, though muscles bulged under Torrin's tunic and Galen was lean and agile. Matt could see a strong resemblance between Torrin and his mother, and Matt wondered fleetingly if Gertrude had been affected by the fire that had spread through town when Kerwin tried to kill Matt.

Finally, Torrin turned back to Matt. "So, why did you leave Sunfield, Matt? Mother wrote me and said that you just disappeared and that there had been a fire. What have you been up to?"

Matt looked to his friends for help, but they were looking at him in alarm.

"Much has happened, Torrin."

Matt did not know how much to reveal, but it was clear his response did not satisfy Torrin.

"Where have you traveled? You've been gone for many months, right?"

"Look, Torrin," Matt said hastily. "We're looking for an old woman named Ellyn. We heard she came here from Borden to visit her daughter. Can you help us find her?"

"Sure! Of course. I know this city like the back of my hand."

A few minutes later, Torrin left, promising to see what he could find out about Ellyn and agreeing to meet up with them the next day.

"Well, that was close," Hal commented.

Galen nodded in agreement. "You need a story, Matt. Torrin seems trustworthy enough, but he may not be very discreet. It is likely that either the council or Malik have spies around here. The rumors we've been hearing of strange beasts and magic make me suspicious of everyone in Aresburg. You are most likely in danger. Again. As always."

"What should Matt say, then, when he asked where he's traveled and what he's been doing?" Arden asked.

"Maybe you went away to train," Hal said, twirling a knife on the tabletop.

"That's half true," Emmon said. "Galen has been training us."

"That will work for now," Galen said with a nod. "Let's say that you've been training for several months and came to Aresburg to observe the port. A lot of soldiers-in-training do that to watch raiding methods."

"All right, then," Matt sighed.

"All right, then," Galen said with a slight smile.

CHAPTER TWELVE

When Torrin finally arrived at around noon the next day, he was red-faced and excited.

"I think I found her! Or at least I think I found where she is living."

"How did you find out?" Matt asked eagerly.

"I did some asking around and started to hear talk of a crazy old woman who's called Ella or Ellen. This morning I asked around the guard. Seems that an old, half-mad woman came zigzagging into the city about a week ago. One of the guards had seen her before and thought her name was Ellyn, but she wouldn't answer any of their questions, and she just wandered about the city unresponsively. Does that sound like her?"

Matt hesitated. "I don't know. I've only seen her once before."

"It sounds like a good lead," Arden said. "Thanks, Torrin."

Torrin beamed and took a small bow. "So, what do you say? You want me to take you to her?"

"That's why we're here," Galen said, nodding at Matt.

"Let's go," Matt declared.

Torrin led them into the crowds on the main street of Aresburg. His size made it easy for him to push through the crowds. When they neared the southern end of the city, Matt could hear the sounds and smells of the port not far ahead.

"It should be here," Torrin said as they turned onto a quiet street.

He walked passed each cottage, his lips moving as he silently counted, and then he stopped in front of a small, stone, flat-roofed house.

"I think this is it," Torrin said.

They all gathered around the door and stood looking at each other.

"Should we knock?" Arden suggested.

Everyone nodded and stepped back, leaving Matt standing alone in front of the door.

"Your show, Matt," Galen said quietly.

Matt stared at the wooden door hanging crookedly on its hinges, open slightly, as is if inviting him to enter. Matt took a deep breath and knocked loudly, then stepped back and waited. For a moment he thought no one was going to answer. Finally, the door creaked and opened with agonizing slowness to reveal a rotund woman with crooked teeth and wrinkled eyelids that sagged so much they nearly covered her eyes. She smiled toothily and her eyes disappeared completely in the crinkles that formed at the corners of her eyes. She held a broom in her right hand.

"Can I help you?" she asked in a gravelly voice.

"Er…, hello," Matt stammered.

This was definitely not the woman that he was looking for, but maybe she knew where Ellyn was.

The woman set her broom against the wall, clasped her hands. "What can I do for you?"

"Do…do you know Ellyn?" Matt asked.

The woman's eyes suddenly appeared, sharp as daggers, and the smile disappeared.

"Ellyn? Who's Ellyn?" she growled. "You come to my door asking about some other woman. Out of here, you disrespectful buffoons!"

She concluded this statement with an angry snarl, grabbed her broom, and began making violently sweeping motions at them, as if to sweep them off her doorstep. The door slammed shut inches away from Matt's nose. He turned to Torrin who was wearing an expression of mortified alarm.

"Something tells me that wasn't Ellyn," Emmon commented.

Arden giggled and then Matt joined in, and eventually they were all laughing. Matt laughingly shoved Torrin, though he did little to move Torrin's mass.

"I thought you said you knew where she was!" he said with a grin.

Torrin shifted awkwardly, obviously embarrassed and not as amused as the rest of them. "This is where the guard told me to look. Idiot. I'll get him for this."

"It's not a problem, Torrin," Galen said cheerfully, but he was watching Torrin. "It was very funny. Did the guard give you any other possible addresses?"

"He did mention one other possibility," Torrin said slowly and then started the other way down the street. "Follow me."

They followed him, grinning, but were careful not to let him see that they were still amused. He led them to the port this time. Matt could smell the unfamiliar, unpleasant scent of fish. He had only been along the ocean shore once before when he had gone to Condern to deliver a message for Kerwin.

"You can hear and smell the port for many minutes before you reach it," Torrin said as if ready Matt's mind. "Here we are, the port of Aresburg. You can see the canal right over there."

He pointed to a wide opening where the canal waters joined the rolling waves of the sea. The canal was at least ten large boat lengths wide and stretched far into the distance going inland through the city. Seagulls were thick in the air, continually circling and then diving for the fish remains on the docks. Fishing boats lined the docks, dumping nets full of fish into huge wooden barrels. Men and boys rolled the barrels back and forth between the dock and the storehouses that lined the streets. And there were so many sounds – men yelling, birds shrieking, barrels rolling, boats banging against the docks.

"Torrin!" a man called, leaning against the wall of a building. "Lend a hand at Twenty. I hear they're overloaded with goods."

"Can't you see I'm busy, Schooner?" Torrin retorted with a smile. "Go on and help them yourself. Captain Nick will have you swabbing decks for a month if you don't get moving."

The man called Schooner gave him a dismissive wave. "Eh, get on with ya, Torrin. I'll see you around later."

They moved away from the port through town again, until eventually, Torrin stopped in front of another small house and nodded decisively.

"This has to be it. I'm sure of it."

"You're positive?" Matt asked. "Because personally I'd rather not encounter another broom-wielding old lady."

"Terrifying experience," Galen agreed solemnly, his eyes twinkling as he patted Torrin on the back.

Matt knocked again, and after a brief moment, a pretty young woman opened the door. Her eyes, vivid blue and intelligent, looked at them appraisingly.

"What do you want?" she said.

Matt was suddenly tongue-tied. Fortunately Galen stepped up and smiled politely.

"We're sorry to intrude, ma'am. We're here searching for someone. A woman named Ellyn. We happened across her in Borden a few months ago." Galen hesitated briefly as the woman's eyes widened and then continued. "At that time, she spoke to Matt here, and she mentioned something about his parents. Recently, the shopkeeper in Borden who employed her informed us that she had left to come here to Aresburg. We merely wish to know if she lives here and if so, if we might speak to her. Do you know of her?"

She remained silent and Galen added quickly, "We don't mean to intrude."

She studied Galen's face for several moments before answering. "I know her very well. I am her daughter. My name is Catherine."

"And I am Galen," he said with a smile, bowed slightly, and introduced the others.

Matt smiled at her uncomfortably and looked down at his boots. Both Torrin and Hal appeared to be very taken with her good looks.

"Is Ellyn here?" Galen prompted quietly.

Catherine nodded. "My mother arrived nearly a week ago. She did not seem quite right and she was babbling something about responding to my letter. I never sent a letter. She has not been well ever since she came here."

Matt plucked up the courage to speak. "When I saw her in Borden, she told me that she…she said 'it burns within you' and then said something about my parents. Like she knew them."

As he trailed off, Catherine looked at him sympathetically and nodded slowly. "It is impossible to tell at this time whether she knows them or not. If you don't mind me asking, why do you wish to know? Where are you from?"

"That's just the thing," Matt answered. "I don't know where I was born. I don't know who my parents are."

There was a short silence before Catherine answered. "I am very sorry. My mother might know something. She has a way of recognizing strange things in people that they do not see. She is an herbalist and healer, and she knows many things about the natural world that others do not. She has taught me many things about herbs and healing, but often," Catherine smiled slightly, "she puzzles me."

"May we see her?" Galen asked.

"You seem honest enough." Catherine pursed her lips. "You may come inside, but I must warn you that she is not at all well."

She pushed open the door and beckoned them inside. Matt stepped into room lit only by a small window on the left wall. There was an old table in the center of the room surrounded by several chairs, and the walls were lined with jars of plants and herbs.

Matt was reminded of Vivona who had always sent Matt to collect exotic plants to brew her concoctions like the one that was said by the wizard council to be keeping Malik and Kerwin alive. But there were happy touches that made the home comfortable and welcoming like the colorful drapes and wall hangings. To the right of the room, there was a short hallway leading to another room, but the door at the end of the hall was closed.

Catherine walked across the room to the small hearth beside the table.

"Would you like some tea?" she asked.

"We would be grateful for it, if you can spare some," Galen answered for all of them.

"Please sit," she said as she hung the kettle over the fire and then began mixing a handful of dried plants which she placed into the kettle. A delightful smell filled the air.

Catherine placed the steaming mugs on the table and said quietly, "My mother is in a very distressed state. The last time I saw her she was perfectly normal.

Matt thought back to Ellyn had spoken to him in the street. She had seemed a bit strange, but she had been coherent.

"I think that she has lost her mind," Catherine continued. "I don't know if she will be able to tell you what she meant by what she said you. She is in the back room. Would you like to see her now?"

Matt nodded and followed Catherine down the small hall to the closed door. He followed her hesitantly into the dark room, his eyes slowly adjusting to the light. In the corner, was a small bed where a woman lay, staring unseeing at the ceiling. Her frizzy, graying brown hair was a mess around her face, but it did not hide the wrinkles that creased her forehead and the corners of her eyes, or the dark green eyes that he remembered so clearly.

"Is that her, Matt?" Emmon asked.

"That's her," Matt breathed.

Ellyn did not move from her trance-like position, still staring at the ceiling with her vacant eyes.

"When she first came to me, she was talking nonsensically and constantly. Eventually, though, she stopped and she has been this way ever since," Catherine told them.

"Can I go to her?" Matt asked.

Catherine nodded and Matt walked across the small room and knelt beside the bed. Ellyn did not appear to know he was there as she stared unblinking at the same spot on the ceiling. Tentatively, he reached out his hand and gently touched her wrist. Instantly, she shot up in the bed and Matt fell backward.

"Clean! Broom...where is it. Oooohh, oooh," she moaned clutching at her head.

Emmon and Hal helped Matt to his feet and pulled him away from Ellyn.

"Borden...no, Catherine. Aresburg...yes, yes. Must clean. Oh, no, oh no. Must go....no time. Must go," Ellyn wailed.

"What happened?" Matt said.

Catherine was at her mother's side, trying to soothe her. Ellyn moaned and screamed a stream of words, until at last Catherine was able to coax her to lie down. She began staring at the ceiling again, muttering quietly under her breath.

Galen frowned. "I think she recognized your touch, Matt. Did you have contact with her in Borden?"

Matt nodded. "I almost ran into her. Yes, I…"

Catherine turned to face Matt, scrutinizing him. "She must have been able to sense something about you. Something different or important. Just as she did when you saw her in Borden."

A shiver went down Matt's spine.

"I think some tea might be nice," Torrin muttered, nervously smoothing down his sandy hair.

"Yes, let's go back to the kitchen," Catherine suggested.

They all followed Catherine out of the room, except Galen and Matt, who lingered a moment longer.

Galen turned to Matt. "What are you thinking, Matt?"

"I was wondering if maybe I could heal Ellyn using the Water Stone."

Galen shook his head. "It may be too dangerous. You could damage her mind more than it already is." He lowered his voice. "I think she may be touched by magic in some way. I mean, the fact that she could recognize you both times is a little strange, don't you think?"

"My mother often does strange things, and more than once I have wondered about magic," Catherine said, suddenly standing beside them again. "She would often wander into the mountains outside of Aresburg and disappear there for days. She never told me why she went there. She has always had many secrets."

She pulled the blanket around her mother's shoulders, and Galen and Matt moved into the hall.

"Catherine and Ellyn know of the existence of magic," Galen said softly. "But listen, Matt, I think that something bigger is going on here. I believe this is more than just a coincidence."

"Do you think it has something do to with Malik?"

"Who's Malik? What are you talking about?" Torrin interrupted from the end of the hall.

"Is it impossible to get a moment of privacy?" Galen demanded, pushing past Torrin.

Matt followed him, but Torrin grabbed Matt's shoulder. "Wait, Matt. You've been avoiding my questions and I think you owe me some answers. What are you doing here, what is wrong with that woman, and who is Malik?"

Instantly, Emmon was at Matt's side, pushing away Torrin's arm. "I'd leave him alone, Torrin. Trust me, you don't want to know."

Torrin glared at Emmon, but Matt said, "He's right Torrin, you really don't want to know. It's a long and complicated story."

"Try me."

Matt turned to Galen, who nodded resignedly. "We have to tell him, Matt. He has helped us find her. You might as well tell our hostess, too, while you're at it."

Matt scanned the faces of his friends. Galen, Emmon, Arden, and Hal. They all shared the secret of their journey and were bound together by what they had experienced. And now two more would know.

"All right," Matt sighed. "You'd better sit down."

Matt told them about the past eight months. His friends occasionally added details to the story. Catherine and Torrin listened intently. It felt strange to relive it. The years before this journey to save Mundaria meant nothing to him – they only held memories of an unhappy life, now made extraordinary. Matt still had a difficult time believing it had all happened to him. He finished the story with the wizard council and his desire to find his true parents.

Torrin and Catherine were silent. Torrin had gone pale and was staring at Matt as if he had never seen him before. Catherine merely nodded.

"It sounds like you've been busy," she said with a smile.

"And we still have a lot to do," Matt replied.

"So what will you do now?"

"Try to find a way to talk to your mother. And find the Wind Stone."

CHAPTER THIRTEEN

"What do you suppose horses think about?" Arden mused as she and Matt groomed their horses.

Matt ran his brush down Striker's sleek black side and shrugged. Murph, sitting on Striker's head, chirruped as if he knew exactly what Striker was thinking.

"Probably about how many oats they're going to get," Matt said. "That's the main thing that Hal thinks about, too."

"Oh, give him a break," Arden said, but laughed.

"Speaking of which, I brought some oats," Emmon said as he entered the stables, carrying two wooden buckets of oats.

He poured them into the troughs in front of the horses, wiped the sweat from his brow, then picked up one of several buckets of water that he had brought in earlier, and dumped it into the water trough. Matt poured another bucket into the trough, but as he poured it, it splashed onto Arden.

"Hey!"

"Sorry, that was an accident," he said with a grin.

Before he knew it, she had picked up a bucket and thrown the contents at him. She was smiling happily.

"Hey, yourself!" he said.

He picked up another bucket of water and threw the contents at both of them. They retaliated by jumping on him and they all landed in a stack of hay. Laughing, Matt pushed them up. They were all drenched, their hair plastered to their skulls, and dirt and straw stuck to their wet clothes.

"You have hay in your hair," Arden told Matt and leaned over to brush it away. Her breath was warm on his face.

"Uh...thanks," Matt said with a weak smile.

"Come on. Let's go," she said as she helped him up.

Matt felt slightly dizzy as he followed his friends down a small side street that led back into the heart of the city, but he tried not to think about it.

"Do you want to find Galen?" Emmon suggested.

Galen had spent the past two days talking with Catherine and trying to decipher what Ellyn was saying. Ever since Matt had put his hand on her, Ellyn had begun to break out of her trance at random intervals and start babbling gibberish. Galen was intent on finding out what she had to say. He also seemed quite interested in what Catherine had to say, but Matt was pretty sure that didn't have anything to do with what she might know about Matt's parents or the Wind Stone.

"We could ask around about the rumors of flying beasts," Arden offered.

Matt and Emmon agreed, and Arden tucked Murph into her satchel. They set out toward one of the local marketplaces that Torrin had shown them. It was a lively place. The dusty streets were lined with shipped goods and barrels of smoked fish, unlike Gremonte where the streets were lined with stalls of colorful handiwork made by artisans. Here, men gathered around taverns, muttering about shipwrecks and raiders.

Matt, Emmon, and Arden snaked through the crowd trying not to attract attention to themselves since most teenagers in Aresburg were at work in the port.

Matt tried to stand as tall as he could so he looked more like a man. He had grown a good deal during the summer months, but he was still was not as tall as Hal. He and Emmon sidled up behind a group of somber-looking men. Arden moved to the shadows across the street since her presence was even more noticeable.

"There have been twenty raids in the past month," one man complained.

"And port security is only getting worse," the second agreed. "I say it's about time our guards were properly trained."

Matt and Emmon nodded as if they were part of the conversation. The men turned to look at them and a heavy silence followed.

"Have any of you heard the rumors about flying beasts?" Matt asked casually.

The men looked at him curiously, but did not answer.

"I hear there have been more sightings recently," Emmon put in. "In Dirth, livestock has been stolen."

"Aye," one man said with a swift glance over his shoulder. "Strange things have been happening all over the region."

Matt and Emmon leaned in.

"People have been disappearing," another man whispered. "And there have been more and more sightings of those beasts you were talking about. There's talk of a search for them. So they can be exterminated."

Matt's heart started beating very rapidly against his rib cage.

"Do you know where they've been seen, then?" he whispered.

The man shifted uncomfortably but just as he opened his mouth to speak he was interrupted.

"Matt! Emmon!"

Hal was weaving through the market toward them. Impeccable timing, as usual. The men backed away and disappeared into the crowd. Arden appeared beside Matt, looking frustrated. Hal reached them in a few quick strides, looking extremely pleased.

"What are you three up to?" he asked, the smile still plastered on his face. "You should see the guard here – it's completely different than Ridgefell."

As they walked away from the market onto another street, Hal rattled on about the guard and how they defended the port, but had no training. Suddenly, a large, bulky man came rocketing down the street, missing Hal by inches and causing him to stumble.

"Out of my way, boy," the man growled angrily.

He spat at Hal's feet, glaring and cursing at him. Hal's face turned scarlet with anger and he stepped toward the man with his fists raised.

"Hal," Arden said warningly, but it was too late.

Hal grabbed the large man's shirt and pulled him toward him.

"Get your hands off me!" the man yelled.

A crowd had begun to gather. Hal gradually relaxed his grip on the man's shirt and just when looked as if Hal had calmed down, he punched the man hard in the stomach. A gasp rippled through the crowd as the man staggered backward. Cursing angrily, he punched Hal squarely in the jaw. Hal fell onto the stone street. Sounds swelled through the crowd as the man turned to walk away, but Hal jumped back onto his feet.

"Get back here!" he yelled, his cheek an angry red.

The hulking man did not respond, so Hal let loose a wild cry and jumped onto the man's back, forcing him to the ground and pinning him down. The crowd cheered as the fighters rolled through the street, throwing punches. The man jerked his head backward, butting Hal in the face. Hal loosened his hold on the man, and he was up in an instant kicking hard at Hal.

Hal rolled away toward the crowd and stood up. The man was now facing him, hatred in his eyes. Matt watched Hal's eyes flick over the man, sizing him up and deciding what to try next. Matt jumped forward, knowing he had to stop the fight before it was out of control. He grabbed Hal's shirt, something that ordinarily he would never dare to do, and pulled the larger boy.

"Stop it, Hal!" he yelled. "Stop it!"

Hal grunted. "Get off, Matt."

"No."

Hal turned his angry gaze on Matt, placed his hands on his chest, and pushed him with all his might. Matt flew against the wall of a building and slid down onto the dirty street. He blinked dazedly, vaguely aware of the pain in his back and head. Emmon and Arden each grabbed an arm and lifted him to his feet.

"You all right?" Arden asked.

"I'm fine," he answered, frustration boiling inside.

"Good try, but I don't think anyone can stop Hal right now," Emmon told him.

Matt steadied himself against the wall, watching the fight. They were circling each other. The hulking man started toward Hal, his right arm swinging at Hal's head, but Hal dove underneath his arm and came up behind the man. Before he could turn, Hal was kicking the back of the man's knees, and he crumpled to the ground. The crowd cheered and groaned simultaneously. Hal turned to the crowd and smiled.

But the man was not finished. He was on his feet again, punching Hal hard in the ribs. Hal began pummeling him in the chest and face. The fight continued until they were both bleeding and hunched over, breathing raggedly. But within seconds, they were at it again.

"This is going too far," Matt muttered.

The crowd was yelling wildly and it seemed to be growing larger by the moment. Hal hit the man several times in the face and when the man doubled over, Hal grabbed his arm and twisted it up over his head. The man groaned in pain as Hal held his arm, pushing against it, and then managed to grab his other arm and hold it next to the first. The man leaned over as Hal pulled him forward by his arms.

"I'm done, I'm done," the man slurred. "I don't have no more fight left in me."

Hal ignored him and began to kick and knee him in the face and upper body. The man grunted and groaned, but Hal continued for a several minutes before throwing him onto the street.

"Matt, look!" Emmon said.

Galen and Catherine were walking together down the street, talking and smiling, but the smile slid off of Galen's face as he looked up to see what the crowd was yelling about. He sprinted forward just as Hal gave his downed opponent another hard, unnecessary kick in the head.

"HAL!" Galen yelled above the din.

Hal turned his head only slightly and then turned back to his fallen opponent, ready to kick him in the head again, but before he could there was a loud bang, and he was rocketed backward onto the street. Galen stood twenty feet away, his hands extended as he held an enormous, shimmering magical shield in the air between Hal and the fallen man.

"What are you doing?" Galen yelled again.

Matt had never seen Galen so angry. Galen was always so even-keeled and easy to laugh, but now he was irate. Anger radiated from him. Nor had Matt ever seen him demonstrate such power. Galen was very secretive about his magical abilities, but now his magical strength was fully visible. The muscles in his arms were clenched and powerful as he continued to hold the shield.

"Is that what you've been trained for? To be a mindless brute?! Is it?"

Hal stared up at Galen, his face pale. Galen's expression went from uncontained rage to disgust as he dismissed the shield.

"Calm down, Galen," Hal muttered, glancing around at the crowd of people surrounding them.

"Calm down? Is that what *you* did?"

Hal's face was growing red again and with a powerful push off the ground, he shot to his feet to face Galen.

"You never learn! Do you have any sense?" Galen said in disbelief.

He turned to help up the fallen man, but Hal ran at him, fists clenched. Galen whirled around with his hands extended and there was another loud bang. Matt felt the ripple of magical energy rush through the air and collide with Hal's chest, sending him sprawling again.

Galen did not even look at Hal. Instead, he turned to Hal's opponent who was barely conscious and was being lifted by the crowd, and said quietly, "Please accept my apologies for my friend's behavior."

Without another glance at Hal, Galen strode away. Matt, Emmon, Arden, and Catherine wove through the crowd behind him. When they were away from the crowd, Galen looked around to find Matt, grabbed his shoulder and pulled him alongside. As they turned the corner, Matt glanced back and saw Hal still sitting alone in the street.

"Idiot," Galen grunted as they made their way toward Catherine's home. "He's made our presence known to the whole city. That's exactly what I was trying to prevent. By morning, there won't be a soul in Aresburg who doesn't know who we are and what has happened."

Catherine opened the door, looking pale, but steadfast as she ushered them inside her home. Matt suddenly realized how cold and wet he was. Although it was warmer in Aresburg than it had been further north, the air was still brisk, and he was grateful when Catherine started a fire. Matt, Emmon, and Arden sat at the table, conversing quietly and occasionally glancing at Galen who sat at the other end of the table silently drinking a mug of tea.

Nearly an hour later, there was a knock on the door. Catherine opened it, and Hal stood in the doorway looking downcast.

"Come in, Hal," Catherine said kindly.

Hal hobbled into the house, glancing sideways at Galen. Galen's eyes followed the boy as he lowered himself gingerly into the chair beside Matt. Catherine picked up a cloth and dabbed at Hal's bloody lip and forehead, then dipped the cloth into a thick ointment in a jar and wrapped it around Hal's raw, bleeding knuckles.

"I'm sorry, Galen," Hal muttered when Catherine had finished.

Galen looked at Hal intently. "I hope you understand what you have done. You have made us recognizable to the entire city. You think Malik doesn't have spies? And what of the council? If either of them have men here in Aresburg, they now know that Matt is here. Do you understand the danger that you've put him in? Put all of us in?"

Hal nodded glumly.

"Besides," Galen continued. "You can't beat a man senseless just because you can. You're old enough to know that. You could have killed him, if you had continued to kick him in the head like that. I don't care what he said or did to offend you, it isn't worth killing someone over. I just wish you'd use a little judgment."

Hal remained silent. Galen asked Matt if they had found out anything about Samsire or the strange reports of creatures, and Matt told him what little they'd learned. Galen had also been unsuccessful talking to Ellyn, but Matt caught him glancing sideways at Catherine as if he believed it had been time well spent anyway.

As evening began to settle in, they bid Catherine good night and walked back to the inn. As soon as they entered the inn, murmuring began and it was clear that the story of Hal's fight had already spread through the city.

One man clapped Hal hard on the back and said, "You're a strong lad, my friend. We could use you around the port to scare off the raiders."

He looked around at Hal's companions. His eyes grew wide when they fell on Galen, and he hastily pulled his hand away from Hal's back. The rest of the crowd watched Galen, fearful and impressed. But Galen ignored them. Matt guessed that growing up as a mergling among the elves of Amaldan had made it easy for Galen to ignore staring. He led them up the stairs without a word and disappeared into his room. Matt fell asleep wondering if Galen's and Hal's notoriety would help or hinder them.

CHAPTER FOURTEEN

The first boom shook Matt awake. He blinked his eyes open, staring around the darkness of the room. Hal was snoring loudly, but that was not what had woken Matt up. Emmon, too, was sitting up in confusion, trying to locate the source of the noise. A second boom followed. It was blocks away from the inn.

It sounded like a building was collapsing. Matt jumped out of bed, grabbing his boots as he ran to the door, Emmon was right behind him.

"What's going on?" Hal demanded.

"Something's happening out there!" Matt called back as he and Emmon ran out of the room.

They ran down the stairs and into the tavern. Galen and Arden were already at the door. None of them wore their cloaks, but Matt did not notice the cold air. His heart was pounding, and for a reason he could not explain, he knew that something unnatural was happening - something to do with him. Galen led the way as they ran through the street. After a moment, Matt realized that they were headed to the port. In the darkness, the tethered boats lining the dock looked sinister.

Near the canal, a plume of what looked like dust rose above one of the storehouses. Stones covered the path and Matt realized that the building had collapsed, the walls shattered inward.

Galen stepped forward slowly, motioning for them to stay back. Matt swallowed, his hand clenching instinctively around the pouch that held the Fire Stone and the Water Stone. Galen moved cautiously, stopping a few yards away from the building. He stared at the collapsed building for a moment, shaking his head.

"Matt, you have to see this!" he called back.

Matt started to move toward Galen when he saw a dark figure emerge from behind a stack of crates near Galen. The figure held a hand out toward Galen.

"Galen, look out!"

The dark figure moved his hands and a murky blackness streamed toward Galen. Without pausing to think, Matt ran forward, extending his own hands. Magical power coursed through him, fueled by the Fire Stone and the Water Stone and surged in front of Galen, forming a fiery magical shield that repelled the deadly attack. The figure recoiled violently, retreated down the canal, and ran into the night.

Matt lowered his hand, his heart pounding and his hands shaking,

Galen put a steadying hand on his back. "Thank you, my friend."

"Who, or what, was that?" Emmon said.

Matt knew the answer, but Galen said it for him. "One of Malik's men, no doubt. Which means that we're in the right place...But right now, we have something else to worry about."

Matt followed his gaze and sucked in a breath as he looked at the collapsed building. It had not just collapsed. Something had landed on it and that something was a huge creature. A giant bird of prey, like an eagle or a hawk, but with a twenty-foot wingspan. It was breathing heavily and despite its size, it looked frail.

Matt stepped forward, strangely drawn to it, just as he had been drawn to Sam. Nobody tried to stop him. As he climbed over the edge of the fallen wall, the creature's eye opened. A sharp black eye narrowed in on Matt and Matt froze.

Then, Murph the morphcat was suddenly there, jumping down from the nearest rooftop. He was bright white in the darkness, and he glowed as he scampered over the rubble toward the bird. The tiny morphcat began to chirrup loudly, climbing across the creature's wings. The giant bird's eye shifted from Matt to Murph, and for a moment, Matt thought that it was going to make a quick snack of the morphcat, but Murph suddenly let out a high-pitched wailing noise, and the creature angled its giant head back toward Matt. It blinked at him and then opened its beak.

"It's you," it said in a whisper of a voice. "He found…you."

Matt stood very still.

"You are the One," the bird breathed. It locked eyes with Matt. "The Wind Stone…you must save us."

The creature stared at him for moment longer, then its head drooped, its eyes closed, and it lay still. The canal was silent, except for the whistle of the wind. Murph climbed up to the creature's head, sniffing its feathers mournfully.

"Is it…dead?" Arden whispered.

Murph stood upright, his eyes wide, and he leaped into the air. Frantically, he began to chirrup, jumping through the rubble. He seemed panicked and afraid. Arden lunged for him, but his fur turned black, and with a bounding leap, he disappeared into the darkness.

"Murph!" Arden called after him.

But the morphcat was gone. Matt stepped back from the creature and looked at Arden. She shook her head, as confused as he was. Galen grabbed Matt's arm and pulled him away.

"We have to get out of here before people start coming," he said quietly.

A crowd was already starting to form along the canal, but Galen quickly ushered Matt and the others away from the collapsed building, trying to blend in with the crowd. They started to move away when a lone woman stood in front of them. Her hair was disheveled, she looked unsteady on her feet, and she wavered precariously as she staggered forward. Matt realized with a start that it was Ellyn.

"It is happening," she declared in a chillingly clear voice.

Her gaze locked on Matt and for a moment he could see that she was fully aware of her surroundings. Matt met her gaze, momentarily transfixed by the clarity in her eyes. Just as quickly, though, a dazed and unfocused look swept over her face and she stumbled forward. Galen lunged and caught her before she fell, but it was apparent that she had fallen back into the fog in her mind.

"What is she doing here?" Hal hissed.

"Never mind that now," Galen replied curtly. "I'm going to take her back to Catherine's. You four go back to the inn. Stay together and keep your eyes open. I'll meet you there."

Matt did not question him. He could tell that Galen was troubled. Walking back to the inn, Matt looked around cautiously, still feeling the magical power that he wielded against the mysterious stranger burning inside of him. When they reached the inn, they sat down at a table, waiting in the silence of the empty tavern. Matt was jittery as he tried to understand what had just happened.

"Do you think Murph will come back?" Arden said quietly.

Matt shook his head. "I don't know. He seemed…scared. No, upset."

Arden bit her lip. "I think he knew that creature."

She was right, Matt realized. None of them spoke again, lost in their thoughts, until Galen finally opened the door of the inn. He sat down at the table.

"Well, this complicates things," he finally began.

"What was that all about, Galen?" Emmon asked.

Galen considered it for a moment. "Whoever that man was, the one who attacked me…I think he attacked the creature, too. There's no other explanation for someone who knows Dark magic to be there at that moment. The only people I know who have knowledge of Dark magic are those who work for Malik. Which means it's not safe here."

"Well, if it was safe, we wouldn't be here, would we?" Arden commented with a grin.

Galen smiled at her and continued, "So, there's obviously a reason that Malik has people here. That creature…must have meant something. I believe it's important somehow…"

"It said something about the Wind Stone before it died," Matt said. "It said I had to save them. Whoever 'they' are."

They sat in silence. Arden played absently with her long braid and then sat up straighter. "It also said that 'he found you'...Do you think it was talking about Murph? Finding you in Gremonte?"

Hal scoffed loudly. "Murph? He's a silly little morphcat, Arden!"

"Be quiet, Hal," Galen told him. "We can't rule out anything." He sighed. "I wish we could find a clear answer to all of this. Why did Ellyn sneak out? Catherine didn't even hear her leave. And she was so aware of everything for that brief moment."

Matt rubbed his eyes tiredly. None of this made sense – it was all a jumbled mess in his brain. Galen slapped the table and got to his feet.

"Let's go rest. That's all we can do at the moment."

Matt gratefully climbed back up the stairs, the image of the giant bird still in front of his eyes. What was it? Where had it come from? And why had it appeared in Aresburg?

If only Sam were here.

CHAPTER FIFTEEN

Lucian surveyed the barren terrain of the Endless Fields. He had been camped at this spot for two days now, waiting for the council's contact to emerge. Any time now, he should appear in the darkness to give Lucian news about the Commander of Shadows. This particular spot in the Endless Fields was strategically stationed several miles from the Black River since the river was often considered the outer boundary of Malik's domain.

Lucian had left Karespurn the day after the wizard council had given him his assignment. He had ridden straight to Perth, a small town on the edge of the Borg Forest and the Endless Fields and the only settlement in the immediate area. From Perth, he had ridden through the Endless Fields, the very same fields on which the Battle of Vanishing Shadows, the battle that caused Malik's initial demise, had taken place.

But now he stood uncertainly beside Innar in the darkness for the second night of waiting. He wondered if the messenger had been discovered and killed by Malik or his Agurans. It was eerily quiet. Lucian gripped his staff tightly. He dared not make a fire for fear of attracting attention, so he stood, with only the company of Innar and the darkness.

Another hour passed without an appearance and Lucian's unease increased. Perhaps it was all a plot by the council, positioning him so close to Malik's territory to be caught and killed so he could no longer question their authority.

Suddenly, Innar whinnied, his ears twitching.

"Calm, Innar," Lucian murmured, scanning the darkness and holding out his staff.

There was a rustle in the dry grass and despite his inner warnings, Lucian created a small ball of shimmering white light that he held in an extended palm. It illuminated the space in front of him, revealing a very thin man crouched in the darkness.

"I come with tidings of things great and evil," the man whispered.

Lucian lowered his staff. The man matched the council's description – tall, thin, sallow face with black, shoulder-length hair. He had also spoken the code-phrase that identified him as trustworthy.

"Tidings?" Lucian answered and spoke his own code-phrase. "A bright light in the darkness."

The man nodded and approached him. "I'm happy to see you, whoever you may be. I've been trying for days to get out of Marlope and I barely evaded the guards. Come now. Get a fire going. You're too far for any spies to see the flames."

Lucian consented, noticing the man's sunken cheeks and the exhaustion evident in the dark circles under his eyes. His cloak was tattered and his pack empty. He huddled beside the fire reaching his arms out for the warmth.

Lucian pulled half of a loaf of bread from his pack and tossed it to the man. He ate it ravenously, as if he had not eaten for days.

He took several long swallows from Lucian's water skin and put it down with a gasp.

"What's your name?" he asked.

"Lucian. I was once on the council."

The man nodded appreciatively. "I know a little magic myself. A few simple invocations. That's all the council says I'm able to perform. My name's Byrd, Special Contact to the Great Council of Wizards."

"Ah, I see," Lucian said, noting his flair for theatrics. "What information do you have then?"

He shook his head. "Nothing good. Terrible news, in fact."

"What is it?" Lucian pressed impatiently.

"They've gone. Left Marlope."

"Who has?" Lucian said, not believing his ears.

"The Commander of Shadows. He has gone."

"Gone? He can't have just disappeared. Where has he gone to?" Lucian demanded.

The man shrugged. "I wouldn't have even known he was gone, except that I work as a messenger for the men of Marlope. About a week ago, I was sent to deliver a message to the head of the guard who was said to be in the tower. The tower was full of men, so I did not notice a change. But I passed the place where that woman stays. Vivona, the potion-maker. She was not there and Kerwin never lets her leave the tower because she's so valuable to him.

"So I kept walking until I reached the strategy room where the recipient of the message was supposed to be. A guard told me that he was on the next level."

He paused, his brow furrowed.

"Go on," Lucian said as gently as he could.

"Yes, so I climbed to the next level. I noticed that the doors to the Commander's chamber were open. I glanced in, but there was nobody inside."

"So?"

"The Commander of Shadows never leaves his chambers unless he is surveying something in the city," the man told him.

"Then that was where he could have been," Lucian said. "Is that the only thing that told you he has gone?"

Byrd nodded.

"Then it is very likely that he is still in Marlope."

"It felt…different," the man argued weakly.

Lucian shook his head skeptically. He had studied Malik's tactics for years. It was highly unlikely that he would leave Marlope at this point, without a single one of the Stones of the Elements or the Immortality Scroll.

"Is that the only 'terrible news' you have to share?" Lucian asked with a sigh.

Byrd shook his head gravely. "I'm afraid not. There's much more."

Lucian waited patiently for him to begin speaking again.

"For weeks now there have been strange noises and much activity around the garan pits. I have tried to investigate, but the guards would not let me near. A few days ago, there were a lot of comings and goings in and out of that area. I managed to blend in with the crowd and…and I finally saw. I did not see much, but I saw what I needed to."

Lucian began to tap his knee. Byrd took another swallow of water.

"I saw most of the garans disappearing into the tunnels of Marlope. To the secret exits. I do not know how many there were but there were many. Hundreds. Thousands, maybe. And they were on the move."

"Why did you not say this before, instead of a theory about what might or might not be true?" Lucian cried. "How long ago was that? Where were they headed?"

"Well, it's taken me many days to get here. I glimpsed them as I left, but I do not know where they were going."

"Was this before or after you assumed Malik was no longer in Marlope?" Lucian asked urgently.

"After."

Lucian sighed. That was good. It was more likely that Malik's absence from his chamber was to survey the garans before they left. Lucian was still convinced that Malik would not risk leaving his stronghold at this point.

The garans were something else entirely. And Lucian could guess what their destination was. He thought back to the cryptic words in the wizard council's records. High magical activity in the south.

He stood up and tightened Innar's saddle, threw his provisions into his pack, leaving some for Byrd, and fastened his staff to Innar's saddle.

"Where are you going?" Byrd demanded in outrage.

"You must tell the council of what you have learned," Lucian ordered as he mounted Innar.

"What about you? That's your duty!"

Lucian smiled grimly. "I have another task to attend to."

He kicked Innar and set off into the darkness. Matt and the others were, once again, in great danger.

CHAPTER SIXTEEN

By the following morning, Matt was no closer to making sense of the previous night's events. At least Hal and Galen seemed to have patched up their differences. They did not speak to each other at the morning meal, but Galen was cheerful again. Hal's right cheek had an enormous purple bruise and his lip was puffy. As they finished eating, the door to the inn was flung open and Torrin entered, breathless.

"Hey, Torrin," Matt said.

"I heard what happened yesterday," Torrin said immediately. "I thought you were trying to keep a low profile."

At first, Matt thought he was talking about the creature at the canal, but then realized that he was talking about the fight.

"Well, that's not going to happen now, is it?" Galen remarked.

"Still, good work, Hal," Torrin replied. "The whole city's been talking about it."

Hal raised his chin and smiled slightly until Arden elbowed him. His smile faded and he glanced at Galen.

"Anyway," Torrin continued. "I was wondering if the lot of you wanted to come down to the port, and I can show you where I work if you'd like. There was a big fuss this morning – some crazy beast crashed into one of the storehouses last night. Nobody knows what it is."

Matt and Emmon exchanged looks. It was the perfect opportunity to get a closer look.

"Sure, that would be great!" Matt answered and the others all nodded enthusiastically.

"Go ahead," Galen told them, and as Torrin move to the door, he said in a low voice, "I'm going to Catherine's to try to talk to Ellyn. Maybe I can find out why and how she was at the port last night. Meanwhile, see what you can find at the canal. Any clues could be helpful."

Within a few minutes the teenagers were on the way to the port with Torrin, and Galen walked away in the other direction.

"So what do you do at the port, Torrin?" Arden asked.

"Depends on the season. During the spring and summer I'll go off on a trading ship. We usually go to Portsmouth or other small village along the shoreline. But during the cold months, we mostly stay in the canal receiving long-traveling ships or cataloging goods that we've collected."

He paused, his eyes glinting. "And then there's the race."

"Race?"

"Every year as fall becomes winter, there's a grand boat race down the canal. The canal is long and wide and obstacles are set up all along it. Each team gets its own set of raiders. It's a grueling game, but the winners gain standing in the town and that's good for trade. I'm with the crew of the reigning champions," Torrin said proudly. "This year's event is only a few days away."

The men along the docks cast sidelong glances at them as they walked by. Matt's hand moved uneasily to the throwing knife that he had concealed at his hip. He forced himself to relax, watching

Torrin's easy smile and manner. They walked a little further, through a maze of storehouses, each with a sign telling what it contained, until the line of buildings abruptly ended at the dock.

Matt paused to look at the magnificent sight. There were dozens of great ships with masts as tall as towers. Ornate prows protruded from the ships – wooden carvings of colorfully painted women or strange creatures watching over the ships like faithful protectors.

The stone path along the canal was swarming with men lifting crates and carrying them onto the ships. The ships were alive with activity. Boys Matt's age were crawling up the masts to the crow's nests, washing the decks, or hanging by ropes from the sides of the ships while they painted the wooden hulls.

It was an amazing sight. Matt had never seen anything quite like it, and he could tell that none of his friends had either. Torrin laughed at their expressions.

"Nothing quite like it, eh? I remember the first time I saw it. The most glorious place there is, I'd wager," he said.

Matt preferred the quiet magic of the Amaldan Forest, but this was still magnificent.

"Come on, then," Torrin said cheerfully. "There's a lot more to see."

They followed him down the crowded docks, taking in every sight, sound, and smell of the canal. There seemed to be endless stacks of crates and giant nets of fish being loaded on and off ships.

"There are only a few more ships setting out before winter," Torrin explained. "But they're being loaded with goods to trade."

Torrin cleared his throat uneasily as they approached the collapsed building. A crowd was gathered around it. Matt craned his neck to see. The creature, the giant bird, had somehow been cleared away.

Matt tried to imagine moving it. It must have taken several dozen men and many ropes to lift it. Where did they take it? Little remained of the scene from last night, only piles of rubble. Hundreds of barrels of fish had been stacked in the collapsed storehouse and they had all broken open when the creature fell on the building. The odor filled the air.

"The foul beast!" a man growled. "It's a good thing it's dead. Otherwise it might have gone after any one of us."

"There were attacks in Dirth, more and more creatures have been sighted out near the mountains, and now this," another muttered. "We ought to gather a hunting party and go after them now, before they attack us!"

Matt was dismayed. The creature had been frightening to approach, but it had spoken to Matt. It had a voice and a mind, just like Sam.

"Come on," Emmon said bleakly and Matt knew he was as saddened about the bird as he was. "There's nothing else to see. They've already cleared everything away."

They moved away from the building, sorrow weighing heavily on them. Arden looked around, scanning the rooftops.

"No sign of Murph?" Matt asked her.

She shook her head. "I think he'll show up eventually, though. It seemed like he had grown fond of us."

Matt smiled at her, and they followed Torrin along the canal until he stopped.

"See that beauty there? That's the *Lady Gemma,* the ship I work on."

He pointed to a large ship about two docks down. It had two tall masts with a complex web of ropes and rigging that swung across the entire ship like a gigantic spider had made its home there. The ship's sides were long and sleek, and the ship looked like it could move quickly and smoothly through the water. A ramp was secured to its side and several men struggled to carry wooden crates onboard.

"Come on," Torrin beckoned to Matt, Emmon, Arden, and Hal. "I'll introduce you to Captain Nick."

They followed him to the *Lady Gemma* where he stopped and called up to one of the men unloading the crates.

"Hanson!"

The man looked down. "Torrin! Haven't seen you in a few days!"

"Is the captain up there?" Torrin called back.

In response a very tall, slim man emerged from below deck and leaned over the rail of the deck, smiling.

"Torrin!" he exclaimed. "It's about time you showed your face!"

"Hello, there, Captain. I've got some people here you might want to meet."

Captain Nick's long legs took him down the ramp in several enormous strides.

"This is Matt, Emmon, Arden, and Hal," Torrin introduced them. "I've known Matt since he was only a baby. Haven't seen him in several years and he turned up here in Aresburg."

"I'm Nick. Say, aren't you the fellow who fought old Bill yesterday?" he said, shaking their hands in turn and pausing at Hal.

Hal nodded. "Yes, sir."

"Call me Nick."

"Yes, Nick," Hal repeated.

"Why don't you stay here and help catalog the crates, Torrin. I have to take the *Lady Gemma* up to Dock Sixteen to unload a few dozen crates of spices. It's too far to carry them, and the port is too crowded because of that creature. How about our new friends take the ride with me?"

Matt hesitated. He had never been on a boat before. But Torrin clapped him on the back.

"Go on, Matt. You'll have the time of your life. I have to go work. Have fun!"

Torrin walked away to help another crewmember lift a heavy crate, leaving Matt and the others standing uncertainly in front of Nick.

"Well, come on, then!"

Nick led them up the ramp to the *Lady Gemma,* and Matt could already feel the gentle swaying of the ship even in the quiet canal with the boat fastened safely to the dock.

"This is Hanson, my first mate."

Hanson nodded to them and turned to Nick. "Shall we shove off, sir?"

"Yes. Tell the men to get us off. I'll take the wheel, Hanson."

"Aye-aye, Captain," Hanson replied and yelled over the side. "Hey, you scallywags! The captain calls for shove off!"

A scramble of men made their way aboard while others untied the many ropes that secured the *Lady Gemma* to the dock and threw them up to the sailors on the deck.

"Watch out for the sails moving about and enjoy the ride," Nick yelled to Matt and the others as he moved off to steer the ship.

The teenagers watched as the sailors ran to the ropes and unfurled the sails. Immediately, a ripple of wind filled the billowing sails. The ship groaned as Captain Nick wrenched the wheel around.

"Dock Sixteen, here we come!" Nick yelled.

The *Lady Gemma* lurched to the right. Matt gripped the rail that ran along the edge of the boat and tried to keep his balance. The air was crisp and smelled salty. Seagulls clucked impatiently above them, searching for fish to scavenge from the sailors.

Matt tentatively let go of the handrail. It was a liberating feeling, standing so high above the water and the port, but every unexpected movement of the ship made him clutch the rail again.

"It will take us a few minutes to get down to Dock Sixteen," Hanson said. "Would you like to see below?"

"Er...I think I'll stay up here," Matt replied, nervous.

Emmon and Arden shook their heads vigorously, but Hal said, "I'll take that challenge."

Hanson gave him a slightly puzzled look. "Right, then. Follow me."

Hal swaggered after him into the small opening that led below deck. Matt grinned at Emmon and Arden, all marveling at Hal's untiring bravado.

"Well, Hal is back, taking dangerous challenges, defeating dark and dangerous places," Arden said with a twinkle in her eye. "It's not like these sailors do it every day. I mean, what would they do, without Hal here to fight their demons?"

"Still," Emmon said, shaking his head. "I wouldn't want to be stuck down there."

They leaned against the wooden rail, watching the ships go by. The sounds that clamored around the storehouses faded into the background. It felt very peaceful.

"Hey! Back off, there!" Nick yelled suddenly.

They turned to see Nick cursing angrily at a large ship with brightly decorated sails that sidled up alongside the *Lady Gemma*. The sailors of the ship were smirking at the men on the *Lady Gemma*. With a sudden, violent turn of the wheel, the other ship rammed into the side of the *Lady Gemma*.

The *Lady Gemma* careened to the side, tilting toward the water. Matt, Emmon, and Arden, who were all leaning on the handrail, went flying across the deck and rammed against the side-guard on the other side of the boat. A rope with a pronged hook on the end of it soared past Matt's head from the *Lady Gemma* onto the other boat and hooked onto their guard rail. Emmon nearly followed the rope over the rail.

"Emmon!" Arden yelled.

Matt flung his arms around Emmon's middle and pulled him back onto deck.

"Sabotage!" Nick yelled in outrage at the offending ship. "The race is still days away, and you're already attempting sabotage?!"

The other captain grinned wickedly and turned his wheel sharply.

"Hold on!" Nick yelled to his passengers, but too late.

The ship collided violently with the *Lady Gemma* again. Matt did not brace himself in time and as the ship lurched to the side, he was thrown into the air. He bounced over the top of the guard rail, but he managed to catch hold of guard rail on his way over it. Water hit him in the face and his fingers slipped. The boat rocked again and he lost hold of the rail. As he fell, he glimpsed something to his left and he reached for it – it was the rope that had flown overboard that was now attached to both ships. The rope went taut beneath his hands as the ship returned to its upright position.

"Matt! Where's Matt?" Matt heard Emmon's voice.

"I'm here!" Matt yelled back. "Over the side."

"Gifford, take the wheel," he heard Nick say.

Emmon and Arden's anxious faces appeared at the rail, and Nick joined them as they stared helplessly at Matt.

"Slide back toward us, Matt, and we'll try to lift you back on board."

Matt began to shuffle along the rope toward the *Lady Gemma*. He could already feel the rope burns forming on his hands, but he gritted his teeth and kept moving.

"Raider!" Matt heard an angry growl behind him. "Ya askin' fo' trouble, ya no-good, rottin' raider!"

Matt looked back and saw a large, muscular man waving his fist at him. The man lowered himself onto the other side of Matt's rope with a jagged knife between his teeth and a dangerous glint in his eye. Matt could not believe he was being chased by a man with a knife just because he had fallen overboard. The rope sagged with the man's weight, and Matt began to slide down the rope toward the other boat.

"Come on, Matt!" Arden yelled.

The man was coming closer by the second. Matt did not know if he could reach the *Lady Gemma* before the man reached him. Matt looked back at the pleading faces of Emmon, Arden, and Nick and then back to the angry eyes of the approaching man.

Matt suddenly remembered the knife he had hidden at his hip. Daring for a moment to let go with his left hand, he reached for the knife and yanked it from its scabbard. He pulled his arms up over the rope and began chopping at the rope between him and his pursuer. A few strands of the rope splintered away and unraveled. Matt sawed at it again and more strands snapped off. Unable to hold the weight any longer, the rope snapped completely. Matt's half went flying back toward the *Lady Gemma.* He grabbed the rope with both hands just before he collided with the side of the boat, and he managed to hang onto it on impact. Unfortunately for the other man, the rope carried him into the dark waters of the canal.

The sailors on the other boat swore angrily at Matt, but he paid no attention as Nick, Emmon, and Arden pulled up his rope. As he reached the edge of the ship, they pulled him over the guard rail and he fell onto the wooden deck.

"That was amazing!" Nick said ecstatically, grabbing Matt's shoulders with his enormous hands. "I've never seen anything like it! You have to be one of my raiders for the big boat race!"

"I…I don't know," Matt stammered, unsure of what to say.

"What's going on?"

Hal and Hanson had emerged from below deck, and Hal was staring at Matt accusingly.

"Hanson!" Nick exclaimed excitedly. "Young Matt here is going to be one of our raiders for the race. He's a natural."

"I am?"

"Sure. You handled that situation perfectly."

"Well, he's definitely a natural at finding trouble," Emmon grinned.

Nick talked the remainder of the journey to Dock Sixteen. Hal, however, was silent and Matt could feel his stony stare focused on the back of his neck.

"Whatever happens with the race," Arden whispered, "you've already accomplished something – I don't think I've ever seen Hal so jealous."

Once they reached the desired dock, the sailors on board and down below on the dock secured the *Lady Gemma,* and a ramp was attached to the side of the ship. Nick led the teenagers to the stone path that ran along the canal. Torrin was there, breathing heavily after his run from the other dock.

"I saw that you ran into some trouble," he said breathlessly.

"Saboteurs," Captain Nick replied. "Fortunately, our *Lady Gemma*'s made of sterner stuff. Not a scratch on her. And Matt, here, has proven himself to be a worthy raider. He'll join the team for the race."

Torrin responded by nearly knocking Matt flat with a hearty clap on the back. "Well done, Matt! I serve as a raider, too! That's great news. Has Nick explained the rules to you yet?"

He and Nick launched into a lengthy lecture of the rules of the race. Matt listened quietly, amused by their enthusiasm. It was difficult to keep track of their explanations, but Matt got the basic premise. There were no rules. It was a brutal game of speed and strength. The raiders were responsible for preventing the sabotage of their ship and, more importantly, for distracting other ships while the raiders' crew sailed their ship to the finish line first.

"Well then, Matt," Nick said with a brilliant smile. "We'll be training for the next few days. Torrin will let you know when."

With those final words, the captain turned back to his ship

"Listen, I've got to work, but you should go and have some fun," Torrin told them. "Really excellent work, Matt."

They walked silently down the canal back toward their inn. Matt was shaken. He knew he should have told Nick and Torrin that he didn't even know if he'd be here in a few days. And that he couldn't swim. He had been so happy that they had wanted him on their team that he hadn't been able bring himself to tell them. He knew the others were thinking the same thing.

Galen was already at the inn, sitting at a table and scribbling in a journal. He looked up when they entered, smiling broadly.

"What's going on with you lot?"

They joined him and Matt explained what had happened at the port. Galen's smile grew bigger as Matt told him of Nick's insistence of him joining the crew for the boat race.

"You better get your sea legs fast, Matt," Galen joked. "The race is a fantastic event to watch. You'll have fun."

"I'll have fun embarrassing myself, you mean," Matt argued. "Beside, how can we know if we're still going to be here then?"

"You'll do fine. Torrin will help you out. We can stay a few days as long as Malik's men or the council's men don't show up."

"But Galen, Matt can't swim," Arden said as she met Matt's glance.

"Did you find anything out from Ellyn today?" Matt said quickly.

Galen shook his head, but pointed to the journal he had been writing in. "She's talking a lot more now, but she is very difficult to understand. Something happened in Borden. I know that. She didn't say a word about last night – it's like it never happened."

He sighed. "Basically, I'm still working on it."

CHAPTER SEVENTEEN

When Matt started toward the canal the next morning, he fully intended to tell Torrin and Nick that he was not going to join them for the race. He was convinced that he could not be of any help to them. And he couldn't swim, which Arden had reminded him of several times in the past twelve hours.

Also, he did not want to stay here any longer than they had to. The encounter with the bird creature and Malik's spy had been disturbing, and he had a feeling that it would not be long now before they would be forced to flee.

"I think you would be great in the race, Matt," Arden told him as they walked. "I'm just a little worried about how you would survive if you fell into the water."

It was just the two of them, Galen was at Catherine's, and Emmon and Hal were trying to find out as much as they could about the bird creature.

"It's not worth it, anyway," Matt replied. "There are more important things I should be doing. Besides, I'll just make a fool of myself."

"You don't always have to be saving the world, you know," Arden said. "And you would do better than you think. Actually, you'd probably end up accidentally setting half the boats on fire."

"Hey!" Matt protested with a laugh.

Arden did have a point. It was nice to take a break from running from Malik and his henchmen and the wizard council. Even though he could not shake the feeling that they were in danger even at this moment, he was enjoying walking freely in the city with Arden at his side. He turned to her, but before he could speak, a tiny object dropped onto her shoulder.

"Murph!" Arden exclaimed.

The morphcat jumped back and forth between her shoulders by climbing over the top of her head. His fur was a variety of colors, but was changing so rapidly that Matt found it hard to distinguish one from the next. Arden reached up and plucked him off her shoulder.

"Murph, where have you been?" she said and then turned to Matt. "He seems anxious about something."

Murph broke free of Arden's grasp and leapt up onto the roof again, looking down at them anxiously.

"I think he wants us to follow him," Matt said. "Come on!"

They ran after the bounding morphcat and soon realized that he was moving toward the port. Matt's heart pounded – something was wrong. As they rounded the corner, he felt something burning in his pocket. He realized with a start that it was Sam's feather, glowing blue and green and emanating heat. At first, a thrill of happiness surged through him. Samsire must be close. But the feeling quickly evaporated as he understood exactly what that meant.

"Oh no," he whispered, his stomach twisting.

He sprinted along the canal to the docks. A crowd had gathered again, but he pushed past the bodies to the front and then he stopped, horrified by what he saw – huge leathery, black wings laying flat against the stone path and brightly colored, feathered legs tied together with ropes.

It was Sam.

The alorath squirmed as more than a dozen yelling men held him down and others hit him with paddles. His snout had been muzzled with rope and he could not speak. Matt stood motionless, wanting to scream Sam's name, wanting to rip apart his bonds with magic. But as he squeezed the feather in his hand, Sam rolled his head around to look at him. His sharp blue eyes were not angry, but carefully restrained. Matt suddenly understood. Sam was here to find him, he was here for Matt.

Sam was not going to jeopardize Matt's safety by further angering or scaring the people of the city. And Matt could not either.

"Matt…" Arden breathed beside him.

"Get Galen," he told her. "Please!"

Arden cast one last desperate look at Sam and then sprinted away. Matt did not move. His heart was in his throat as the crowd around him jeered at Sam, cursing the strange creature that had appeared in their port. Matt felt numb, aware of nothing but Sam's presence.

After Samsire had been completely bound, the men brought forward a huge, flat wagon. Amid cheering from the crowd, several dozen men lifted Samsire onto the structure and began to roll him away. Sam overhung the wagon on every side, his body dragging on the ground as they pulled him along. A parade of people followed them. Matt struggled to stay in front as they approached a large building with huge wooden doors. Matt realized it was used to bring ships in out of the water for repairs.

A group of guards motioned for the crowd to move away as Sam was pushed inside, but Matt lingered by the side of the building, waiting.

Eventually, the crowd disappeared, and Matt was alone except for the guards who stood stoically in front of the doors. He could not believe that this was happening. Why had Sam come here?

"Matt!"

Galen and Arden came running down the path. Galen tilted his head toward the doors.

"He's in there?"

Matt nodded, not trusting his voice, and Galen stepped up to the guards. "Excuse me, but we need to talk to the person in charge here. We have an…interest in that creature. Who do we speak to?"

The guards shifted uneasily and one of them finally said, "Baxter's inside. We could let you in to talk to him, I guess."

He pulled open a small door to the side and they filed inside. The cavernous room echoed as the door closed behind them. Samsire was still tied to the flat wagon, his body heaving up and down with every breath. Matt resisted the urge to run to him and he could feel Arden doing the same. She put her hand into his and squeezed it. A large, portly man stepped out from behind a ladder, looking at them skeptically.

"What are you doing here?"

"You're Baxter?" Galen asked.

"Yeah, I'm a port monitor. What do you want?"

Galen nodded toward Sam. "We want him."

The man laughed. "You want that thing? Stop jesting! It's a beast."

"Look, have you ever heard of the Wizard Council of Karespurn?" Galen said, leaning close to the man's face. "Well, I work for them. Anything unnatural, any creature like that, have to be reported and delivered to them. And trust me...they are not the kind of people you want to disobey."

The man's face went pale. Whether or not he knew the council, the effect was the same.

"I don't have any authority. This creature will probably be killed...more likely held for ransom for a time, to see if we can draw out any more of the feral things from the mountains and be done with them once and for all."

Galen considered him for a long moment and then said, "What if we were willing to provide a sum? Then, would you hand the creature over to us?"

The man paused. "I might. How much are you offering?"

Galen did not hesitate. "One hundred gold pieces."

Matt and Arden looked at each other. Where was Galen going to get that kind of money? The man seemed to be thinking the same thing.

"How do I know you're good for it?"

"Give us a few days. You get your money and we get the creature. In the meantime, you feed him and loosen those ropes a bit so he can breathe."

Baxter smiled. "Deal."

He and Galen shook hands, and Galen turned away, nodding for Matt and Arden to follow. Matt squeezed his feather, hoping

Sam would know that they were doing their best. When they stepped back out onto the path, Matt and Arden rounded on Galen. Even Murph looked at him as if demanding an explanation.

"Where are you going to get that much gold, Galen?" Arden asked.

"I'm not going to, Arden," Galen said with a grin. "Matt is."

Matt blinked at him in confusion and Galen grinned more broadly. "The boat race gives a prize of one hundred gold pieces to every crew member."

"What if we don't win?"

Galen shrugged. "Then we will break Sam out ourselves. But it would be better if we could stay on good terms with the people here. That's what Sam was trying to do by not fighting. We have to try."

Matt nodded, a lump in his throat. He would do anything for Sam.

The next few days passed quickly for Matt. Each day, Torrin took him to the port and they went out on the *Lady Gemma*. On the third day they left the canal. Unlike the water in the canal, the sea was rough and riotous.

Matt was awestruck by the beautiful, endless blue-green waters so like the Water Stone that hung at his neck, but he hated the constant rolling of the waves. It reminded him of what Lucian had once told him about the Water Stone. That water had two faces, one calm and one wild. Torrin and Nick taught Matt a few new knife techniques and some useful skills such as ship-hopping, one of Matt's least favorite tactics, and how to defend the ship with large, shield-like planks.

Every day he returned to the inn exhausted. Emmon and Arden came with him each day to watch and urge him on. Always lingering at the back of Matt's mind was Samsire, held captive like an evil beast.

CHAPTER EIGHTEEN

By the time race day arrived, Matt was more than ready for it. He set out for the port early that morning with Torrin. They were met by a spectacular sight. Seven immense boats were lined up side by side across the canal. The port was already swarming with spectators. Matt and Torrin walked to the first dock where small rowboats were taking crews to their ships. By the time Matt and Torrin climbed up the side, most of the crew was already onboard.

It seemed to take ages for the race to start. Matt stood on deck, nervously fingering the long knife that Nick had loaned him and testing the strength of the guard planks and ropes. The port grew even more crowded as the race drew closer, and he felt his stomach flutter nervously.

"Right then, Matt," Nick said as he adjusted the rigging on one of the sails. "You remember what to do?"

Matt nodded. The crowd began to quiet down and Matt saw that a temporary stand had been constructed at the edge of the canal where a man was addressing the crowd. Matt could not hear what he was saying, but the crowd cheered jubilantly. The man then turned to face the line of ships.

"This is it," Torrin told Matt.

Suddenly, the man raised his arm and threw it down. At the same time, Captain Nick yelled, "Pull the anchor! Release the sails!"

The *Lady Gemma* leapt forward as the wind filled her sails. Matt sprinted to the side of the ship. The other six ships were clustered around them and one of them pulled alongside. Matt could see the leering raiders preparing to attack the *Lady Gemma*.

Matt's heart began to race as the raiders drew their knives, preparing to jump onto the *Lady Gemma*.

"Matt!" Captain Nick yelled. "Do something about that ship coming up behind us!"

"Yes, Captain!" Matt yelled back.

Matt looked back at the ship trailing them and called to Gifford, the third raider for the *Lady Gemma*.

"What do we do?" Matt said as the ship nearly rammed into them.

"We jump! Torrin can handle that ship there."

Matt's stomach was clenched into a knot. He hadn't told any of his shipmates that he couldn't swim.

"Come on!"Gifford called as he scooped up a bucket, took a mighty leap, and landed easily on the other ship.

Taking a deep breath and a running start, Matt sprinted to the edge of the ship and kicked off the edge, propelling himself forward. He cleared the gap and tumbled onto the deck at the feet of a sailor. He sailor looked down at Matt and opened his mouth to yell, but before he could say anything, Matt jumped to his feet and shoved him forcefully in the chest, sending him sprawling. Matt ran to join Gifford who was making his way toward the wheel.

Matt remembered what Torrin told him. The point was to distract and interfere with the crew, not to damage the ship.

Matt dodged around sailors until one looked him in the face and yelled out to the captain, "Raiders!"

A group of sailors whirled around and faced Matt and Gifford.

"Hold them off for as long as you can," Gifford told him, grabbing a bucket of water sitting on the deck. "I'll try to distract the captain."

Before Matt could answer, Gifford sprinted off toward the wheel, leaving Matt to face the men alone. Their eyes flickered toward Gifford's departing back, but Matt stood in their way and drew the long knife Nick had given him. He would have preferred to have Doubtslayer in his hand, but both Nick and Torrin had insisted that a sword was an inappropriate weapon for a raider.

Matt's opponents advanced on him quickly, and Matt hopped from foot to foot, remembering Galen's advice to never focus on one opponent when there are many. Men lunged from either side, but Matt danced out of the way, hoping that Gifford would hurry up and distract the captain. He could not continue this dance much longer, and three of the men had now drawn their knives.

Without looking for Gifford, Matt ran toward the center mast hoping to make his opponents follow. The ship jerked violently to the right and Matt nearly slipped down the deck.

"Run, Matt!" Gifford yelled.

Gifford was running toward him. The captain was drenched with water and tied to one of the smaller masts. The unmanned wheel was spinning back and forth.

Several of the soldiers ran to their captain while the others chased after Gifford who had already run past Matt. Matt ran after him. The ship they were on was turning rapidly away from *Lady Gemma*.

As they drew closer to the edge and to the departing *Lady Gemma*, Gifford grabbed Matt's arm and propelled them both over the edge. Time seemed to stop as they flew over the large gap of water and finally landed on the deck of the *Lady Gemma*.

Laughing triumphantly, Gifford slapped the deck, jumped to his feet immediately, and hurried to help the other sailors. Matt pushed himself up and watched as the ship behind them careened into another ship, halting them both in the middle of the canal.

"Ho, there, Matt!" he heard Torrin call. "Where have you been?"

Torrin was holding a wooden plank in front of the sailors to protect them from projectiles coming from the ship beside them. Matt snatched another wooden plank off the deck and crouched beside him.

"We're neck and neck!" Torrin yelled as a rock hit his plank. "We have to do something!"

Matt peered out from behind his plank. The other ship was very close and Matt recognized its brightly decorated sails as the ship that had tried to sabotage the *Lady Gemma* days before.

"Let out more sail!" Nick ordered.

Hanson and the others responded quickly to the order and the boat leapt forward. Unfortunately, so did the other ship and it once again pulled even with the *Lady Gemma*. It was so close that Matt was afraid they would attempt to ram them again. If he could get aboard he might be able to do something, but the ship deck was higher than the *Lady Gemma's* and he could not make the jump.

"Throw me over," he said suddenly to Torrin.

"What?"

"Throw me onto the ship. I'll try to get them away from us!" Matt said.

Torrin dropped the plank and flung Matt across the water. Matt landed hard on the deck.

A sailor grabbed him.

"Raider!"

He punched Matt in the stomach and threw him across the deck. Matt clambered to his feet, dove toward the center mast, and scrambled up the wooden slats to the mast until he reached the crow's nest. Two men were scaling the mast below him.

He remembered the way Gifford had distracted the other boat with a bucket of water. He did not have a bucket, but he had something more. Knowing that the men below were fast approaching, Matt grabbed the pouch around his neck and let the magical power course through him. He extended his hand and water flowed from his hand, wetting the sails in front of him and temporarily forcing the wind from them. As the sails deflated, the ship faltered.

Matt grabbed a rope that hung down to the deck, stood on the rail of the crow's nest, and swung out over the gap between the two ships. As he swung over the deck of the *Lady Gemma*, he let go.

He plummeted downward, the wind rushing in his ears. His boots hit the wood, and he rolled across the hard deck until he came to a stop, spread-eagle, on the deck. The crew of the *Lady Gemma* suddenly erupted in cheers as they cleared the finish line with the other ship several yards behind.

Matt stood up, but was nearly knocked over again as Torrin hugged and lifted him with a triumphant yell.

"We won! We won!"

Captain Nick was there, shaking Matt by the shoulders. "Well, done! I knew you would make an excellent raider. The *Lady Gemma* wins again!"

The celebration onboard lasted for more the ten minutes until finally, Nick breathlessly declared, "Let's bring her in, mates!"

As they pulled up to the dock, the crew of the *Lady Gemma* was greeted by a sea of cheering people. Matt stood behind Torrin's broad back, his face burning in embarrassment. The rest of the crew bowed and waved to the crowd.

All that Matt could think about was that soon Sam would be free.

When he reached the dock, Hal shook his hand, Emmon pushed him playfully, and Galen gave him a broad grin and a pat on the back. Arden threw her arms around his neck.

"Like I said," she said happily. "You're a natural at finding trouble!"

CHAPTER NINETEEN

Malik paced back and forth along the rock outcropping, stopping to face the shadow before him. His spy's message was clear. While things were still progressing as planned, the boy was now in Aresburg. But Malik knew better than to think that the boy knew what he was doing – he had succeeded so far on nothing more than luck. It would not last, not against the power that Malik wielded.

And even if by some stroke of luck the boy did manage to uncover the Wind Stone, his triumph would be short lived. He would revel in what he thought was a victory, but it would be brief. Soon the boy would have to reckon with the force of Malik's power, and the Stones of the Elements would be stripped away from him. The Stones power would belong to the Commander of Shadows once more.

"My lord!"

Kerwin climbed up the slope behind the Commander, looking up at him nervously. Kerwin was becoming a nuisance, but Malik knew that at least for now he needed him. There would come a time when his dependence on Kerwin would end. When the Stones were his again.

"The captain is ready to move again, my lord," Kerwin told him, bowing deeply.

"Very well, Kerwin," the Commander replied. "Give the order. I will be down momentarily."

"Yes, my lord."

Malik waited until Kerwin had walked away before he turned to face the shadow again. "Tell your sender that everything must be in place. Do not disappoint me."

He waved his hand in front of the shadow and it shot back up into the air, disappearing into the night. The Commander of Shadows started to leave, but staggered. This journey was weakening him. He needed to have Vivona make another batch of potion. Soon, he would no longer need her, either. Soon, he would be in control of Mundaria.

* * *

Matt and Arden stood behind Galen as he knocked on the door of the storehouse where Samsire was being kept. Matt clutched the bag of coins that he had been given after the boat race. He was barely able to contain his excitement at seeing Sam free again.

Baxter opened the door, surprised at their appearance. At first he did not seem to recognize them, but then he pulled the door open and gestured for them to come in.

"I didn't think you would show," he muttered as they stepped inside.

"Well, here we are," Galen said. "And we have your gold."

The man's eyes lit up. "You have it? Let's see it, then."

Matt held out the bag of coins. Galen took it from Matt before Baxter could and he reached inside, pulling out a handful of coins. Galen flipped one in the air and Baxter caught it greedily, running his fingers over it to make sure that it was real.

"One hundred of them," Galen said. "It's all yours when you release the creature."

"Give it to me now and the creature's yours."

"That's not our deal," Galen countered, pulling the bag back. "Creature first and then you get your money. Otherwise you get nothing."

Baxter's eyes followed the bag longingly. His face grew flushed, and he seemed to forget himself for a moment.

"I-I don't have that kind of authority."

Galen's face hardened. "What do you mean?"

Baxter turned even redder. "The city is in charge of the beast. I'm just supposed to keep it alive until they decide what to do with it."

Anger surged through Matt as he realized what Baxter meant. "You can't release Sam, but you were going to take the money anyway?"

Baxter took a step back, holding out his palms. "Look, I...I was going to try to figure something out."

"You're a crook," Galen accused. "Do you have any idea how important this is? We tried to be accommodating. But you lied to us, and you tried to steal from us."

Matt stepped forward, anger boiling inside of him, but Arden was suddenly pulling him toward the door.

"Um, Matt? You might want to step back."

Matt heard a strange tone in her voice and turned to look at her. She was pointing over his shoulder toward Sam, and Matt realized that Sam's legs were free of the ropes and he was standing upright.

"I think he's about to make a break for it," Arden whispered with a grin

They retreated to the door as Sam began to pump his wings. And then his mighty wings lifted him to the roof.

"See you soon, Matt!" Sam bellowed joyfully as he broke through the roof.

Matt laughed in amazement as wooden planks rained down. Sam flapped in the air above them for a moment and gave Matt a toothy grin before flying over the city.

"Did you untie him?" Matt whispered to Arden as he helped her to her feet.

She nodded and held up her knife, her eyes gleaming.

"The beast!" Baxter suddenly yelled and then whimpered pathetically.

Galen looked up at the ceiling, grinning. "You'll have a nice time explaining this, I'm sure. You should have taken the deal."

Baxter just whimpered again. Matt's heart soared with happiness, but he felt a pang of pity for the man. He might be a crook, but he didn't deserve to suffer the backlash from Sam's escape. Sighing, Matt tossed the bag of coins on the floor beside Baxter.

"For repairs. But try a little honesty next time."

The guards outside were staring up at the sky and did not even notice them as they passed.

"Thanks for that, Arden," Matt said as they walked.

Arden grinned. "Sam told me he'll meet us in the mountains tomorrow."

"The mountains?"

"That's where everything seems to be happening, don't you think?" Arden replied.

"I agree," Galen said. "Ellyn has been disappearing into the mountains for years, and we may be able to learn more there than she's able to tell us yet. Let's head over to Catherine's, Emmon and Hal are meeting us there."

"Come in," Catherine said with a smile when they knocked on her door a few minutes later.

"I have an idea, Cat. May I have just a few more minutes with your mother?" Galen said.

They all filed into the house and sat around the table while Galen disappeared into the back room. Murph jumped from lap to lap, until Emmon placed a hand on him, and then he chirruped loudly and immediately fell asleep. Within minutes, Galen reentered the room, grinning broadly. They watched him as he pulled back a chair and sat down.

"Well, come on, Galen," Arden said. "We all know you're dying to tell us what you found out."

Galen's grin grew wider and he nodded. "It is rather exciting." He turned to Matt. "Unfortunately, I haven't learned anything about your parents, but I did learn something that is equally important."

Matt nodded, trying not to show his disappointment.

"Well," Galen continued. "Ellyn has constantly said that 'it had found her' and 'it burned her.'"

"Burned her?" Matt said, his hand automatically reaching for the pouch that held the Fire Stone. "There's not a mark on her, is there?"

"No, there isn't. But then she said something interesting. The 'it' had learned about 'the boy.' That's you, Matt. And she kept referring to whatever had found her as 'it,' meaning it was some sort of creature."

"A creature? Why would a creature go after Ellyn?" Arden asked.

"Because of Matt. I think it knew that she had encountered Matt. And the burning would be…"

"An Aguran," Matt finished hollowly.

Galen nodded. "We know from experience that the Aguran's touch causes a very painful burning sensation in its victim – it likely found Ellyn after we left Borden. Remember how Rock Thompson was able to trail us to Oberdine. We are leaving magical traces behind. I believe that Malik gave that Aguran the power to find anyone who had been in contact with you, Matt by tracking your magical traces."

A chill snaked down Matt's spine. If Galen was right, then anyone who had touched Matt could be tracked.

"There's more," Galen continued. "The important part. Ellyn seemed most upset about something that the Aguran discovered. She kept mentioning her 'secret.' I haven't been able to make any sense of it, but just now she said 'secret hideaway.'"

"What's the secret hideaway?" Matt asked.

All eyes went to Catherine. She hesitated for a moment, her brow furrowed.

"I'm not sure," she said at last. "But it's possible that it's in the mountains. She went there frequently. She would disappear for days and then return unharmed and very cheerful."

"The mountains," Galen said triumphantly. "Exactly. That's where Sam wants to meet us. I think he found something there and that's why he came looking for us. I think that something is in those mountains, but I don't think that they are as dangerous as people think.

"Darrick Wanderer went into the mountains and came out alive, just like Ellyn has always done. They say he went into the mountains to prove that he could come out again since so many people were disappearing. He got hopelessly lost, but he managed to find his way out. He also said that there was something strange about the mountains. Something magical."

Everyone was silent for a moment, but Galen's words made Matt's thoughts race.

"We leave tomorrow morning."

"But you just said that even Darrick got hopelessly lost," Hal muttered.

"Yes, but we have a goal. The mind can overcome magic, if it knows what to look out for," Galen answered.

"I will care for your horses while you are away. It is too dangerous for them," Catherine said as she gathered the empty mugs.

"Thank you, Cat. Thank you for everything," Galen told her quietly, taking her hand.

"Be careful in those mountains," she said softly. "They are unpredictable and treacherous. I will be here when you come back."

Galen smile and turned to leave, but Catherine pulled him back and kissed him on his scarred cheek. Matt, Emmon, Arden, and Hal exchanged glances.

After Catherine pulled the door closed, Galen turned to the others.

"Let's go," he said, his face slightly pink as he cleared his throat.

CHAPTER TWENTY

All Matt could think of that night while he was laying in bed was Samsire flying free somewhere beyond the city. He could hardly wait to speak with him again. His thoughts wandered to the past journeys they had made together and he wondered what mystery awaited them this time.

The air was cold the next morning as they began their trek to the mountains, but the sun was shining brightly. The ground was still wet from a recent rain, and without horses, their boots quickly became heavy with mud.

Galen was in a jovial mood as he shared stories about Darrick the Wanderer. Murph hoped from one person's shoulder to the next, eventually settling down to sleep around Arden's neck. Matt kept scanning the sky for signs of Sam, but he knew they were still too close to the city for Sam to appear.

"We'll probably reach the foot of the mountains by nightfall," Galen mused. "Hopefully, Sam will-"

There was a sudden rustle in the grass and Galen stopped. Matt looked around to locate the source of the noise. Galen reached for his sword. A terrifying, ear-shattering shriek tore through the air behind them.

"Garans!" Hal yelled.

Matt whirled around, drawing Doubtslayer. Two dozen garans bounded toward them. Their long claws and sharp teeth flashed cruelly. An arrow whistled from Emmon's bow and embedded itself into a garan's side. The garans charged them.

Matt yelled and swung his sword as a twisted body leapt at him. He slashed and whirled around as it landed and turned around to attack again. Another garan hit him in the shoulder, forcing him to the ground. It stood on top of him, snarling viciously. It slashed at his chest with its deadly claws but Matt rolled away from it and pushed off the ground.

Magic coursed through him and shocks of energy jolted the garan backward. It crumpled, moaning piteously, but the first garan sank its teeth into Matt's ankle. He yelled out in pain, falling to the ground. The garan let go and then it lunged for Matt's neck. There wasn't time to create a shield. An arrow whistled past Matt's ear and the garan fell in a heap. Emmon was firing arrows continuously, hitting every garan he aimed at.

Matt quickly surveyed the situation to see where he was needed. Hal was fighting two garans. Arden yanked one of her long, dagger-like knives out of the side of another, her face pale but determined. Galen was facing four garans, all dancing grotesquely around him until he was surrounded. Before Matt could help him, Emmon hit two of them with arrows, and Galen struck one down.

Galen tried to rotate his sword to the remaining creature, but the garan, the largest Matt had ever seen, raked its long, sharp claws down Galen's back, cutting him deeply. He wavered unsteadily for a moment, his face contorted in pain, but his sword found its mark. Only a handful of garans remained. They turned to flee, but as they ran, Emmon's arrows found all but two of the retreating beasts.

Galen fell to his knees.

"Galen!" Matt ran to his side.

"S'okay," Galen slurred, but he slumped forward.

Matt caught him and then gently lowered him to the ground. Blood was already soaking through the back of his shirt.

"Heal him quickly, Matt," Emmon urged.

Matt reached for the pouch around his neck and gripped the Water Stone as he placed his right hand on Galen's back. He shut his eyes and focused on the power he held in the palm of his left hand. He reached out with his own magic and plunged into the cool, gentle magic of the Water Stone. He opened his eyes and concentrated on the deep slashes on Galen's back.

Tiny droplets of water fell from his fingertips and gathered in pools over the gashes. The pools seemed to melt into Galen's skin, and almost imperceptibly, the gashes began to close until only faint scars remained.

Matt withdrew his hand and sighed, relieved. "There. Is everyone else all right?"

He examined his friends and healed their superficial wounds. Murph climbed into Arden's lap. He was bright white and trembling, but unhurt. They all sat in silence for several minutes.

Matt felt an unease growing inside of him. Galen had always been resilient. He had fought Rock Thompson through wounds that had been much worse, and then he had responded quickly to healing, waking soon afterward even though he had been near death.

Matt helped Emmon, Arden, and Hal drag a cloak underneath Galen's limp form. They each took up a corner and walked as quickly as they could back into town. When they reached the archway that led into the city, Emmon and Hal, as the tallest, draped Galen's arms over their shoulders. Galen dangled limply between them and his boots dragged against the stone, but few people gave them a glance.

"Come in," Catherine said urgently, when she opened her door.

Matt helped Hal carry Galen through the door and Catherine quickly shut the door behind them.

"Put him in the back room."

They laid him on the bed in the tiny back room. Galen moaned quietly, but did not wake.

"What happened?" Catherine demanded as she followed them in.

"Garans," Matt answered numbly. "They attacked us on the plains. One of them got Galen on the back. I healed him, but he never woke…I've never seen Galen like this."

Catherine pursed her lips. "Can you think of anything that could have weakened him?"

Before Matt could answer, Arden spoke, her voice scarcely a whisper.

"Rock Thompson." She paused for a moment. "When Galen battled Rock in Oberdine, he should have died. There was no way he could have survived those wounds, but Matt healed him and he lived. The dwarves in Oberdine told us that anything healed by magic would be weak for a time, that it takes the same amount of time to regain strength as it would if the person had healed without magic."

Catherine nodded, looking very worried. "If he was indeed about to die, he would still be very weak. He may not have realized it, but once he was injured again, it became worse than an ordinary wound. I will do my best to help him."

Matt suddenly remembered how tired Galen had seemed after the attack by the council's men on the way to Aresbrg and again after using magic to stop Hal's fight. They sat around the table near the fire, speaking little while they waited anxiously for Catherine to emerge.

"I did what I could for him, but it is up to him, now," she said quietly when she finally joined them. "You can stay here if you'd like."

They nodded gratefully. Hal dropped off to sleep first, followed by Emmon and Arden. Eventually, Matt laid his head on the table, too, unable to fight the fatigue any longer.

* * *

"Leave me," Chief Golson ordered. "I'm tired of your frivolous nagging."

Natalia clenched her fists angrily at her father's ignorant refusal to face the facts.

"Father! How can you say such a thing?"

"I'm afraid, Natalia, that you are creating a problem from nothing. This silly nonsense about the Commander of Shadows must stop."

"Well, you're right about one thing," she said scornfully. "You are afraid. Afraid to face the truth! Don't you remember when Hightop invaded Gremonte, Father? Don't you remember what it did to the city? That was Malik's work and you know it!"

"I think that you have been spending too much time with those outsiders, Natalia. They have made you insolent and delusional!"

"They also saved our entire city from a plague just weeks ago! And they are my friends. I trust them, and I have seen what the Malik can do. Please listen to me, Father!"

"You are not going anywhere, Natalia. It's too dangerous out there. You saw that horrible garan creature that was in the tunnel before it ran away. Those are the kinds of hazards that are up there. Gremonte is the safest place for you. Now, please, I have things to take care of."

Natalia glared at her father and turned on her heel. The guards pulled open the doors and she walked into the stagnant underground air of Gremonte. For weeks she had been begging her father to let her go and join the others on the surface - in the fresh air. She knew she could do little to help them, but she missed their company.

Sighing, she turned down a street and headed toward the library. There, she knew, her last companion remained, Alem. Every evening they would sit on the balcony of the library and she would listen to his stories in an attempt to quell the boredom.

She walked glumly up the stairs of the library and sat down next to the little dwarf, who was waiting for her.

"Did your father refuse again?" he asked patiently.

"Of course. I didn't expect him to agree to let me go. But I had to try."

"Well, then, it looks like you're stuck with me." Alem smiled and patted her hand. "What story would you like to hear?"

"Anything," Natalia replied dully.

"Have I told you the story of Dorn's escape from Southwood Forest?"

Natalia sighed. "Yes. Twice already."

"Oh," Alem said, a frown growing on his small, round face. "What haven't I told you, then?"

"I don't know," Natalia said in exasperation.

She brushed her hair off her face and stared up at the skylight in the roof of the library to stare at one of the few patches of sky visible in the underground city.

"Where do you suppose Emmon, Arden, and Matt are now, Alem?" she said wistfully.

"Well," the dwarf said, rubbing his beard. "I believe a few weeks ago your father's soldiers reported that they were in Borden."

"Two days ago he told me they were in Karespurn, but that can't be right. Matt was trying to get away from Karespurn," Natalia argued.

"Ah, yes, well I'm sure they're safe."

He fell silent, but Natalia continued to stare up at the sky. The stars seemed so far away, but they twinkled encouragingly. She thought of the days that she had spent with her friends.

"I miss the surface, Alem," she muttered, struggling to keep the bitterness from her voice. "Everything is so alive there, not like this dark cave we live in. There are trees and grass and wind and…life."

Alem sighed, but remained silent, letting her vent her frustrations to him. Natalia glanced at him and saw that his eyes were clouded.

"I remember when I was a young dwarf," he finally said. "I had just recovered from the great sickness, and I begged for stories of Dorn. I was tired of sitting around. I wanted adventure. I waited and waited for something amazing to happen to me like in those stories in my books. But nothing happened."

He was quiet, lost in memory.

"Well, what did you do?" Natalia encouraged.

He smiled impishly. "Instead of waiting for adventure to find me, I decided to go searching for it. That's the only way you'll ever find it."

CHAPTER TWENTY-ONE

Matt opened his eyes and lifted his head from the table, looking around blearily. Catherine was standing beside him with her hand on his shoulder.

"What is it? Is Galen all right?" he said, sitting upright.

He was still in the hard chair that he had occupied the previous night. The sun was shining weakly through the window, but it was still early. Hal and Emmon were still asleep at the table but beginning to stir. Arden was awake, a sleepy Murph on her shoulder.

"He is fine. He is awake, Matt," Catherine said, smiling slightly.

"Is the fever gone?" Arden asked her hopefully.

"Mostly. But he is still very weak. He is asking for all of you."

They followed Catherine into the small backroom. The light was dim but Galen's face was visibly pale. His eyes were closed, but his breathing was easy. As Matt walked over to his bedside, his eyes opened and a crooked smile grew on his face.

"You all look like you're going to a funeral," he said.

"And you look like you're fit to battle all of Marlope," Matt retorted. "How are you feeling?"

"Fabulous," he said, grinning again. "I've seen worse."

"Well, don't even think about getting up and climbing those mountains," Catherine scolded him. "You shouldn't overexert yourself."

"We'll wait for you, Galen," Emmon said supportively

"No." Galen spoke emphatically. "I thought I was stronger. But I was wrong. After every fight we've been in during the past few weeks I've felt the weakness, but I pushed it away. Now it has stopped me, but I will not let it stop you. There is far too much at stake. Plus, there's something else that I've decided I must do."

To everyone's surprise, he turned to Hal. "Hal, what do you think about the Aresburg guard?"

"The...the guard? It's one of the worst I've seen, I guess. They've only been trained to fight off ship thieves, and even that training is pretty poor. The sailors are better fighters than the guard."

"My thoughts exactly. Something needs to be done about it. I think those garans we're a scout party, and I think there are more garans on the way. Many more. And if they attack, Aresburg needs to know how to defend itself."

"So, you're going to train the entire Aresburg guard?" Matt asked skeptically.

"We must. This is no longer a private war between you and Malik, Matt," Galen said quietly, his eyes very serious. "The world can no longer remain ignorant of Malik's evil. Soon it will affect everyone in Mundaria if we don't stop it everywhere. Those garans were right outside of Aresburg's walls. This city needs to be able to defend itself. I have to try to train these soldiers. I have a feeling they will be eager to learn."

"I will help you," Hal said suddenly.

Everyone turned to look at him and he reddened.

"That's right. I said I'll stay and help."

Matt glanced at Galen, but he could not read his face.

"Listen, Galen," Hal said. "You told me that it was time I showed some responsibility. You were right, and that's what I'm going to do."

Matt exchanged a bewildered look with Emmon and Arden. Hal had never been this dependable.

"Okay. You can help. But understand that we don't know how much time we have, so it will be hard work."

"I can handle it," Hal assured him.

"Good," Galen said and then turned to Matt. "You have to go to the mountains. There is something there that is very important to Malik, possibly the Wind Stone. If so, we must do everything we can to keep him from getting it."

"I'll go, Galen," Matt said.

"I'll go, too," Emmon added.

"Me, too," Arden said.

Galen smiled. "Thank you. Find Samsire, he will know what to do. Camp in places where you can see everything around you and don't travel after the sun sets. Remember what we've learned about those mountains. They're more treacherous than most."

"We'll be fine, Galen," Matt said with a smile. "Try to take care of yourself. Stay out of trouble."

"I don't know. You haven't been a very good role model for me," Galen grinned, and then his face became serious. "Be careful, Matt."

With a final goodbye, Matt, Emmon, and Arden, with Murph on her shoulder, filed out the door. They walked somberly through the city.

"Okay, let's try this again," Emmon said. "Let's hope we can get a little further down the road this time."

"No garans would be nice," Matt agreed.

As they trekked toward the mountains, Matt glanced at his companions, thinking about their first journey together. He smiled as he remembered how they had happened upon him and Sam in the Glade Forest outside of Sunfield. It was the start of a very long trek, but Emmon and Arden had never voluntarily his side. They were steadfast and loyal. And they had a knack for helping him find as much trouble as possible.

"What are you smirking about, Matt?" Arden asked him.

"Do you remember when you and Emmon found Sam and me in the forest?" he said. "Your scream scared every bird in the forest."

"Hey!" she exclaimed indignantly. "It's not every day you see a giant, feathered beast. Who can talk, no less."

"Yeah, and I broke Matt's nose. Who knew that we would end up friends," Emmon said with a smile.

By nightfall, Matt's legs ached and weariness clung to his bones. They made camp at the foot of the mountains and lit a small fire.

"Do you think Galen's right?" Emmon said suddenly. "Do you think there really are more garans on the way?"

"Probably," Arden said. "I don't think we were supposed to find those garans."

"I think they found us," Matt countered.

"Either way, Malik's been very quiet lately, hasn't he? He's either planning something big," Arden speculated. "Or he finally keeled over and died... which is highly unlikely."

"What strange thing do you think is in these mountains?"

"All I can say is I hope it's not another Oberdine," she said, sticking out her tongue. "I'd rather not go underground again."

Matt glanced up at the stone giants before them, wondering what mystery they held. Somewhere, Samsire was up there waiting for him.

They started early the following morning. Matt led the way up the rolling hills that quickly turned into steep, rocky slopes covered in pine trees and craggy and narrow ravines that they had to go around. Finally, they found a less treacherous slope and slowly ascended the mountainside. The air was becoming considerably colder. Matt stopped at the top of a steep face, breathing hard.

"Do you see anything yet?" he gasped as Emmon and Arden joined him.

"Nothing but a perfect place to camp," Emmon said, pointing to their left.

A small alcove was hollowed out of the hard stone, forming a perfect protective ledge that overlooked a small ravine. Without a word, they made their way to the spot, confident that it met Galen's orders. Matt pulled out his package of food and with numb fingers, passed out bread and hard cheese.

"What do you think Galen-" Matt started to say but was cut short by a gasp from Emmon who had stood up abruptly.

"Did you see that?" he said.

"See what?" Matt asked, standing up next to him.

"On the other side of the ravine. There was…something over there. I saw something move."

"An animal of some kind?" Matt said.

"It looked like a horse."

"A horse? In these mountains?" Arden said skeptically. "No one from Aresburg would dare bring a horse up here, and a horse wouldn't just be roaming around on its own."

Emmon was not convinced. "It was white. The whitest horse I've ever seen."

Matt looked at his friend's bewildered face and put his hand on his shoulder. "Come on. Let's have something to eat and we'll keep an eye out."

Emmon agreed, but he remained watchful. Eventually, Arden tucked Murph into her pack, curled up on her bedroll, and fell asleep. Matt stayed awake with Emmon.

"We have to get to the other side of that ravine, Matt," Emmon said. "I think there's something important over there."

"We'll try. I'm just not sure if that is the direction we should be heading."

"I know it is," Emmon said simply. "I'll take first watch."

Matt drifted off into an uneasy sleep, and soon Emmon was shaking him for the second watch. Matt positioned his back against the wall, shivering in the folds of his cloak. The moon was nearly full and cast an unnatural glow on everything.

Murph crawled out of Arden's pack, and after a moment of deliberation, climbed up onto Matt's shoulder. The morphcat stared dutifully into the wilderness around them. Matt smiled and scratched the creature's head. He pulled out Sam's feather, but the normally glowing blue and green strands were dull and lackluster again, just like they had been when Matt and Sam were many miles apart. Maybe the magic of the mountains was interfering with Sam's magic. Or maybe it was something else.

Murph suddenly leapt off of Matt's shoulder, hissing as his fur turned jet black. Matt's heart hammered. He stood up slowly, looking around for whatever was making Murph so nervous. The trees were only shadows in the darkness and he could not make out any movement. But an unnatural chill had fallen over everything. Matt took a step out of the alcove and his heart skipped a beat.

A sinister, dark cloud of thick mist moved through the air in front of the rocky outcropping. Matt reflexively took a step back as several tendrils of mist twisted like snakes toward the alcove where they had made camp.

"Emmon, Arden, get up!" Matt shouted.

CHAPTER TWENTY-TWO

Matt flung his pack onto his shoulders as the other two leapt to their feet and looked around in a panic. The arm of mist was already bending around the side of their camp. They snatched up their things and stumbled forward.

"This way! Hurry!" Matt exclaimed.

They scrambled along the edge of the ravine, desperately searching for a way down. They found an area with less foliage and skidded and tripped down the side of the ravine. The arm of dark mist followed them like one of Malik's spectral shadows. They ran as fast as they could with Murph scampering alongside.

"Over there!" Arden gasped, pointing to a more gradual slope up the opposite side of the ravine.

They sprinted up the slope, breathing heavily as they reached the top. Matt glanced back at the strange, dark fog. The tendrils were still moving toward them. His heart thumped wildly against his ribs.

Without knowing why, Matt was more terrified than he had ever been. He knew instinctively that the mist was evil and deadly, and that they could not defend themselves against it. Their only hope was to outrun it.

They ran as fast as they could into the dense maze of trees. Matt did not look back, but he knew it was still there. Then, a roaring sound reached his ears.

"A river," Matt exclaimed.

They hurried toward it, but it was too deep and too fast to cross.

"We'll be swept away!" Emmon yelled above the thunder of the river. "We have to find a better place to cross!"

Matt looked back. The mist was still seeping through the trees, but they had a little time. They ran along the river bank searching for shallower, slower water. Emmon grabbed a long, fallen branch and stopped to test the depth of the river. The stick sank.

"What about there?" Arden said suddenly, pointing ahead of them.

A fallen tree stretched across the river, forming a bridge from one bank to the other.

"Do you think it'll hold?" Matt said.

Emmon pushed up and down on their end of the tree, testing its strength. "It looks like its rotting, but I don't think we have a choice."

Matt glanced back. The mist was only a dozen yards away. They did not have time to hesitate.

"Let's go!"

Murph bounded along it first and then Emmon. Matt pushed Arden on before him and then followed. He carefully shuffled his feet along the slippery log, trying to ignoring the rushing of the water beneath him and the mist reaching out behind him. Emmon was near the opposite bank when Matt heard the groaning.

"Move!" he shouted.

But the log was already splintering. There was an earsplitting crack, a scream, and the log gave way beneath their feet. He plummeted through the air, his body slicing through the freezing water.

The rushing water blinded him. His lungs felt like they had turned to ice. He struggled madly to get to the surface, but the rapids would not release him. The current dragged him further and further down the river. He fought desperately to reach the surface.

The rapids roared in his ears as he felt air on his face. He caught a glimpse of Emmon. Matt struggled to keep his head above water, but was pulled under again and his body scraped across the rocks. Water filled his mouth, but he pushed downward against the water until he was back on the surface.

Emmon was trying to tell him something, panic on his face.

"Wate…all," he garbled through a mouthful of water.

Matt fought against the rapids, rolling around in the churning water. His head broke the surface again and he caught sight of the river ahead of them. The water suddenly disappeared. A waterfall. That was what Emmon was trying to tell him.

He tried to push against the water, tried to steer himself to the bank, but the current was too strong. He slammed into more rocks, but he could not grab onto anything. He was carried closer and closer to the waterfall.

He seemed to fall for an eternity.

When he finally hit the water pain rippled through his body. He sank to the bottom. He was no longer buffeted by the fast-moving water, but he did not have the strength to fight to the surface so far above him. His lungs were screaming at him.

Without thinking, he reached for the pouch around his neck and let his magic meld with the magic of the Stones. He felt power and strength surge through him. He pushed hard against the bottom and shot to the surface, gasping for air as he broke through the water. A gentle current carried him downstream. He paddled awkwardly, trying to stay afloat. Emmon swam toward him, his golden hair plastered to his forehead.

"Where's Arden?" he gasped.

Matt looked around wildly. He finally spotted her lying along the shore near the base of the waterfall. Emmon swam toward her as Matt pushed himself toward shallower waters and then waded quickly to where Emmon had pulled Arden onto the bank.

"Arden?" Matt said urgently.

She did not respond. Matt grabbed her limp hand.

"Is she breathing?"

"I don't know. I don't think so," Emmon cried frantically. "She must have breathed in water."

Matt stared at Arden's pale face. The coldness around him seemed to intensify. He thought of all the days they had spent together. Her sharp wit, her happy smile, her courage and determination, her uncanny ability to see understand what he was feeling. He had to do something.

His mind raced. She had breathed in water. Water. He could do something about water.

Emmon stared at him as he groped for the pouch. Thankfully it was still there. His frozen fingers fumbled to open it and he withdrew the Water Stone. The blue-green stone seemed to join soothingly with his palm. He lifted his other hand, shaking violently, and held it above Arden, unsure of what he should do.

He shut his eyes, releasing himself to the power of the Water Stone. He thought of the water that was pooling in her lungs. He put his hand on her throat and reached out with the magic that rippled through his body, imagining the water escaping from her mouth.

Emmon gasped and Matt opened his eyes. Large droplets of water began to form on her lips and then float into the air, gathering into a sphere of water over the hand that held the Water Stone. Matt and Emmon watched, transfixed.

Finally, the water stopped forming on her mouth. Matt let the orb of water fall to the ground and he held his breath, but she did not move. Her hair was lying chaotically around her face and her lips were blue.

Matt stared at her desperately, his rapidly beating heart sinking. He realized how much she meant to him. Murph appeared suddenly and curled up beside her, whimpering softly.

Suddenly, a shudder racked Arden's body. She took a gasping breath and her eyes fluttered open. Emmon yelped happily and Matt let out a strangled sigh. She smiled faintly.

"I guess that log didn't hold," she whispered, lifting a weak hand and wiping her hair off her face.

"Don't do that again," Matt said in an emotional voice. "You scared me out of my skin."

"I'll try not to," she said, eyeing the stone in Matt's hand. "Help me up?"

Matt and Emmon pulled her to her feet and she stood shakily for a moment. Emmon grabbed her in his arms and hugged her happily. Matt's stomach twisted into a knot. Arden turned to him and hugged him. They both shivered in the cold. He held her for a moment and then released her reluctantly. Murph bounced happily at their feet.

"Well, it looks like we got away from that mist," Arden said.

Matt and Emmon nodded. They stood uncertainly for a moment before searching through their packs to find salvageable goods. Nearly all their food was ruined, and the rest of their belongings were soaked through. As Matt stuffed his things back into his pack he heard Arden trembling behind him.

"Here," he said taking her hand in his.

He focused on the warm Fire Stone against his chest and urged it to spread. It warmed his body and radiated from his hands. He took her other hand and within minutes she had stopped shivering. She smiled at him gratefully.

"We might as well walk a bit," Arden suggested, her face still very pale. "Just in case whatever that thing was, comes back."

Arden was unsteady on her feet, and Matt walked behind her, watching her closely as they walked along the riverbank. He couldn't stop thinking about how afraid he had been. His gaze settled on Emmon. Emmon and Arden had always been close and Emmon tried to protect her from every threat, but how far his feelings for her went, Matt did not know.

The traveling grew increasingly tiresome and soon they could go no further. Arden fell to her knees on the sandy bank. Matt and Emmon followed suit and within minutes they were all asleep on the shore of the river.

CHAPTER TWENTY-THREE

"The troops are assembled, sir!"

Galen smiled and nodded. "Thank you, sergeant."

The soldier scurried away, leaving Galen to survey the soldiers who stood in neat rows of twenty across the plains directly outside of Aresburg. It had been several days since Matt, Emmon, and Arden had left for the mountains. Galen felt a little stronger every day, and he and Hal had been working with the Aresburg's army. The day Matt left, Galen had convinced Catherine that he was well enough to speak to the head of the guard, Idris, and tell him what needed to be done.

The captain of the guard had laughed at first at Galen's description of the garans, but after Galen showed him the scars on his back, Idris had consented to listen. Galen told him of Malik, though he avoided mention of Matt, and warned of an impending attack. Idris remembered Galen's performance in halting Hal's street fight. And just like that, the commander gave Galen full control over training the guard.

"What should we do now?" Hal asked, standing beside Galen.

Galen examined the guards. Two groups, each with twenty rows of twenty men. It was only a small portion of the complete guard, but Galen had been working with different groups at different times during the day. Although they had only been training for a few days, Galen had noticed a significant change in the soldiers' skills and their confidence. They held their swords more firmly in their hands and they moved with more assurance.

"Let's run through a quick attack sequence in pairs," Galen told his younger companion. "You help the left half. I'll take the right."

Hal nodded dutifully. The men had been surprisingly responsive to Galen's orders, although he was years younger than many of them. Hal had been an able assistant, obedient and respectful to Galen, and helpful to the men. Even Galen was forced to admit that Hal was a very skilled fighter and a good teacher.

As Hal strode toward the left half of the troops, Galen stepped forward to address his group. "Break up into pairs. I want you to practice that swift uppercut sequence that I showed you yesterday. Go to."

The soldiers obediently split up into pairs. Galen walked through the groups, watching as one side systematically executed a series of superficial side strikes before quickly swinging their sword into a swift uppercut. The other soldier would block each stroke, but attempt no attack or interference in the sequence. They all seemed to remember the moves fairly well, pleasing Galen with their progress.

He was passing a particularly speedy pair of soldiers when he heard the clattering of swords and an angry yell.

"What are you doing?" a soldier yelled.

Galen whirled around and saw that one of the soliders had dropped his sword, and his face was red with anger.

"What's going on here?" Galen demanded.

The first soldier lowered his sword looking slightly confused, but the one who had dropped his sword raised an accusing finger.

"He's not obeying orders, sir. He nearly skewered me at the end of his sequence."

"I'm sorry, sir," the first man said immediately. "I was trying to follow the sequence, but I just…"

"Reacted," Galen finished, allowing a smile to creep onto his lips. "There is nothing to apologize for about that."

The soldier, expecting punishment, looked at Galen in surprise. His companion's mouth dropped open in outrage.

"What your name?" Galen asked the first soldier.

"Sanford, sir."

Galen nodded. "Hal," he called. "Bring your troops over here. I want to give a little demonstration."

Hal quickly gathered his soldiers and they formed a circle around Galen.

"We've been doing a lot of work with sequences to get you all used to using a sword properly," Galen began. "But there is more to being a good swordsman than knowing moves. You have to know how to apply them to different situations. So, Sanford, here, has volunteered to spar with me so I can show you what I mean."

Sanford paled visibly. He opened his mouth to protest but no words came out.

"Good," Galen said with a smile. "Let's begin, then."

The circle of soldiers backed up, giving Galen and Sanford a sizable area in which to spar. Sanford gripped his sword tightly as Galen drew Lightningstrike from his scabbard. He looked at the sword fondly as it had saved him from many threats. Before approaching the terrified Sanford, Galen rotated his shoulders, testing his back. He no longer felt any pain. Matt had done an excellent job of healing him.

Galen let Lightningstrike hang loosely in his hand as he approached Sanford. He turned to Hal, who stood at the edge of the circle, and nodded for him to start the demonstration. So much had happened since he had done the same for Hal and Matt and the others in the training room in Hightop's palace.

"Ready, begin!" Hal called.

Galen merely raised his sword and then he waited for Sanford to make the first move. Sanford hesitated, unsure if he should be intimidated or not. But that was how Galen liked it. He liked to keep his opponents guessing as much as possible.

Finally, Sanford lifted his sword and began to execute the sequence that Galen had taught them. He swung first at Galen's left side. Galen parried easily, but allowed the sequence to continue without interruption. Sanford brought his sword down, but instead of blocking it, Galen quickly sidestepped it and his opponent's sword whistled past his shoulder. Then Galen twisted, and in one fluid motion, knocked the sword out of Sanford's hand, rolled around behind him, grabbed his shoulder, and held Lightningstrike at his throat.

The crowd stared in stunned silence while Sanford hung helplessly in Galen's grasp. Galen released him and flipped up Sanford's dropped sword with a kick of his foot. He caught it in his opposite hand and turned to the group of soldiers.

"You cannot perform a sequence expecting it to go as planned. It is impossible to battle an opponent without him hindering your plans in some fashion. You have to be prepared to *react*. Don't expect a garan or an enemy soldier to wait for you to finish your sequence properly."

He handed the sword back to Sanford. "Now allow me to perform the same sequence this time and when I come in for the swipe, I want you to sidestep as I did."

Sanford mutely took the sword and assumed a ready position.

"Ready, begin!" Hal called once more.

Galen languidly went through the steps of the sequence. As he swiped, Sanford sidestepped to the right then dropped his sword.

"We're not finished yet, Sanford. Fight me. Use your instincts."

Without waiting for a response, Galen swung Lightningstrike. Sanford parried, but did not strike back. Galen hammered him with a series of blows, but purposely left time for Sanford to strike back, an opportunity he never took.

At last, Galen struck Sanford's blade with a fierce uppercut. He held his sword there for a moment, waiting. Sanford's sweaty face broke out into a determined grimace, and he brought his own sword streaking toward Galen's chest. Galen responded by leaping backward and then, as Sanford's sword passed by, he leapt back in, kicking Sanford hard in the chest and sending him sprawling to the ground. Galen returned his sword to his sheath and pulled the exhausted Sanford to his feet.

"Well done, Sanford. Thank you for your help," he said and turned to the soldiers. "That is what I want you all to do. Feel each strike and react to the situation. Don't just follow a set of moves.

Trust your instincts." He turned to Hal. "Why don't you take them for a minute, Hal?"

Hal nodded and turned to address the troops while Galen pushed through the crowd, ignoring the awed expressions of the soldiers. He walked to the archway that led into Aresburg where the head guardsman, Idris, was watching approvingly.

"Where did you learn to fight like that?" Idris asked him as he approached.

Without thinking, Galen ran his fingers over the scar that marred his right cheek, given to him by Rock Thompson when Galen was still a boy. He often had to remind himself that his mortal enemy, whose murderous actions had driven Galen to train so vigorously, was now dead.

"Oh, here and there," Galen answered dismissively.

"Well, you've inspired the soldiers. I've never seen them train so diligently. And that young man, Hal, right? He's very skilled for one so young."

Galen smiled. "He's a natural swordsman. You should see what some of my other young companions can do. You wouldn't believe your eyes."

Idris looked at him skeptically, and Galen made a mental note to have Matt set his cloak on fire and have Emmon pin his tunic to the wall with an arrow.

"Where did you say you were from again?"

Galen hesitated. He did not consider Amaldan a home to return to, but it was the place of his birth.

"Up north," he answered.

"And that's where you learned of this Malik creature?" Idris asked uneasily.

"I have been spying on him for the past five years. It is a shame that most of Mundaria does not know of his evil. I have no doubt that he is planning something and that it is imminent. I must do what I can to make sure that all of Mundaria is prepared."

Idris was quite pale as he whispered, "And those garans?"

Galen placed a hand on his shoulder. "Don't worry. That's why I'm training your troops. If the garans come, we will be ready."

Galen began to walk back toward the soldiers to relieve Hal.

"Oh, Galen?" Idris said.

Galen stopped and turned to look at him.

"They are your troops now."

CHAPTER TWENTY-FOUR

Light penetrated Matt's eyelids, but he did not open them right away. It felt so good to lay here even though his clothes were stiff and cold.

When he finally opened his eyes, blinking against the bright sunlight, enormous golden eyes were staring down at him. Beneath them was a huge hooked beak that looked capable of crushing boulders. The rest of the massive head was covered in fluffy, golden feathers.

"Wha-?" Matt breathed.

The creature standing over him was only slightly smaller than Samsire. Gigantic wings sprouted from its back and its front feet were like the claws of a bird. Fur like golden velvet covered its hind legs, which looked like lion paws. A long tail with a fluffy, brown tuft extended from its hindquarters, and it swished back and forth lazily.

Matt yelled in alarm and Emmon sat upright with a startled grunt. The creature grabbed Matt's foot with its talons, dragged him across the sandy bank, and lifted into the air. Matt's head brushed against the ground as the creature flew higher until Matt was dangling upside down several feet above the ground. The blood rushed to his head and pounded loudly in his ears. The creature hovered there, slowly beating its wings to stay aloft.

"Emmon, do something!" Matt shouted as Emmon scrambled to his feet.

The creature bent its head down and thrust its leg forward until it was staring Matt in the eyes again. Matt stared back, acutely aware of his rapidly beating heart. In the creature's eyes he saw intelligence, wildness, and suspicion.

"Hey, let go of him!" Emmon yelled from below.

To Matt's surprise, the creature turned its head to face Emmon, and its eyes narrowed dangerously. Emmon reached for his bow and gripped it so tightly his knuckles were white. His hand reached for his quiver of arrows.

Then the creature opened its beak and spoke.

"I would stand still if I were you. You're next on the menu."

Matt tried to reach up to free his foot from the creature's grasp, but it shook him reprovingly.

"Didn't I say for all of you to stay still? You're ruining my meal."

"What are you?" Matt whispered disbelievingly.

"Why, I am a griffin, of course, you scrawny, little human," the creature half squawked, half growled. "Now, be quiet. I don't like it when my food talks back to me."

It moved Matt closer to its beak.

"Hey, birdbrain!" Arden yelled, now standing beside Emmon. "Yeah, I'm talking to you."

The griffin glared at her, but merely flapped its giant wings.

"You call yourself a griffin?" Arden continued as Emmon edged behind her, reaching for his quiver. "If I plucked out those puny feathers of yours everyone would see that you're only a big chicken."

The griffin ignored her and moved Matt closer to his beak.

"Stop!" Matt yelled. "We mean no harm!"

"Harm? How many times must I say that you are nothing but a snack?"

In response, an arrow whistled so close to the griffin's head that Matt saw it skim the top of both of its feathered ears.

"Next time it goes through your head," Emmon said, his bowstring already pulled back again.

"You wouldn't want to eat us anyway," Matt added, sensing their advantage. "My alorath friend would tear you to pieces." He managed to reach a hand into his pocket and pulled out Samsire's feather. It was once again shimmering. "See? Proof."

"An alorath, you say?" the griffin said, its voice interested.

"I would be that alorath," a deep voice said.

Matt's heart soared as he craned his neck and saw Samsire standing on the shore. The griffin's grip on Matt's feet weakened and Matt dropped to the ground hard.

The griffin immediately reached out with his claws to grab Matt again, but Matt flung up a magical shield between them. The griffin reared back, but then calmed down in an instant. Matt could have sworn he saw the creature's eyes soften.

"Sam, you know this creature?" Matt asked, looking over at the alorath.

"Yes," Sam replied, lumbering over to Matt. "And he would do well to remember it.

"Should I release?" Emmon said, not relaxing his bowstring which was still aimed at the griffin's head.

"You can put down your bow, elf," the griffin said. "I was never really planning on eating any of you. Throwing you one by one off a cliff, perhaps, but not eating you. You creatures have a terrible flavor."

Emmon glanced at Samsire, who nodded, and Emmon lowered his bow. Matt watched the griffin warily. The creature sat back on its haunches like a docile dog, its tail still swishing back and forth.

"Now, what I would like to know is what are you doing here in my territory?" the griffin said.

"We're here with Sam," Matt answered, his voice cold. "You should let us go."

The griffin exhaled in disgust. "I have every intention of letting you go. What disagreeable creatures you are!"

"Disagreeable?" Matt argued. "You're the one who nearly ate me."

The griffin's eyes flashed dangerously and it raked its talons through the sand.

"I'll ask again. What are you doing here? This is not a welcome place for humans."

"They are here with me, griffin," Samsire growled. "That should be enough."

The griffin clawed at the ground again, his gaze unchanging. Matt glanced at Emmon and Arden, and they nodded. Sam gave him a small nudge. He had to tell the griffin why they were here.

"Do you know of the Commander of Shadows?"

The griffin squawked loudly and flapped his wings violently.

"You dare to speak of that foul spirit in my presence? If you tell me you are spies of his, I will definitely eat you without hesitation."

"Believe me, we're the farthest thing from spies," Matt assured him. "My name is Matt, and I am the One of the Prophecy of the Elements."

CHAPTER TWENTY-FIVE

The griffin squawked again, but this time in humorous disbelief. Matt was now used to this reaction so he focused on the Fire Stone sitting on his chest. He lifted one finger and a flame sparked into existence, hovering above his skin. The griffin's golden eyes stared at it in surprise.

At that moment, Murph bounded from the trees onto the shore. Matt half expected the griffin to snatch up the tiny morphcat. But instead, the griffin straightened up and stared at the little creature almost reverently.

"Morphcat," he murmured. "It is you…Then you found him."

Murph scampered up Matt's arm and settled on his shoulder. He gave a little chirrup for good measure.

The griffin was silent, eyeing Matt warily. Matt waited for him to speak.

Finally the griffin said, "My name is Gusren."

"Gusren? Can we call you Gus?" Arden said.

The griffin glared at her, but said nothing. Samsire let out a low rumbling noise, something akin to a chuckle.

"We're here because we know that there's something that Malik wants here, and we don't want him to find it," Matt asked him. "Will you help us?"

As Matt waited for the creature's response, a screech tore through the air. A familiar hawk swooped down toward them.

"Is that Raumer?" Arden said.

The hawk flapped its wings as it landed on Matt's other shoulder. It took no notice of the griffin, but flapped its wings impatiently until Matt took the small piece of folded parchment from his beak.

He unfolded it. "It's from Lucian."

"What does it say?" Emmon asked.

Matt read the letter out loud, struggling to decipher the hurriedly scribbled writing:

Matt,

I hope this letter finds you well. I apologize for not contacting you sooner, but the council sent me to meet with one of their contacts from Marlope. The contact told me grave news. An immense squadron of garans is moving south, toward Aresburg. I am riding through the mountains north of Aresburg and the garans are not far behind me. This force is too large for the sole goal of capturing you, Matt. The destruction and captivity of Aresburg is imminent if something is not done. Please send Raumer back to me with a response as soon as you can.

-Lucian

Matt stopped reading and looked at Emmon and Arden in alarm.

"Galen was right. There are more garans on their way. The garans we fought was a scout party."

"We have to hurry, then," Emmon said. "We have to warn Galen."

"He already said he would be training the guard," Arden argued. "We can't leave without finding what we're looking for."

Raumer pecked at Matt's head impatiently.

"All right, all right!" Matt said, reaching for the pen and ink he had stowed in his pack.

He quickly scribbled out a reply on the back of Lucian's note:

Lucian,

Emmon, Arden, and I are in the mountains, as well. Galen and Hal are in Aresburg and are already training the troops. We fought a group of garans a few days ago. We are in the mountains trying to find what Malik is searching for, perhaps the Wind Stone. We are with Sam and a griffin, hoping they can both help us in our search. I hope our paths cross soon.

-Matt

He gave the note back to the hawk and Raumer promptly flew off into the sky. Matt turned to his friends.

"We have to find the secret of these mountains as quickly as we can," he said and then turned to Gusren. "You'll help us, won't you?"

"Come on, Gus," Arden pleaded when the griffin remained silent..

"Griffin…," Samsire growled.

"It appears that I must."

"What about Lucian?" Emmon put in. "Do you think he can get past that fog?"

Samsire growled again. "You've seen the fog?"

Matt nodded. "It nearly got us. We tried to cross the river and almost drowned, but we escaped."

Sam and Gusren exchanged a worried glance.

"It's getting closer," Gusren muttered. "Our magical defense of the river will not last long. And with garans coming…"

The griffin trailed off and turned to Matt. "We know all who enter our valley. Your friend is not far away. I will not allow him to lose his way. He will find you."

"We?"

The griffin ignored the question. "The only way I can help you is to fly you deeper into the valley. Though it is humiliating for me to carry anyone, I will help Samsire carry you. I will carry the elves."

Murph jumped over to Arden's shoulder, and Emmon and Arden grabbed their packs and climbed up Gusren's outstretched wing onto his back. Arden smiled nervously at Matt as he climbed onto Samsire's neck.

The griffin kicked off from the ground with his powerful hind legs like he was pouncing on his prey. He pumped his feathered wings and shot through the air. As Samsire rose into the air, Matt laughed happily. Despite the urgency of their journey, it was good to be flying with his friend again, and to at last have a moment together.

"I missed you Sam," Matt called above the wind.

The alorath flapped his wings joyfully and emitted a low, guttural sound like a purring cat. They flew silently for a minute, enjoying each other's presence.

"Sam, what's going on down there?" Matt finally asked.

"There is no alorath colony, Matt," he replied. "I found something else, though. A whole community of magical creatures."

"I'm so sorry there are no aloraths, Sam," Matt said, stroking his feathers. "What kind of creatures did you find? More griffins?"

"Many more than just griffins. It's like nothing you've ever imagined," Samsire said. "Malik has been hunting them for some time, now. He knows that the creatures are a powerful threat to his goal to control Mundaria. Humans have always been afraid of these creatures and for hundreds of years they mistreated them or killed them, until finally, many years ago, when their numbers had dwindled they gathered together in these mountains.

"They hide here in this sanctuary for protection from humans because they are no match for a world united against them. I should warn you, they do not like humans very much."

Matt digested this for a moment. He thought of all of the clues and mysteries they had puzzled over. It all made sense now. The wizard council had found signs of high magical activity in the area. A sanctuary of magical creatures would cause just that.

But if they were so safe in the mountains, why were they suddenly appearing in places like Dirth and Aresburg? What was driving them out?

"Sam, what was that fog?"

Sam did not answer at first. His silence felt chilling and ominous.

"It's Malik's doing, Matt," Samsire finally growled. "It has to be. It's Dark magic. It's devouring the mountains. First the lake was gone. Then the pastures, where the creatures used to feed. Any time a creature has wandered into the fog, or flew over it, they were pulled in. And they never come back out.

"The creatures in the sanctuary are near starving. They can't leave to hunt for fear that the fog will devour them. Their magical protections are dwindling. They've managed to protect the river, so they still have water to drink and fish to eat, but they won't last much longer."

"Malik created the fog?"

"Malik or one of his men. He's trying to draw the creatures away from the sanctuary and separate them so that he can kill them one by one. They're weakened now. They won't stand against an army of garans."

"He just wants them gone? Because he thinks they can stop him?" Matt asked, puzzled by the effort.

"There's something else, Matt. The creatures understood what was happening. They realized that they could not fend off this new threat. And though they have little contact with the outside world they are very aware of the magical world. They knew that the first two Stones of the Elements had been discovered. They knew that the person who wielded them could help them. So they sent one of their own to track you down, Matt."

Sam grinned. "I guess that little morphcat was more than just a snack."

"Murph?" Matt exclaimed. "They sent Murph to find me?"

"Evidently morphcats can track magical pathways."

Matt's mind was reeling. He thought about how Murph had practically jumped on them in the tunnels of Gremonte. Then there was the garan and shadow that had attacked Galen. Malik must have realized what was going on and sent the garan after Murph.

"I don't really understand why Malik is doing this. The creatures just don't seem to be that great of a threat to him."

"Because, Matt, hidden in this very same valley, protected by the magical creatures, is the Wind Stone."

CHAPTER TWENTY-SIX

The Wind Stone was here. The thought sent a thrill through Matt. So that was why Malik was after the creatures, because they were standing in the way of him and the Wind Stone.

Sam angled through the valley, following the curves of the river. The griffin in front of them slowed and began to circle down into a misty forest area below. This mist was different than the insidious darkness that was spreading through the mountains behind them. The griffin landed heavily, and Emmon and Arden nearly bounced off his back. Sam landed beside them, and Matt slid down.

They stood in front a dense grove of pine trees. The mist settled above the top of the trees like a protective ceiling hiding the sanctuary from prying eyes.

Samsire turned to the griffin and jerked his head dismissively. "You go on, griffin. We will be there in a moment."

The griffin glared at the alorath and padded slowly toward the trees. The branches seemed to bend out of his way as he approached, and they returned to their original positions as he disappeared.

"Ignore that cantankerous griffin," Samsire said. "He has been searching the mountains for you ever since I told them you were on your way. So, he is actually very glad to see you, but would never let you know that."

Matt quickly told Emmon and Arden everything that Sam had just told him.

"The Wind Stone is here?" Arden whispered in amazement.

The alorath nodded. "I'm sure that Cosgrove and Pryor chose to hide it here because of the magic that whistles through this valley. There's probably not a safer place in Mundaria."

"Take us in, Sam," Matt said, anxiety growing inside him. "We have to hurry. If the garans are coming, we have to move quickly."

The alorath jerked his large head toward the wall of trees. "The branches only move for those who possess some sort of elemental magic. Hold onto me if you can't pass through, but you should all be able to."

The branches bent away just like they had done when Gusren had entered the grove. It reminded Matt of the entrance into the Heart of Amaldan, the lair of the elves. It seemed that trees served as strong protectors.

As they made their way through the valley, the trees began to thin and the mist seeped into the gaps between the boughs. Matt felt increasingly unwelcome as they drew closer to the mysterious sanctuary. Murph jumped onto Arden's shoulder, bouncing excitedly. Matt wished that he could borrow some of his enthusiasm. Sensing Matt's reluctance, Samsire nudged him forward encouragingly.

Suddenly, the valley opened before them. Creatures, small and large, darted across the rolling expanse of grass. Matt, Emmon, and

Arden stood rooted to the spot as they stared in amazement. At the far end of the valley was an iridescent grove of trees.

Matt's gaze first fell to a small pond to their left where an eight-foot long creature was dragging itself from the water. Its body was long and floppy like an otter. It turned toward the newcomers, and Matt gasped as he saw the long tusks that protruded from its mouth. It had stubby legs, like flippers, but cruel claws scraped against the rock as it pulled itself onto the bank. Its tail was covered in long hair like that of a horse and it swished constantly back and forth.

Two more plodded onto shore beside it, each eyeing Matt, Emmon, and Arden with intense mistrust.

They heard a neighing to their right, and a horse, as white and pristine as falling snow, joined them. A spiral, silver horn sprouted from its brow. A unicorn. It snorted, its nostrils flaring. As it ducked its head, its long silvery mane glowed even in the muted light. Others appeared from the trees behind it. There were also horses with thick fur, rather than the usual horsehair, each black, brown or spotted, with matching wings protruding from their backs.

Other creatures were not as pleasant looking. One creature had three heads. The majority of its body was the body of giant cat with its center head covered in a thick golden mane, and it bared sharp teeth. The head on the left was a dark serpent, its red, forked tongue flicking. The third head was a goat, and Matt involuntarily took a step back as it snorted and a small jet of flame escaped from the nostrils.

Another creature also had a cat body, though its pelt was a golden red. Instead of a cat's face, it had the face of sneering man surrounded by a wild mane. Its tail was enormous and armored like a scorpion's tail, which Matt suspected was complete with a poison stinger.

As the creatures stared at them silently and suspiciously, the sound of hooves pounded against the stone. A new group had joined them. Each creature had the torso of a man, but the body of a horse. Centaurs. The leader, dark-haired and muscular, spotted them and his eyes narrowed venomously.

"Intruders!" he yelled.

A sudden shrieking filled the air as the creatures from the pool raised back their heads. It was not like the piercing shriek of the garans, but a hollow sort of lament that chilled Matt's bones. In response, there was a cawing of birds and Matt looked up to see a flock of giant birds streaking down from the craggy cliffs that walled the valley. Their wingspans were enormous.

Matt realized with a start that they were same kind of birds as the one that landed on the building in Aresburg. They looked like giant eagles. There were other birds, too, some considerably smaller with the head of terrifying women. Others appeared to be griffins, like Gusren. And there were normal-sized birds with brilliant red and gold feathers, like fire.

After they had gathered around them, the creatures fell strangely silent, and Matt could hear his own heart pounding. He nervously grabbed the pouch around his neck as Gusren stepped forward to speak.

"These are the unsightly beings that I encountered at the front of our valley. They are friends of the alorath."

"Why have you allowed them to enter the sanctuary, alorath?" the first centaur demanded angrily. "They are human filth."

Matt, Emmon, and Arden stood silently as the creatures began to crone, roar, and caw in agreement. The unicorns hoofed the ground ferociously.

"Let's drive them out," one said. "They should never have gotten this far."

"Drive them out? Then they will just tell the rest of their human friends about us and they will come for us," growled the large cat with the scorpion tail and human face. "Let us kill them."

The three-headed cat reared back and its goat mouth shot a jet of flame into the air. The unicorns neighed and the giant birds flexed their talons.

"W-wait," Matt stammered.

The creatures erupted in sounds of distorted laughter. Matt turned back to look at Sam, Emmon, and Arden. He had been separated from them by a group of centaurs holding bows and arrows in their strong hands. Sam's eyes told Matt not to be afraid, that he had the strength to do this.

"Let's dispose of them quickly," another griffin urged.

"Let's wait to see what they have to say first," one of the winged horses countered. "They look friendly enough."

"Friendly?" cackled one of the birds with a woman's face. "You like anyone who will stroke your feathers!"

"The harpy is right. All humans are harmful," a unicorn agreed. "We all know that."

"Well, don't forget about Ellyn," the horse replied. "She's the only human we seen in many years, and she is not harmful."

Matt was tempted to ask about Ellyn, but the unicorn's response stopped him.

"Do not forget the old days that drove us here. Humans are destructive. They killed thousands of our brothers and sisters."

"That is not fair," Matt yelled above the fray.

The creatures fell silent and each turned their head or heads to look at Matt who stood with his fists clenched at his side.

"You do not know who we are or what we want," he said, struggling to keep his voice level. "Why do you assume we're harmful? I've proven that I am friend to an alorath."

"That alorath was an intruder, too," the scorpion-tailed cat said.

"Calm down, manticore," one of the winged horses soothed. "Any magical creature is welcome here."

Matt dragged his eyes away from the sneering human face of the manticore and focused his gaze on the grove of trees that stood at the end of the valley. He could feel the power radiating from there, and he knew that that was where the Wind Stone lay waiting.

"You would do well to let me through," he said loudly.

"Let you though?" a harpy cackled. "I would rather peck out your eyes! You impudent little boy!"

"I have had enough!" the manticore growled. "You're mine, human!"

It ran toward Matt's with its sharp claws extended and scorpion tail twisting. Matt's hand automatically went to Doubtslayer, but he stopped. There was no way he could defeat these creatures with normal weapons. He also did not want to harm them. They would most certainly trample him if he did and they would cease to listen to him. But he could prove himself to them by other means.

He allowed the flood of raw magic and energy course through him. When the manticore was nearly upon him, he flung up his hand and conjured a shield. The manticore rammed into it, and without effort, Matt felt the magic of the Fire Stone, released the shield, and threw fire at the manticore. The manticore screamed as his mane went up in flames.

But Matt still had control of the fire, and he quickly drew the flames back into his hand. The manticore's mane was burnt to a charred crisp, but the creature was otherwise unharmed.

It was suddenly deadly quiet. Matt raised his hand over his head, with the ball of fire still hovering above it. After a moment of silence, the unicorns neighed angrily, and the creatures from the water shrieked eerily once more. As they all began to close in around him, Matt realized that he may have overdone it. He quickly extinguished the flame in his palm.

"I am not a little boy. You may be creatures of the elements, but I am master of the elements," Matt said calmly, hoping he sounded stronger than he felt. "I do not wish to harm you. I want to protect you. From the Commander of Shadows. From Malik. You need me. That is why you sent the morphcat to find me."

The unicorns raised their horns from their threatening positions aimed at Matt's stomach and the three-headed creature stopped breathing fire. Murph jumped from Arden's shoulder onto

Matt's head. Matt knew he likely looked ridiculous wearing the tiny creature as a hat, but the effect was immediate.

"You," one of the centaurs said in an awed voice. "How can a human boy be the one of the Prophecy?"

"It seems that that is, indeed, the case," Gusren said, looking around the assembled creatures.

The griffin glanced sideways at Matt, as if urging him to go on. Surprised at the griffin's support, Matt searched for the right words.

"I know what is out there. I have seen the fog. It nearly overtook us. It is Dark magic and it will not go away. It will keep growing and gaining strength until you have all starved, or until you are so weakened that you will not be able to fight against the garans that Malik has sent to attack, first Aresburg, and then you.

"That is what he wants – he wants you all to die. If you want to survive, you must let me help you. I know that the Wind Stone is here. I can wield it. It is the only way to destroy the mist. It is the only way you will survive.

"I promise I will help you."

The creatures were silent, and then they began to whisper among themselves.

One of the winged horses flapped its wings agitatedly and said, "We should let him through. The others can stay here, but he should pass."

There was some dissent among the creatures, but at last, they parted reluctantly. Matt glanced at his friends and they nodded. He took a deep breath and stepped forward, acutely aware of the mistrusting gazes of the creatures surrounding him. He felt very small as he walked through their ranks, but he forced himself to meet every gaze. One of the brilliantly feathered birds, a phoenix, shot ahead of him, guiding him toward the grove of trees at the end of the valley.

The wind whistled through the valley as the creatures and Sam, Emmon, and Arden disappeared from Matt's view. He kept his eyes glued on the grove of trees ahead of him. He was so close. Finally, he would claim the Wind Stone.

After what seemed like an eternity, his feet carried him to the edge of the trees. The phoenix dove around him, circling him, and then perched on one of the trees. Matt turned to the wall of trees, searching for a way through. He ran a hand along the crumbling bark as he walked along the wall. A few yards away, the trees formed an arch, but branches stretched across the opening, blocking his way through.

Matt ran his fingers along the border of the arch. It was just like those he had had to cross to reach the Fire Stone and Water Stone. His fingers fell into carvings in the wood. The first was a dancing flame, the second waves of water, the third a spiral of wind, and the last, a tree.

Matt pressed his fingertips against them. They suddenly began to glow. He stepped back as the branches blocking the entrance eased apart. The archway was open, and the light faded from the symbols in the wood. The wind whistled through Matt's hair as he faced the opening. He could not see the Wind Stone, but he could feel the power. With a deep breath, he walked through the archway.

His eyes adjusted quickly to the dim light, and he saw that he was standing in a large circle of trees. In the center was a single tree stump. On it laid the Stone, a deep, translucent blue stone with wisps of rolling gray storm clouds. He walked slowly to the stump and tentatively reached for it. As he grasped it in his hand, he felt the iciness of the stone's surface and a rush of power. He examined it curiously, thinking about air magic. It was as if he were holding a storm in his palm. Flashes of lightning bounced across the interior of the Stone, dark clouds swirling.

The power of the elements was now his.

CHAPTER TWENTY-SEVEN

Innar neighed in exhaustion as he pushed across the river. Lucian leaned forward in the saddle and patted his neck encouragingly. To their left, an enormous waterfall pounded the pool of water below.

When they reached the opposite bank, Lucian carefully scanned the sand, looking for any kind of clue that the teenagers had been there. Mixed among the large animal footprints, one of which looked like Sam's, were a number of human tracks. Lucian was sure those were Matt's boots. As he pulled Innar to a halt, something caught his eye.

A single arrow was buried in the sand, only the tip showing. An arrow of Amaldan. Emmon and Matt and Arden had come this way. Perhaps the arrow was a result of their encounter with the griffin Matt had mentioned in his letter. Lucian stowed it in the pack fastened to Innar's saddle. He hoped that there had not been trouble. They could not afford any delays. The army of garans was marching close on his heels.

Lucian climbed back into the saddle. He would follow the river, since it held the only clue to where Matt and the others might be. He urged his exhausted horse onward, and he struggled to sit upright. He had been riding nearly nonstop for many days trying to outrun the garans. And now, it seemed, he had just a little farther to go.

They continued along the river until it curved into a deep valley. Peering down the valley, Lucian could see the sheer rock faces surrounding it. The foliage was sparse through the middle of the valley, but there was a dense wall of trees lining either side. A strange cloud covered the valley several hundred yards in. It looked solid and seemingly impenetrable. Lucian knew immediately that it was his destination.

The valley was eerily quiet. His nerves were on edge, and he warily scanned the mountains surrounding him. There was something sinister here. He rode on uneasily until the mist lingered above him. He pulled Innar to a stop in front of the wide grove of trees, as thick as the mist above.

He dismounted and Innar whinnied in relief. Lucian patted the horse's neck and walked stiffly to the tree, running his hand along the tree trunks. There was a loud crunching and the branches knitted more tightly together. A magical entrance. Lucian looked up and saw Raumer circling around him, unable to enter the misty area from above. Frowning, Lucian brandished his staff and pointed it at the trees.

"Open. Allow me to enter," he commanded.

Nothing happened. The only sound was the whistling of the wind. Lucian lowered his staff, but he did not step back. He was certain that Matt was behind that grove, and he would not rest until he reached him.

He summoned his remaining energy and focused it in his staff. Jabbing his staff forward like a sword, he sent a ball of concentrated magical energy at the wall of trees. There was a deafening bang and the branches quivered slightly, but they remained as impenetrable as ever. Lucian drove his staff into the ground in frustration. He had not ridden all this way for nothing. But perhaps there was someone or *something* listening on the other side. Perhaps if he tried a less aggressive tactic.

"I implore you to allow me to enter," he said loudly.

He stared at the trees for a while longer, but they yielded no response. Then he heard a loud, unnerving noise like the hollow cry of a dying animal.

CHAPTER TWENTY-EIGHT

Matt made his way out of the trees to the valley floor, gripping the Wind Stone tightly in his left hand. The phoenix flew from its perch as he emerged, and it began to circle above him, marking his progress for the other creatures of the sanctuary to see.

Finally, the creatures came into view. As Matt approached them he straightened his back and then strode purposefully through their ranks. The unicorns and centaurs parted reluctantly, but the manticore with the scorched mane refused to move. Matt stepped around it, knowing it was not worth the confrontation.

"Matt!" Arden cried and she rushed toward him with Emmon close behind her.

She flung her arms around his neck. He hugged her back and she let go of him, carefully studying his face, as if she thought he might have changed in those brief moments.

"Did you get it?" she whispered.

But before Matt could answer, there was movement behind him, and Gusren was standing over him.

"Well, human?" he asked in a low rumbling voice. "I think you have something you owe us."

To emphasize the griffin's point, the manticore flexed its scorpion tail threateningly, and the three-headed beast breathed a jet of flame from its goat's mouth.

Samsire lumbered over to Matt, butted him playfully with his head, and looking down at him encouragingly. Matt smiled at the alorath, grateful for his presence. It would have been much more difficult to face the crowd of creatures without Sam.

"Human!" a griffin suddenly screeched.

Matt first thought that it was talking to him, but he realized that the griffin had come from the entrance to the sanctuary.

"There is another human demanding entrance into the sanctuary," the griffin squawked. "It won't go away."

"It is not Ellyn?" Gusren asked.

"No. It is a man."

"Send the harpies to peck out his eyes," the manticore growled viciously.

At this the harpies cackled in agreement and Matt felt a sudden rush of dread. A man. Had someone followed them here? Lucian, of course. Matt hurried forward before the harpies could fly.

"Wait!" he said. "What did the man look like?"

The griffin looked highly affronted that Matt was interfering but said, "A tall man riding a bay horse. He carries a staff."

"It's Lucian," Matt said urgently as the harpies clawed at the ground. "He's a friend." The creatures looked at each other skeptically and Matt added urgently, "He's a wizard. He doesn't wish you any harm. He's been fighting against Malik. Please let him in."

The creatures considered this, and after a moment's hesitation they all nodded. Gusren flew leisurely to the trees and disappeared among the branches. Matt, Emmon, and Arden waited nervously until finally, the griffin reappeared, walking now. Lucian followed behind him, pulling Innar's reins and looking thoroughly exhausted. He gazed at the creatures in amazement, but did not look alarmed. When he caught sight of Matt and the others, his expression still did not change, but Matt saw relief in his eyes.

"Lucian," Matt said, placing his hand on the wizard's arm. "Are you all right?"

Lucian smiled and his gray eyes twinkled. "Yes, tired is all. I have been racing the garans night and day." He looked around again. "What is this place?"

"It's a sanctuary for magical creatures," Samsire answered him from above.

"Ah, hello, Samsire, my friend," Lucian said. "I did not notice you among so many fascinating creatures. But yes, that makes perfect sense."

"What does?" Arden asked.

"This place," he answered looking around once more. "It's exactly what Malik would like to destroy."

The creatures examined Lucian with intense mistrust.

"Why are we allowing more of them into our home?" a harpy shrieked.

Many creatures sounded their agreement, pounding the ground and growling. They were only quieted by an even louder, more ferocious roar. Flames flew from Samsire's claws, and he glared menacingly at the now silent creatures.

"I've put up with this for long enough," he growled. "You will listen to what the humans have to say. Without their help, you will die."

"Lucian, tell us what you know," Matt said quietly.

"There is a vast army of garans traveling south. They were less than half a day behind me, but they will go to Aresburg first. If they destroy Aresburg, their path is clear to anything in this region. I must assume that this sanctuary will be the next place they visit."

"So you have led the garans here?" one of the unicorns neighed.

"No," Lucian answered. "They are not following me, they are on a mission to take control of Aresburg. I cut through the mountains in the hope of arriving in Aresburg before they do so that I may warn the people living there. The garans will not reach Aresburg for at least another day."

"We must go, then," Emmon said urgently.

"It will take us days to get back. We'll never make it in time," Arden pointed out. "Unless Matt can make the wind carry us or something."

Lucian turned to Matt, his eyes darting to Matt's hand. "What is that?"

"The Wind Stone was at the end of the valley."

Lucian smiled. "Ah. I wondered if this might be something more than just a haven for magical creatures."

"The only reason you have it, human," a centaur said, "is because of us. You cannot leave. You promised to help us, to get rid of the fog."

"Fog?" Lucian muttered. "I am assuming you are not referring to the cloud cover that protects the sanctuary from prying eyes, is that correct?"

"You are right," Arden said and then quickly explained how the fog had pursued them.

Lucian nodded gravely. He gestured for Matt to come closer.

"I do not think that it would be wise to clear the fog just yet," he said quietly. "You need them, Matt, just as much as they need you. This army of garans is too great for Aresburg to face on their own. Can you imagine your advantage if you had an army of magical creatures at your side?"

CHAPTER TWENTY-NINE

Matt considered this for a moment. Lucian was right. He could not let this opportunity pass. Taking a deep breath, he stepped forward.

"No," he said clearly. "I cannot leave. But I am not going to fix the fog. Yet."

They stared at him with new hatred. "What are you saying human?"

"I'm saying you still have to do something for me before I can help you."

One of the centaurs let out a yell and galloped toward him. Before Matt could react, the centaur crashed into him. He felt a blinding pain as his head hit the ground and his shoulders fell under the creatures' hooves. He opened his eyes to see a sharp arrowhead aimed at his throat.

"You two-timing human!" the centaur growled.

Out of the corner of his eye, Matt saw Samsire prepared to rip the centaur off of him, but Matt shot him a look of warning.

"Explain yourself, human!" the centaur roared. "Or I'll shoot you in the throat."

The harpies were cackling wildly, eagerly it seemed.

"Kill it now, centaur," one of the unicorns urged. "It is a foul beast and a traitor."

The centaur seemed to consider this as he pulled his bowstring back farther. Matt felt a rush of anger. He was not an *it*. He was trying to help them and the rest of Mundaria. As anger rushed through him, so too did magical power. He felt wind surge from his hands, wind so powerful that it blasted the creature off of him. The centaur flew backward, releasing an arrow at Matt as it did. He flung up his hand again and instantly summoned a shield without even thinking about it. The arrow bounced harmlessly off of it.

Matt scrambled to his feet, breathing hard, the magic still coursing through his body. The centaur had returned to a standing position, looking quite angry. Lucian, Emmon, and Arden stood steadfastly behind Matt.

"Look," Matt said, his voice rising. "Just listen to what I have to say. I need your help. Aresburg needs your help. Please, help us fight the garans."

Bedlam broke out again. Yelling, cawing, growling, roaring, screeching. Matt angrily stomped his foot, seething. They were not listening.

"Do you not understand?" he tried to yell over the din.

They did not stop. Matt felt the blood rushing in his ears. He would not give up. Galen, Lucian, Aresburg were all counting on him. He would not fail. He needed to get their attention somehow. His mind raced. He could use magic, but what would make them notice? Fire? No, it was too risky. But now he had air magic on his side, as well.

Matt tried to remember what Lucian had told him about the powers of air magic. It controlled wind, but also all properties of weather. Hot and cold, snow and rain, lightning and tornados. That was what he needed.

Matt looked up at the mist hiding the valley. The sun was shining behind it. Gripping the Wind Stone very tightly, he closed his eyes and concentrated. He wanted clouds. Dark, rolling, storm clouds to block out the sun. He opened his eyes and stared at the sky. Power rushed from his outstretched hand, spreading through his body and into the air. Within seconds it was colder. Clouds began to gather behind the mist, blocking out the sun completely.

The creatures fell silent.

Finally, they turned to Matt who was trembling slightly from the power that he had just exerted. He had never used magic this powerful. It was so unlike the Fire Stone and the Water Stone. He faced the creatures, relieved that they were now silent.

"It is very cold, isn't it?" he said quietly. "That is what it will be like always if Malik gains power."

"The Commander does not affect our home here," one of the unicorns snorted derisively. "We live beyond his reach."

"You thought you did. You have for many years," Matt replied. "Until the fog nearly suffocated all of you. Malik is getting stronger, and he will become stronger still, if we fail. The garans are not coming for Aresburg. Conquering Aresburg will just make it easier for them to reach you.

"They are coming for you. They have been sent to destroy you and this sanctuary. Malik wants you dead. Aresburg is just a stopping point. But if Aresburg falls, you will be destroyed."

The creatures were silent, but Matt knew that he had not yet reached them. He took another breath.

"One of Malik's Agurans found Ellyn. She was trying to protect you, but she was tortured and she has been lost in its evil."

"Ellyn? That traitorous human!"

Matt shook his head. "Ellyn did not betray you. But Malik has irresistible methods of persuasion. I've seen what he can do. When Malik is finished with this place, it will be cold and dead. Everything will die. Every plant, tree, and animal will wilt and die. The fog is just the beginning of the kind of Dark magic that Malik can wield.

"I am the One of the Prophecy of the Elements. I can wield the power of the elements, but I cannot stop Malik alone. And he will not stop until all of Mundaria is his. If Aresburg falls, you will be next. And after that, nothing can stop Malik."

He paused. "We can only stop this army of garans if you help us. We can only help you if we stop the garans. I say we do exactly what Malik fears. We form an alliance. We become united against him in magic."

He felt his anger and adrenaline slowly ebb away. The bitter cold began to subside and the great dark clouds began to disperse, allowing the muted light to once again shine through the protective mist.

"What do you say?" Matt asked hopefully, trying to hide how drained he felt.

"I see great power in you human," Gusren the griffin said loudly as he stalked through the throng. "It would be unwise to have you as our enemy."

Matt fought back a triumphant smile, and nodded solemnly at the griffin. Some creatures shifted uneasily and indecisively, but many of them bobbed their heads in agreement. He waited until agreement had spread through the sanctuary. He felt victory surge in his chest.

"Thank you," Matt said. "Your help will not go unnoticed."

"It better not," Gusren said. "You agree that as soon as this battle is over, you will destroy the fog, correct?"

"Yes. You have my word."

Gusren stared intently at Matt. "What will you have us do human?"

"Wait at the edge of the plains between the mountains and Aresburg," Matt replied. "Samsire will come to you with more instructions later."

"Fair enough. We will do as you ask."

Matt felt almost faint with relief. Lucian put a steadying hand on his shoulder. It was time to return to Aresburg. Emmon was right, though, they had to get back to Aresburg as quickly as possible.

"Samsire?" Matt asked. "Are you up for another flight?"

"I thought you'd never ask," the alorath grinned. "I can fly to Aresburg easily, but I can't carry all of you and Innar."

"We would be grateful if one of you would help us get to Aresburg," Matt said to Gusren.

"We have done enough for you human," the manticore growled.

"I will take you," Gusren said. "If the alorath carries that despicably plain horse creature and two of you humans, I can carry the other two of you."

Several of the other creatures snorted in disdain, but the griffin ignored them.

"Thank you," Matt said.

Matt climbed onto Sam's back and Arden climbed on behind him. Lucian and Emmon climbed onto the griffin. Samsire pumped his great wings and rose into the air, delicately grabbing Innar in his claws. They rose through the trees and above the mist. Matt let the wind beating against his face and the elegant movement of Sam's wings, calm him.

Gusren labored under the weight of his passengers but kept pace with Sam. They would reach Aresburg in no time. The tall treetops blurred together in a lush, emerald carpet as they sped over the mountainsides. Arden held tightly to Matt and the warmth of her grasp distracted him from the beauty of the passing landscape.

Before long, Aresburg was visible ahead, and Samsire and Gusren both descended, flying low to the ground.

"I'll stop here," Samsire finally said. "I don't want to get too close to the city. Better not to cause alarm again."

He slowed, carefully releasing Innar onto the ground before landing a few yards away from the horse. Matt and Arden slid off the alorath's back as Gusren landed beside him.

"Thank you, griffin. We are most grateful," Lucian said courteously.

Gusren grunted and turned to Matt. "You have caused quite a bit of trouble among the animals. I think you might actually taste nice with a wash."

Without another word, the griffin shot back into the air toward the mountains. Matt hoped they lived up to their end of the bargain. They did not have much of a choice.

"I'm glad you finally turned up, Matt," Samsire grunted. "I've never been with a more cantankerous lot of animals. What took you so long?"

They quickly told the alorath all that had happened since he had left them in Gremonte.

"Okay, so go then," Samsire said as soon as they had finished. "Go warn Galen, Hal, and the rest of the city. I'll be here if you need me."

They jogged to the city walls. When they reached the arch that covered the entrance into Aresburg, Lucian chuckled as he read the quote from Darrick Wanderer.

"Ah, yes. In my first days with Galen, he talked incessantly of Darrick. I never thought he'd stop talking about him. I can't imagine what he would have done if I had told him that I knew Darrick well."

"You knew him?"

Lucian nodded with a mischievous grin on his face. Matt smiled as he pictured Galen five years ago as a teenager, chattering excitedly about Darrick. He could easily imagine Lucian's expression of strained patience, one that Matt had seen many times after asking one too many questions.

"What business do you have in Aresburg?" a guard asked them, stepping in front of them.

Matt glanced at Emmon and Arden. The guards had never before challenged them when they had entered Aresburg.

"We're...we've been staying in Aresburg for a few weeks now," Matt said. "We're with a man named Galen who is still here in the city."

At the mention of Galen's name, both guards straightened slightly.

The first guard smiled. "Go on through."

After settling Innar with the other horses, they made their way to Catherine's.

"Look at that," Arden said, pointing down the street at dozens of soldiers sparring with each other.

Galen stood above the soldiers on an overlooking rooftop. Within seconds he had spotted them and a broad grin spread across his face. He leapt off the rooftop and landed lightly on the street.

"You're back so soon. Did you run into trouble," Galen said, his eyes shifting from Matt to Lucian. "What are you doing here Lucian?"

"I'm afraid I bring bad news, Galen," Lucian said, a ghost of a smile on his lips. "Fortunately, you look like you have been busy, so we may be able to deal with it."

"This is amazing," Emmon said, looking around at the soldiers. "The Aresburg troops didn't even know how to use their swords a few days ago"

"We've been training them," Hal said as he joined them, his voice full of pride. "Ever since you left."

"That is good news. There is an army of garans traveling south toward Aresburg as we speak," Lucian said.

"How long until they get here?" Galen said calmly.

Lucian looked up at the sky. It was barely early afternoon. "They were a half a day behind me when I entered the mountains. They will be going around the mountains, rather than through them, and I have had the privilege of being flown here from the mountains, which greatly shortened the journey. I would guess we have a day and a half before they arrive. Remember that garans do not feel exhaustion or pain. It could be sooner."

Galen rubbed the back of his neck. "How many?"

"A good many. Thousands. I did not have the time to count, but according to my contact most of the garans that were in Marlope have left. But there is worse news even than that. I don't know how he has done it, but Malik had changed some of the garans."

"Changed?" Matt said. "What do you mean?"

"Nearly a third of the garans can now stand as they walk. They are still feral beasts, but they are enormous and they can stand on two feet and bear a sword like a man."

"And then of course, there are their claws, which are as effective as a knife," Emmon said quietly.

Lucian nodded. "Malik has created strong adversaries. The garans are also led by an Aguran. Malik has taken no risks."

Galen nodded, and turned to Hal. "Hal, go to Idris and tell him about the garans. He will start the necessary preparations."

To Matt's surprise, Hal sped off without a word of protest. Normally, he did not like taking orders from Galen.

"What did you find in the mountains, Matt?" Galen asked.

Matt told him about the sinister, dark fog, the animal sanctuary, and the Wind Stone. He held the Stone out for them to see.

"Well done," Galen said, impressed. "We're going to need every bit of help we can get. But you all look like you could use a bit of rest before battle. Come, we'll go to Catherine's."

When they arrived at her door, Catherine ushered them inside, and Galen introduced her to Lucian before explaining the situation to her.

"I should go help Hal and Idris prepare the guard," Galen said.

"Wait," Matt said, stopping him. "I want to do something, if it's all right with Catherine. I want to try to heal Ellyn."

Matt saw the protest forming on Galen's and Catherine's lips.

"No, listen, please. I know I can do it. I have more control now. I feel like the Stones are…listening to me now. They obey me. It's hard to explain. Please. I feel that it is very important that we hear what she has to say and there is no other way to unlock the information in her mind. You've tried everything else."

Matt did not know how he knew this, but the longer he held the three stones together, the more confident he felt about his ability to control the power they held. And now that battle was imminent, Matt was desperate to know what Ellyn was trying to tell them. He looked at Catherine and he could tell that she was struggling with the choice.

"Yes," she said finally. "I trust you. I want my mother back, as well."

Matt smiled, but he felt his stomach clench. "There is a chance that it might not work or that it might even make her worse."

"She cannot be much worse than she already is," Catherine answered.

"If anyone can do it, it's you Matt," Galen said.

They followed Matt into the tiny room where Ellyn lay. Her eyes were shut, but her lips were moving silently, and her brow was furrowed into deep wrinkles. Her frazzled mane of gray-brown hair was scattered about the pillow.

Matt squeezed her limp, cold fingers, took a deep breath, and closed his eyes. The magic surged through his body. He focused on Ellyn, thinking of her ailments. The lost, empty look in her eyes, the tortured, crazed yelling, and the mumblings that escaped her lips. Gently, very controlled, Matt allowed the water magic to flow from him to Ellyn.

He opened his eyes, but there were no water droplets like there had always been when he healed wounds inflicted by swords or garans. But he could feel the magic reaching her, and he continued to hold her hand. An aura of magic seemed to envelop her entire being, blanketing her in unseen strength and nourishing her lost soul.

Finally, she took a great, shuddering breath. A shiver racked her body and then she laid very still, her eyes shut tightly. Matt released her hand and waited. He could feel his friends shifting anxiously behind him. Tense moments passed. And then, her eyes shot open and her gaze flitted across the ceiling in confusion.

"Mother?" Catherine said quietly.

Catherine knelt beside the bed and Ellyn turned to her daughter. A smile grew across her worn face.

"Catherine," she said hoarsely.

Catherine smiled and laughed lightly, hugging her mother.

"How...how long have I been here?" Ellyn croaked as her daughter released her. "Is this Aresburg?"

"You've been here for many weeks," Catherine said gently.

"But I was in Borden..." Ellyn trailed off, her eyes turning to Matt. She motioned for him to come nearer.

"You," she croaked. "What is your name?"

"Matt," he answered. "Do you remember me?"

She smiled. "Of course. I met you in Borden. How long ago was that?"

"Three months."

Her smile faltered and became a frown.

"Ellyn," he said quietly. "What happened?"

She looked around the room, but she did not appear to be alarmed by the presence of so many strangers. She looked at Matt again, studying his face carefully.

"It wasn't long after I had spoken to you. For some reason, I thought of you often after we met in the street."

Matt's heart was now beating very quickly.

"Then the stranger came." Ellyn shuddered involuntarily at the memory. "I left the shop in Borden one afternoon to pick up some more potatoes from the market. By the time I had started back, it was already turning dark and most people had gone into their homes. I was nearly back at the shop when...when it found me. It appeared behind a stack of barrels in the back alleyway. It grabbed me. It was like fire itself, burning my arm."

"It was an Aguran," Galen said. "A creature of darkness."

Ellyn nodded fiercely. "A cloud of darkness surrounded it. It did not speak, but I...I could feel it in my mind. And then my thoughts were covered in the cloud of darkness. I didn't know who I was or what was dear to me. I was lost in the darkness. It wanted information."

She fell silent, her eyes wide and terrified.

"What did it want to know?" Matt asked.

"Oh, no," she said, as if just remembering. "I think I told it everything. All of my secrets. I don't remember anything since then. Just confusion. But...I...I think I told it my secrets."

She looked guiltily at Catherine. "When I was a younger, more adventurous woman, I took a trek into the mountains. I came across a peculiar valley. There was a web of trees, but they parted for me. There is a sanctuary there, a home for beautiful and powerful creatures. They trusted me, but now that beast knows where they are."

She shook her head sadly, but continued. "That wasn't what the creature was looking for, though. It knew I had met you somehow, Matt. I think that is why it found me. It wanted information about you, but instead it found out about the sanctuary."

It was now clear how Malik had discovered the sanctuary and why he wanted it destroyed. The Aguran had learned of it from Ellyn and had thought that Matt knew of it as well. But Matt still had one unanswered question.

"I'm sorry, Ellyn," he said quietly. "It is my fault the Aguran went after you."

"Don't fret, child."

"May I ask you...what you meant when you spoke to me in Borden?" he asked finally. "You mentioned my parents."

"I have always been able to recognize strange things in others that they cannot recognize in themselves," she said slowly. "I suppose that is why I have always been able to enter the sanctuary. Magic seems to like me."

She paused, and then said in a clear voice, "You are a mergling, Matt."

CHAPTER THIRTY

Matt stood in stunned silence, staring at Ellyn in disbelief, unable to process her words. Yet, he knew that she was speaking the truth. Matt looked around the room at his friends. Lucian, Galen, Emmon, and Arden. They looked as bewildered as he felt.

"You're not serious," he finally sputtered.

"I am completely serious," Ellyn said calmly. "You are a mergling. I can feel it." Her eyes looked past him. "Just like that charming and very handsome young man behind you."

Matt turned around and looked at Galen pleadingly. Galen looked down at Matt, his eyes glowing with what could only be triumph. A smile grew on his lips and he nodded almost imperceptibly.

"Thank you, Ellyn," Matt muttered hoarsely.

Lucian placed his hand on Matt shoulder and smiled. "It may not seem so at this moment, Matthias, but being a mergling is a great privilege. Some of the finest people I know are merglings."

"And now we must start preparations for battle," Lucian continued, turning to the others.

Galen nodded. "Emmon, Arden, go down to the port and find Torrin. Tell him what's happening and ask him to gather every able-bodied man. Have him take you to the headquarters of the guard. I will meet you there."

Emmon and Arden hurried from the room, both casting glances back at Matt as they did.

Galen took Catherine's hands in his. "We have to go, Cat, but I'll be back soon."

She smiled and laid her head on his shoulder for a brief moment. Ellyn waved at Matt as he walked out of the room.

Matt's mind was swimming. He needed air. Outside, he leaned against the stone wall and then slid down it to the cobblestone.

"Matthias," Lucian said quietly.

Matt looked up at him, a hollow feeling in his chest.

"Is she right?" he asked.

Lucian smiled. "Yes. I believe she is. It makes sense. Merglings are highly gifted in magic."

Matt nodded reluctantly. He knew it was true, but he did not want to believe it. He had gone from being an outcast to being accepted, only to end up back where he started. He had heard stories about the disrespect and anger directed toward merglings. Hadn't Galen said that his childhood had been miserable just because he was a mergling?

Galen seemed to read his thoughts and sat down next to him. A smile played at the corner of his lips.

"What are you smiling at?" Matt said defensively.

"It's not so bad being a mergling, you know. And don't forget, that you are no different than you were ten minutes ago. You've always been a mergling, you just didn't know it. It's strange to think that I've been traveling with you all this time and we never knew. There's so few us, it's amazing that our paths crossed."

"Not so bad? Look at what happened to you in Amaldan," Matt argued.

"Think of it this way," Galen said. "At least you've already been banned from Amaldan. There's not much else they can do to you. They treat every non-elf like they're inferior, it's nothing personal."

Galen's grin and his lack of bitterness, made Matt feel a little better. Galen punched him playfully on the arm.

"I don't really know what I was expecting Ellyn to say," Matt said. "But I didn't expect this."

"You are ignoring one important detail," Lucian said, standing above him.

"What's that?"

"Merglings not only possess extraordinary magical abilities, they also share the elves' power of earth magic since one of their parents is an elf," Lucian said.

"Right, so now, with the Wind Stone," Galen continued, "you have power over all of the elements. You truly are Master of the Elements."

Matt took a deep breath. All this time he had believed that he would have to learn the magic of the earth from the elves. But he was a mergling. That magic was already his. He now had the power over all four elements that Malik had been seeking for decades. A different kind of energy was flowing through him now that he had the Wind Stone – tranquil and powerful at the same time. He was the one controlling the Stones, rather than the Stones controlling him.

And he was not alone – Galen knew how it felt to be a mergling. Galen stood and held out a hand to him. Taking a deep breath, Matt let Galen pull him to his feet.

"Well," Matt said solemnly. "Don't we have a battle to prepare for?"

Galen grinned. "Right. I have to get to the guard headquarters." His smile faded. "But we may need help against these garans. I'm not sure Aresburg is ready to do this on its own."

"We already have that covered," Matt replied. "The creatures from the sanctuary have agreed to help us. Sam is waiting nearby to relay messages to them."

Galen nodded gratefully. "Good. Tell Sam to organize the creatures and then wait for the sign to join the battle. Their signal to join the battle will be an orb of fire high in the sky above the city which you will provide, Matt. Before Sam leaves for the sanctuary, though, have him fly over the city once or twice. I want the soldiers to get used to seeing creatures. They still don't believe that garans exist and they are in for a nasty shock."

"Right," Matt yelled back as he began running down the street.

When he was outside the city arch, he plunged his hand into his pocket and grabbed Sam's feather. Within seconds Sam appeared and Matt explained Galen's plan.

Samsire nodded. "Right. I'll circle over the city a few times, and then I'll head to the sanctuary. I'll bring them back as quickly as I can."

"And Sam? There's something else too," Matt added hesitantly.

Sam seemed to sense Matt's tension, and he leaned his huge head against him. "Go on. Tell me."

Taking a deep breath, Matt told him about Ellyn. Samsire pulled back slightly so he could look Matt in the eye.

"I always knew it would be something like this. You've always been full of surprises. I knew you'd come up with another one to explain your heritage."

Matt smiled.

"Just imagine what you can do now, Matt. All four elements. Just like me. We are a very powerful pair, aren't we?" he said grinning toothily. His low laugh rumbled through the air and the ground around them.

"I'll see you soon," Sam said and nudged Matt playfully with his nose. "Next time I see you, we'll be in the heat of battle. You be careful, Matt – no unnecessary heroics, okay?"

Matt nodded and rubbed Sam's nose. "You, too, Sam."

Without another word, the alorath flapped his wings and took to the air. He flew low over the city several times, letting out an occasional roar. Matt could see the shocked faces of the guards standing beneath the arch. Matt smiled, waving to the alorath as he flew off into the distance. As Matt walked back to the city, the guards gaped at him.

"Did...did...," one of them sputtered.

Matt smiled. "Don't worry about it. That alorath is the least of your worries."

Matt noticed a definite change in the attitude of the people of Aresburg since word of the garan army had spread. They whispered nervously to each other and few were on the streets.

Matt did his best to ignore the fear that had fallen over the city and walked to the port.

The port was as noisy as ever, but it was now swarming with uniformed soldiers rummaging through the storage buildings for supplies. The *Lady Gemma* was crowded with sailors, but Matt could not spot his friends among them.

"Hey, Matt," Emmon said, suddenly beside him. "Where have you been?"

"With Sam. He's gone to bring the creatures to Aresburg."

"We're going to need their help. Galen's just ordered every weapon in the city," Emmon said. "When Galen's worried, you know there's something to worry about."

Matt nodded, watching the soldiers and sailors pass.

"Listen, Matt," Emmon said. "I want you to know that I'm really proud that you are half elf. I hope it doesn't bother you that you have elf blood in your veins."

"How could I be sad about that when my two best friends are elves?" Matt said with a grin and nudged Emmon. "Where's Arden?"

Emmon looked relieved and pointed at the *Lady Gemma*.

"She's up on deck. She has an idea to use sailors in the battle. Captain Nick and Torrin asked her to talk to the sailors. Who knows what crazy, but, of course very effective, idea she's come up with."

Matt smiled as he thought of Arden telling the sailors what to do.

"Do you remember when you and I and Hal went after the Fire Stone?" Emmon said. "Remember how I didn't want her to come because I was afraid Counselor Lan would skin me alive if she got hurt? She never lets me forget it. It's a good thing I changed my mind about bringing her along. We'd be lost without her."

Matt looked up at the ship, hoping to catch sight of Arden's long, brown hair. Emmon shifted beside him, and Matt noticed that a ridiculous grin had spread across his face.

"What?" Matt demanded.

"You know, you're all she talks about," Emmon said, still smiling.

"What do you mean?" Matt said a little too quickly.

"She likes you, Matt."

"Er...really? How do you know?"

"I just do. You know, you're a little bit slow on the uptake sometimes. "

Matt stared at his friend, the grin still plastered on his face.

"I've known Arden since I was five and she was three. That's eleven years, Matt. She's been with me through nearly every spot of trouble I've ever been in. I've been around her long enough to know what she thinks about and how she feels about things. And especially how she feels about people. Of course, she'd be furious with me if she knew I was telling you this. You know, Arden. Every bit a fighter."

Matt continued to stare at his friend.

"I thought that you...that maybe you...," he said finally, "...that you and Arden were..."

"No, Matt. She's like my little sister."

Matt was silent, letting that sink in.

"Come on, Matt. I know you like her. You're not exactly subtle."

"Er…right," Matt said awkwardly. He tried to hide his embarrassment and searched for something to say to change the subject. "So…what does Galen want us to do?"

Emmon laughed and shook his head. "Right. Galen's down at Storehouse Eleven. Let's go and see."

Matt was relieved to leave the subject of he and Arden behind, but his heart felt considerably lighter. When they reached the storehouse, Galen was issuing orders to several clusters of soldiers.

"How many crates of arrows have you gathered?"

"Nearly thirty, sir," one of the soldiers reported.

"Keep searching. What about swords? How many do we have?"

"Enough for every soldier at least, sir. Probably more. And we've also found a large collection of spears in Storehouse Seven."

Galen nodded his satisfaction. "Let's get everything passed out to soldiers first, then sailors and townsmen. Thank you, you may go."

The soldiers hurried away and Galen walked over to Matt and Emmon. "Well, Matt?"

"The creatures will be here soon. Samsire will lead them."

"Excellent," Galen said. "Now we wait for an army of garans."

CHAPTER THIRTY-ONE

The day grew dark, the hours disappearing with blinding speed. Matt, Emmon, and Arden ran back and forth across the city under Galen's orders.

"Go to the front archway," Galen told them. "You'll find a soldier named Sanford. He'll show you the supply of arrows and bows that we found in the warehouses. Hal, gather some of the soldiers and all of you try to find the best archers. Lucian and I will be with Idris, so come find us when you're finished."

They tracked down Stanford and he directed them to the crates of bows and arrows. Emmon reached into one and strung a bow. He tested the strength of the string, fitted an arrow, and shot it straight into the wall.

"What do you think?" Arden asked.

"Decent bows. I think there are enough arrows here to actually have an effect on the battle."

Hal arrived with three dozen soldiers. Matt and Arden led them outside of the city while Emmon set up targets with the lids of the crates and Hal distributed bows. They watched as the soldiers alternated shooting at the targets, carefully evaluating their range and aim. In the end, after a brief discussion, they decided that only six of the soldiers were poor enough archers to be sent back to the main infantry.

After dismissing the freshly picked archers, Matt and his friends and Sanford walked back down the streets, which were now completely deserted. Hal led them to an old building several blocks away from the port. Galen and Lucian sat inside, talking animatedly over a table covered in papers.

"Ah, come in all of you," Lucian said.

"Hello," Galen said wearily. "Did you pick out the archers?"

Matt nodded.

"Good. Sit down."

They all pulled up chairs and stared intently at Lucian, Galen, and the third man who Matt guessed was Idris.

"We've decided to keep the garans away from the city as much as possible," Galen began. "We'll assemble the troops on the plain and we'll station the archers behind and to the right of the main infantry."

He turned to Arden. "Did Nick agree with your plan?" She nodded. "Excellent. Nick and Torrin will lead a group of sailors from the water and hit the garans from the side. Lucian will signal them with light when it time for them to join the battle. There will also be another, separate group that will come from the left flank and cut the garans off on that side as well. Hal, I want you and Sanford to lead that group."

Hal nodded briskly.

"Matt, when we are ready for the creatures, you will send the ball of fire into the sky high above the city and let it hover there for ten seconds, okay?"

Matt nodded.

"Good. Emmon, I need you to command the archers. Matt and Arden, stick together and help wherever necessary. Now, let's get a few hours of sleep while we can."

* * *

Matt belted Doubtslayer to his waist. He also had his throwing knives, as well as the pouch with the three Stones of the Elements, his most vital weapons.

It was that very dark hour just before the sun begins to rise. He, Emmon, and Arden stood under the archway into Aresburg, squinting in the darkness, their weariness overcome by anticipation. Together, they walked into the dark field with Matt holding a ball of light to guide their way.

The plain was dotted with blazing torches. The army had traveled a good distance away from the city in hope of protecting it from the approaching garans. Some soldiers and townsmen had been left in the city in case the garans broke through the defenses in the fields.

Matt tried to spot any sign of the garans, but it was too dark. They waited in silence. Matt felt like he would be sick if he tried to speak. Emmon gripped his bow tightly, a quiver of arrows on his back and a sword at his side. Arden wore her knives, but Galen had convinced her to take a sword, as well. They joined the lines of soldiers, and Emmon stopped at the archers who stood separate from the main group.

Matt and Emmon shook hands and hugged each other with their other arms.

Matt said, "I'll keep an eye out for you. Look after yourself."

"Same to you," Emmon said as Arden grabbed him in a tight hug.

Matt and Arden left him reluctantly and walked together between the lines. Matt looked at Arden. This was not how he wanted it to end, in battle. He wished he was good with words so he could let her know how important she was to him. He wasn't sure he could explain the strength of his emotions to her, so he said nothing.

Galen and Lucian stood with Idris, surveying the troops. Galen was wearing his sword and a long knife. Lucian carried his staff, but also wore a sword. Their faces were grim when they turned to Matt and Arden.

"It will be difficult to see the garans coming in this darkness," Galen said. "They could be right in front of us at this moment for all we know."

"Lucian, you're the Wizard of Light, aren't you?" Matt said. "Can't you light the way?"

"For a moment, at least, to see where they are."

Lucian lifted his hands into the air. A brilliant white light appeared and then rocketed forward down the plain. In that brief instant, they could see the vast army of grotesque bodies rushing toward them.

The light blinked once, and the night went black again.

A ripple of fear traveled through the soldiers but Galen spoke calmly.

"Only a few minutes and they will be upon us. We are ready."

"Where's Hal?" Arden breathed.

"He and Sanford are already with their legion," Galen answered. "Good luck to us all. Remember, stay close to each other."

Matt looked at Arden, the dim light from the torches dancing across her face. Fear gripped him. Quietly, she reached over and squeezed his hand, and he felt renewed courage and determination.

"Draw swords!" Galen yelled.

CHAPTER THIRTY-TWO

The air was suddenly filled with yelling as swords were pulled from their scabbards as Galen's order spread through the ranks. Matt drew Doubtslayer from its scabbard and scanned the darkness. He could see nothing. The garans would be here any minute. How could they fight their enemies blinded by the darkness?

Feeling desperate, Matt conjured a handful of fire and threw it into the air, and then, drawing on the Wind Stone, he made it spread into a wave of fire, rippling above the plain. The garans were no more than ten yards away.

"Attack!" Galen yelled, though it was hardly necessary.

Soldiers and garans collided, sword against claw. The air was filled with the horrifying shrieks of the garans, the yells and screams of men. Matt edged closer to Arden, his mind racing. How could he keep her safe? They were thrown sideways as soldiers rushed by them. Matt was knocked to the ground, feet kicking him painfully in the head. He fought to his knees, struggling to find Arden.

"Arden!" he yelled.

There was no answer. After a moment, a warm hand slid into his own, gripping it tightly. Not wanting to release her, he scrambled to his feet.

"We have to be ready to fight, they're almost upon us," Arden said urgently.

And then garans were everywhere, snarling and screeching as they surrounded the humans. Matt swung Doubtslayer at the nearest garan, stabbing it in the abdomen as it lunged with deadly claws. He whirled around and stabbed another in the neck. A garan lunged for his throat and Matt raised his hand, conjuring a shield.

The garan bounced away, but Matt let his shield fall too quickly and another garan attacked his side, its claws raking down his shoulder and arm. Matt groaned and dropped his sword. The garan crouched to attack again, but Matt blasted the offending creature with a burst of fire. The garan writhed in pain and ran blindly into the garans around him, spreading the fire to other garans as it went.

Matt grasped his bleeding shoulder as the area around him cleared. The soldiers were fighting ferociously against their cruel, mindless enemy.

"Matt!"

Arden was a few feet away from him, her face horrified as she pointed at the garan army in front of them. Glowing in the fire light, was a cluster of tall creatures that looked similar to the garans, but were twice the size and walking on two legs. They moved clumsily, as if they were walking for the first time, carrying brutal-looking swords and pointed spears.

In the center of these new garans, stood an even taller figure with gray skin and a skeletal body. One of Malik's Agurans.

Several more garans charged Matt. He began throwing balls of fire since the garans seemed to panic at the mere sight of the flames. The larger, upright garans came nearer, and Matt threw fire at them, but without the same effect – the fire did not burn them and they did not appear to be afraid of it.

Onward they marched, only yards away from him now. Doubtslayer hung uselessly from his injured arm. His heart began to beat faster and he scrambled backward, tripping over dead garans. He widened the distance between himself and the giant garans, and plunged back into battle.

Just before he moved to help a soldier fend off three garans at once, he realized that he had lost sight of Arden. He quickly sent fire shooting at the three garans and then looked around wildly, unable to spot her in the fray.

Galen was suddenly there grabbing his arm, pulling him away from the approaching wall of creatures.

"Come on!" Galen hissed. "We've got to move!"

Matt followed him, weaving through the fighting.

"Watch those walking garans. We haven't been able to stop them," Galen yelled.

He pointed to a cloud of arrows raining down upon the garans. Only one of the enormous creatures fell. The others ignored the arrows and continued to plow through the soldiers with incredible strength. The Aguran in the middle was surrounded by a magical shield that deflected the remaining stray arrows.

"They are breaking through," Galen said urgently. "Go to Emmon and warn him and the other archers. Tell them to get moving or they'll be dead!"

Matt set off through the ranks of soldiers. Three garans tore after him, leaping off the chest of a dead soldier. Matt turned as he ran, sending a blast of magical energy into the garans. They were blasted backward. Matt ran faster.

The battle raged in all directions. Men and garans collided in a horrible clash of claws and swords. The ranks of garans seemed to stretch endlessly before them. When one garan fell, another took its place. It did not matter how hard they fought, how many garans the soldiers struck down. The garans kept coming, attacking with mindless ferocity. The creatures knew no thoughts, no fear, only the orders issued to them. Nothing would stop them from pressing forward.

Archers send volleys of arrows streaking down on the approaching garans and solider swung their swords. But the garans claws were swift and sharp. With every attack, more soldiers were struck down and their defenses grew weaker.

Everywhere was the sound of pain and fear.

Within moments, Matt could hear Emmon's voice above the din.

"Aim for the garans, not the walking creatures! They are not falling. And the Aguran has a magical shield!"

"Emmon!" he yelled.

"You are surrounded by garans. They're moving fast," Matt called. "Galen said to draw your swords and drop the bows."

Emmon hesitated for a fraction of a second and then nodded.

"You heard him! Get going!"

The soldiers clambered to obey. Emmon did not drop his own bow but continued to shoot. "Where's Arden?"

"I don't know. We got separated. Come on."

Emmon fitted an arrow into his bow and followed Matt into the battle. It was growing lighter as the sun crept toward the horizon. Matt almost wished for the darkness again as the bodies of the dead and wounded were more visible in the dim light.

"Look!" Emmon said suddenly. "Hal."

Hal led a group of soliders from the west and they pushed ferociously through the ranks of garans. The sight of the reinforcements gave Matt renewed strength, and he and Emmon ran into battle where a group of soldiers were surrounded by a large cluster of garans.

Emmon fired an arrow into the chest of one garan, saving an unarmed soldier. Matt pulled out one of his throwing knives, took careful aim, and threw. The knife burrowed into a garan's side. Emmon's well-aimed arrows felled garan after garan, giving the soldiers the opportunity to fight through the gap.

And then the ground suddenly shook. One of the enormous walking garans was upon them.

"Move!" Matt yelled, pushing Emmon out of the way.

The creature's sword burrowed into the earth where Emmon had stood just a moment before. Emmon fired another arrow and it buried deep into the chest of the creature. It lurched forward, but did not fall. Emmon shot another arrow and another at the beast until, at last, it fell.

Garans came at Matt from both sides. He dived forward, avoiding the first swipe of their claws, but was still trapped between them. Adrenaline surged through him and he barely felt the deep wounds on his shoulder and arm. He lifted his sword just in time to avoid a blow from the garan on the right, but claws dug into his back.

Matt struggled to stay focused as he rolled across the ground, bringing up his sword to stab his attacker. Emmon yelled out, clutching his arm in pain. A giant garan swung its sword at Emmon, barely missing his head.

Matt staggered to his friend's side and flung his second knife through the air. The blade caught the beast in the leg, but Matt knew that it was no good. It seemed to feel no pain. Matt tried fire again, but to no avail. It raised its sword to deliver the killing stroke. Matt struggled to conjure a shield, but the beast brought its sword downward. And then it froze and doubled forward, stabbed from behind. It turned, growling ferociously to face its attacker. Matt saw the opportunity and, yelling wildly, stabbed the creature in the stomach.

Gasping, Matt turned to face their savior. It was Arden. And she was bleeding from a gash on her forehead.

CHAPTER THIRTY-THREE

"Arden," Matt began.

"You're hurt, Matt," she said immediately, grabbing his arm to steady him.

Matt did not answer, reaching for the pouch around his neck. He was immediately calmed by the power rushing up his arm and to his back. In a few moments, Matt felt cool droplets of water settle on his skin and the deep gashes healed completely.

"Not anymore," Matt said with a quick smile. "Here, I can fix that."

He reached out two fingers, brushing Arden's hair off of her face and then gently stroking her forehead until the gash was healed over. He looked at her for a moment, and she smiled before turning back toward the battle. Matt hastily grabbed Emmon's arm and healed him as well, ignoring his amused expression.

"Matt, the sailors," Arden said urgently.

"What about them?"

"They were supposed to reach shore at first light. They need the signal to attack."

"Lucian," Matt said quickly.

"I don't know where he is and we need the sailors. Now."

Matt grabbed her hand and pulled her along, searching for signs of Lucian.

"Look out!" someone yelled suddenly.

Matt whirled around to see a garan charging them. Matt dropped his sword and held up his hands. A new kind of power surged through him, the power of the Wind Stone. Electricity hissing in the air and there was a terrific bang as blue lightning shot out of Matt's palm. It hit the garan's body, throwing it backward with a sizzle.

A triumphant yell drowned out its screams.

"That was great!"

Hal ran toward them. His left sleeve was bloody, but he was grinning. His sword dangled limply at his side and was breathing heavily.

"The charge worked, but we need reinforcements. Where are Torrin and Nick? They were supposed to be here by now," Hal said.

"We need to find Lucian," Matt said, grabbing Hal's arm and quickly healing it.

"Thanks. I saw Lucian near the center a few minutes ago," Hal said flexing his arm appreciatively. "Come on!"

They tore after Hal, fighting garans as they went. At the center of the battle, Galen was struggling to hold off a group of garans and Lucian was in a magical duel with the Aguran. There were flashes of Light and Dark magic shooting between the two figures, and Matt could feel the energy crackling through the air. But every attack Lucian made was blocked by the Aguran's shield. It seemed impossible to bring it down.

Matt ran toward the wizard, jumping over fallen soliders and ducking away from attacking garans as he ran. As he reached him, Lucian dodged an attack from the Aguran.

"Matt," Lucian hissed through gritted teeth. "Get out of here!"

Matt flung up a magical shield, protecting them both from the Aguran. "Send the signal for the sailors!!"

Lucian moved behind Matt and pointed his staff toward the eastern sky. Matt faced the Aguran as it drew a cruel, twisted, silver blade. Matt could sense rather than see the light erupting from Lucian's staff, but Matt's gaze did not leave the Aguran. It swiped at Matt's shield with its blade and Matt felt his defenses failing. Finally, Lucian turned, ready to fight again, and Matt let his shield fall.

There was a thunderous noise as the sailors ran from the eastern shore, yelling. They bore every kind of weapon – knives, swords, clubs, spears. Torrin led them headlong into battle, colliding violently with the garans.

Galen took a final lunge at the standing garan he was battling. Its sword fell to the ground. Galen swayed precariously. His right leg was soaked in blood and he doubled over in exhaustion. Matt ran to his side.

"Garans with swords," Galen gasped as Matt grabbed his arm. "What kind of cruel idea is that?"

He winced, grunting in pain. Matt threw up a shield around them and healed his leg. Matt could feel his own strength beginning to ebb as he used so much magic. He helped Galen stand. Galen wiped the sweat from his face.

"There are still so many garans," Galen said, still taking rasping breaths. "We're losing men quickly."

"Should I call the creatures?"

"Not yet, but soon. Where's Idris?"

Matt gratefully lowered the shield and Galen joined the battle again, swinging his sword at the never-ending procession of garans. Matt tried to ignore the exhaustion that threatened to overcome him, and he began to create and throw balls of fire at the garans near him.

And then he saw that Lucian was on the ground, senseless, and the Aguran was suddenly upon Matt. It held a black, whip-like rope in one hand, its enormous dagger in the other, striking down everything in its path.

In one sweeping motion, the Aguran raised its blade and brought it streaking down toward Matt's head. Matt raised his sword, blocking the blow, but the Aguran's strength was far greater than he had expected and he staggered backward. The second attack was even faster, and Matt jumped out of the way just in time.

An odd chill rippled through the air as the Aguran paused, gazing at Matt. They both knew that it was stronger and more skilled than Matt. But Matt had something he could use to his advantage. The combined power of the elements was more powerful than anything the Aguran could wield.

Willpower and magic surged through Matt, and he flung fire at the Aguran, but the Aguran's whip snapped and the fire died before it could reach it. Matt tried again, but once again the fire was extinguished.

Matt raised his sword and lunged at the creature. He was repelled instantly, landing hard on his back. The Aguran advanced on him, brushing aside the soldiers that attempted to attack it from all sides. It raised its sword above Matt, but before it could strike Matt shot a blast of energy magnified by the strength he drew from the Stones.

The Aguran staggered backward and Matt jumped to his feet. He did not wait for it to regroup, but stretched his fingers outward. A dozen flaming projectiles flew toward the Aguran. They danced across its gray skin, but the creature merely shivered like it was shaking off rain, and the fire disappeared.

CHAPTER THIRTY-FOUR

Matt's mind raced. If fire did not affect it, what would? Water? Desperate, he released a powerful jet of water. It did nothing. The Aguran was almost upon him now, and Matt's heart pounded. This had to end.

Wind.

Matt threw wind so powerful that everyone nearby was thrown to the ground. The wind was like ice, but Matt barely felt it, his blood was running so hot in his veins. The water that Matt had soaked the Aguran with had now turned to ice, freezing the creature in its tracks. The creature quivered and Matt knew that it would break free in moments.

Around him, the garans still snarled and slashed, and soldiers fought bravely and fell. The Aresburg defenses were weakening. The battle had been pushed closer and closer to the city and the garans were beginning to break through. It was only a matter of time before they swarmed through the streets and everything they had been fighting for would be lost. Malik would win.

It was time to call Samsire.

Matt raised his hand to the sky and shot a ball of bright fire above the battle – the signal for the creatures. Ten seconds was all he needed, but it was ten seconds he didn't have. He could hear the ice encasing the Aguran cracking. It would soon be free. Matt kept his eyes on the fire above him, concentrating on maintaining the blaze. There was another loud crack and Matt knew that the Aguran was free.

And then Matt felt an intense burning surging through him, like his body had been plunged into flames. He writhed in pain but could not shake it away. The pain lessened ever so slightly and Matt managed to open his eyes.

The Aguran was holding Matt with only one hand now. The other hand fumbled to get a grip on Arden, who was hammering at the creature's Dark shield with her sword. Its hand closed on her arm and she went limp. Matt kicked ferociously at the Aguran's chest. It did not slacken its hold on him, but it released Arden. Matt knew he couldn't let it grab him with the other hand or all would be lost, but he had no strength to fight it.

The Aguran was suddenly yanked backward as sharp claws closed around its middle and ripped it away from Matt. Samsire roared angrily, flying higher and throwing the Aguran into a crowd of garans. The sky was filled with griffins, flying horses, phoenixes, and harpies. The land creatures came galloping from the north, centaurs shot their bows, and unicorns speared garans on their horns.

"Matt, are you all right?"

Arden helped Matt to his feet. His whole body ached. He looked at Arden's pale face.

"Yes, are you?" he said quickly. "I have to get that Aguran."

"No-"

Matt cut her off. "This is something I have to do. I'll be back."

He ran to the place where Sam had dropped the Aguran. It was hunched over the ground, getting slowly to its feet.

Without pausing to think about what he was doing, Matt knelt down to the ground and plunged his fingers into the soil. It was time for him to connect to something that had always been part of him, but he had never known. Earth magic. Matt reached deeper into the ground and the rich soil stirred in his fingers. He felt a trickle of life.

He nearly fell backward as power moved through his hands into the ground. Without warning, dozens of rope-like tree roots shot from the dirt and snaked toward the Aguran.

The roots wove around the Aguran and grabbed it in an unshakable grip. No matter how much it struggled, no matter how much it tried to slice through them or blast them away with magic, the roots held firm. They wrestled it down, pinning its arms and legs to the ground. The Aguran's shield flickered weakly until it sputtered out of existence.

The Aguran twitched violently as the roots tightened. Its body shivered and a cloud of darkness erupted around it. And then, without a sound, the Aguran stopped moving and was dead.

CHAPTER THIRTY-FIVE

Matt stood above the dead Aguran, his breath coming in short, ragged gasps. He had done it. It was dead.

He tore his eyes away from it and scanned the rest of the battlefield. The garans had abandoned their attack and were now running haphazardly around the plain, chased by sailors, soldiers, and the creatures from the sanctuary.

"Matt," a voice said from his right.

Matt turned to see Torrin standing beside him a broad grin on his face.

"That was brilliant!" Torrin said, gruffly shaking Matt's hand.

Matt smiled. "Thank goodness you came when you did. Otherwise the garans might be in the city by now."

Torrin nodded, casting a wary glance over his shoulder. "Yeah, maybe. Those creatures you brought in were pretty helpful. Terrifying, but helpful."

He gestured toward a griffin that was systematically attacking a group of garans with its claws.

Matt laughed. "Don't let them hear you say that."

Matt picked up his sword and walked with Torrin through the battlefield. The creatures were dealing with the remaining garans, leaving Matt and Torrin to find those who were wounded. Matt stopped to heal a man with a bad slash down his side. As Matt stood up, he was engulfed in a hug from Arden.

"We did it," she said quietly. "You're okay?"

Matt nodded and put his arms around her. He turned to see Emmon and Lucian walking toward them. Matt was relieved that Lucian appeared to be unharmed by the Aguran's painful magic. Emmon clapped Matt on the back and Lucian smiled.

"That was well done, Matt," Lucian said. "You truly are the master of the elements."

Matt felt his face go red, but he was saved the need to respond as Hal approached, carrying Sanford whose shirt was red with blood.

"Any chance of healing him, Matt?" Hal asked hopefully.

Matt immediately knelt to help the semi-conscious man, carefully sealing his wounds, and then he stood, overcome by exhaustion. He wondered how many more men he would be able to heal.

"Where's Galen?" he asked.

"I'm here."

Galen was standing several yards away, his face full of grief.

"What is it?" Matt asked.

"Idris is dead," Galen replied dully. "Many have died."

Lucian put his hand on Galen's shoulder.

"Yes, many have died. It is a great tragedy," Lucian said and then fell silent for a moment. "But we must remember that they died to save us all from Malik's evil. They fought willingly and they have saved the lives of many. We have won a victory against Malik today. He will not be able to walk away from it easily."

Galen nodded sadly, but then patted Matt on the back. "That was some impressive magic there, Matt. Quite impressive. Considering you're only a mergling."

Matt grinned.

"Come on," Galen said. "Let's gather the rest of troops."

Anyone well enough to stand gathered in the center of the field. After much coaxing from Samsire, the creatures joined them, as well. Matt was disheartened by how few of Aresburg's soldiers remained.

Galen stood before them, surveying them all appreciatively.

"We have lost many today and we are saddened by and grateful for their sacrifice," Galen began. "But we have triumphed, as well. Today we took a step toward ridding the world of Malik's evil. Once more we will have peace. But today we have also done something more."

Galen paused and looked around at the faces. "Only days ago, many of you knew nothing of the Commander of Shadows. You could not even imagine what existed beyond the walls of your city. And now, humans stand beside magical creatures, united."

At this the creatures began to claw at the ground indignantly.

"Yes," Galen said. "United. Malik has managed to do something he never expected – force humans, creatures, and magical beings to stand together against him. Do not forget this day. It has been more of victory than you know. Do not live in fear of the Commander, but do live in defiance. That is the only way he can be defeated. Today we have won, let's not forget the lessons we have learned from it."

There was a loud cheer – from human and creature alikewhich continued for several minutes.

"Good speech, Galen," Matt told him with a grin.

Galen smiled broadly.

"Human," Gusren said to Matt. "I believe you have a promise to keep."

Matt nodded and made his way to Sam's side.

"We have one thing left to do, Sam," Matt said wearily. "Let's go."

Sam rose into the air and flew toward the mountains. Matt dozed in Sam's soft feathers, lulled by the rocking motion of Sam's wings and the gentle wind. After an hour of flying, the alorath angled downward and landed at the edge of a valley. Matt slid off of his back. The mass of dark fog was shifting in front of him, one more enemy to face - a sinister and powerful enemy.

"Do you think you can do this?" Samsire asked him quietly.

Matt took a deep breath and nodded.

He stepped forward, pulled the Wind Stone out of the pouch and held it out in front of him. The fog swirled threateningly toward him. Matt raised his hand, clearing his mind of the emotions from the battle. The cooling power of the Wind Stone filled him and he released the magic outward. A gust of wind sped through the valley, streaking through the fog.

The fog reared back like a threatened animal. Matt held steady and the wind continued to buffet it. But the fog still fought, rearing back and lunging forward. Matt released the Wind Stone, watching the roiling vapor. How could he defeat this?

"Any ideas?" he asked Samsire.

The alorath considered the fog. "Since this is of Malik's making, then he would want to make as difficult to destroy as possible. Perhaps you need more power."

More power. Matt pulled the other two Stones of the Elements out of the pouch and held the Fire Stone, the Water Stone, and the Wind Stone on his palm together. He focused his magical power, and dark storm clouds began to gather above the massive fog. Wind whistled through the valley and flashes of lightning shot down into the fog. Matt tapped into the power of the Water Stone and thick rain drops began to fall from the sky. The mist seemed to writhe as the attack continued.

Finally, Matt reached out to the Fire Stone. Heat and electricity burned through the air, mingling with the rain drops. There was a tremendous hissing sound as the fog made contact with the rain, and the electrical energy erupted in an explosion of lightning.

The fog was under siege. It writhed and twisted. Tendrils of dark mist snaked toward Matt, but they were continually forced back by the wind and then devoured by the onslaught of rain, heat, and lightning. Matt did not know how long he stood there, wielding the power of the elements, but after what seemed like an eternity, the fog was gone.

All that remained was the sickly terrain that had been covered by the fog. Plants and trees were wilted and colorless. But they would grow again.

Matt lowered his hands, staring down at the three Stones of the Elements, mesmerized by their swirling colors and their power. He felt a sudden shudder of power and he stared curiously at the

Stones. They were moving together, their edges melting and seeping into one another. A flood of power roared through Matt's arms and he stepped back in surprise, holding the Stones against his chest.

He stared at the Stones, disbelieving. They were moving as if they were the elements themselves, swirling like fire, water, and wind. Matt understood at once what was happening, the thing that he had heard about so many times in the stories about Malik.

The Stones were joining.

CHAPTER THIRTY-SIX

The swirl of color settled on Matt's chest and he felt the raw power pulling him into its sweeping depths. A loud buzzing clouded his ears, drowning out Samsire's bellows, and his vision grew clouded as he stared at the vortex of color. The Stones seemed to sink into him.

He could no longer feel them against his chest, but felt an intense current of magic. It was the wild dance of flames, the roaring rapids of river, the brutal battering of wind washing over him all at once, almost feeding off of him. His own strength, his own magic, his sense of self, was being consumed by the power of the Stones.

Through the haze, Matt's thoughts pounded weakly in his brain. This, he realized, was the cause of Malik's deformation. That was what the stories told of, the joining of the Stones went wrong, disfiguring Malik and burning down the workshop of Loyland, the creator of the Stones.

He would not suffer the same fate. He would fight. Strength and resolve rushed through his body, and Matt felt his own magic push back the magic of the elements. He concentrated all of his energy, and in a sudden blast of light, the indistinct mass that was the Stones shot away from his body and hovered in the air.

Matt lay limply on the ground gasping for breath. Samsire was leaning over him, his blue eyes wide. Matt heard a strange hum. The Stones still moved in the indistinct swirl of color above him. They were taking shape, the colors dancing around, stretching into a long thin shape, and then solidifying into a dark, wooden pole. It fell beside Matt, and he picked it up tentatively. It was a staff, smooth and perfect. It was just the right height with a gentle, sloping top. He grabbed it at the place where the wood curled, feeling the power it held, and he pulled himself upright.

"Matt," Samsire breathed. "Are you all right?"

Matt held the staff wonderingly, looking up at the alorath. "I'm fine. More than fine."

He gripped the staff firmly in his left hand, utterly bewildered by it, but hesitant to let go of it. He leaned on it heavily, exhausted. He looked back at the valley. The fog was gone, the job was done.

"Come on, let's go back," Matt said, wearily climbing onto Sam's back.

Matt barely noticed the flight back to Aresburg as he gripped the staff tightly. So much had happened over the past day, he could not make sense of it all. So instead of trying, he reveled in the peace of flying on Samsire's back, watching the world pass beneath them.

As Samsire landed in the fields, a group of people and creatures circled around them. Matt saw the faces of Lucian, Galen, Emmon, Arden, and Hal, and Gusren at the front. They all stared at him in curious amazement.

"It's done," he announced to Gusren. "The fog is gone. And the people of Aresburg will not bother you. Galen has told them that you are not to be disturbed or trifled with."

Gusren dipped his head. "Thank you, human. I believe that we have now settled any favors owed between us." The griffin hesitated a moment. "You are, indeed, powerful. We can only hope that you succeed in defeating the Commander. Good luck."

Without another word the griffin joined the group of creatures and, as one, they took to the air, flying toward the mountains. Matt watched them go and turned back to his friends.

"What happened, Matt?" Arden asked him quietly.

Matt took a breath and said, "I fought off the fog using all of the Stones. And after the fog was gone, I held all of the Stones together." Matt hesitated, not wanting them to tell them that the Stones had nearly consumed him. "And…the Stones joined. Into this staff." He raised the staff to show them. "This staff used to be the three Stones of the Elements. I think it will control fire, water, and wind all together, just as the Stones did separately."

They all stared at Matt. Matt understood their expressions of awe and fear. He felt the same way. He did not want the responsibility of possessing something as powerful as the staff. But then again, it was either him or Malik.

He gripped the staff tightly. The power of the three elements coursed through him continually as he held the staff, but it now truly felt subordinate to his will. He tried not to think about the terrifying and enigmatic behavior of the Stones when they had attempted to join. To join with him.

Lucian smiled at him. "You did well, Matt. And the rest of you, as well. You all showed great courage."

"Matt," Galen said, clapping his shoulder. "Let's go celebrate."

CHAPTER THIRTY-SEVEN

They spent a short while celebrating with the soldiers and townspeople, but a shadow hung over Matt thought of what they had lost. Throughout the afternoon, the battlefield was cleared and the bodies of the dead were brought to their families. It was unbearable to watch the tears and cries of the families. Matt, Emmon, and Arden walked silently outside the city walls through the dead grass that swayed in the cold wind.

The sky was gray and the air was cold. They had left their weapons back with Galen and Lucian, and Matt felt considerably freer and happier without the burden of the weapons they had wielded in battle.

After a while, they returned to the city, and found Galen, Lucian, and Hal standing under the archway that bore the words of Darrick.

"Come on," Galen said. "Let's-"

"If you say something that requires more work than snoring, I'll feed you to Sam," Matt interrupted.

"I was going to suggest we go see Catherine," Galen said, going slightly red, "but we'll do it the morning."

They all exchanged a grin and followed him down the quiet streets to the small inn they had called their home for the past few weeks. The innkeeper was not at the bar, but sailors and soldiers were dancing on the tables with mugs of ale in their hands. They attempted to coerce Galen and Lucian into joining their celebration, but Galen waved them away. He stopped only long enough to send a message to Catherine telling her that they were all okay, and then he forged a path up the stairs to the comfortable beds that awaited them. Matt was asleep before his head hit the pillow.

Matt slept long and well, despite the sadness that clawed at him. By the time he woke in the morning, the sun was high in the sky. He dressed slowly, his body still aching painfully from the day before, but sleep seemed to have washed away some of the emotional pain. It was a new day and it was time to rebuild. He met the others in the tavern below. The only sign of the raucous celebration the night before were the fallen mugs and upturned tables.

"I'm surprised they're not still at it," Arden said, stifling a yawn. "It sounded like they could go on for days."

The streets were still eerily quiet as they made their way to Catherine's home. A few soldiers passed them, saluting Galen as they walked by. Galen only knocked once on the door before it flew open, and Catherine threw her arms around him and kissed him. Then she stepped back and put her hands on her hips, pretending to be cross.

"Well, you certainly took your time getting here."

Galen, who looked as though he'd been hit on the head, nodded. Arden was unable to suppress a giggle and Galen turned red.

"Er...right. Can we come inside?"

They all followed Galen and Catherine into the small house and Catherine poured tea for everyone.

"I'm sorry so many were lost," she said quietly. "I could hear the battle from here." She shuddered. "Thank goodness you all made it out alive."

Silence fell around the table.

"How is your mother, Cat?" Galen asked.

"Oh, she's well. She's been asking about all of you incessantly," Catherine replied. "Would you like to see her?"

They followed her into the tiny back room where they found Ellyn sitting in her bed, knitting merrily.

"Hello!" she cried delightedly. "I was wondering when you would come back. We've had so little time to get to know each other."

She beamed at them and put down her knitting. "So, tell me," she said. "Did my information help you?"

"Yes, most certainly," Lucian said. "Without the knowledge you gave Matt about his heritage, he would not have known how to defeat the Aguran general.

Ellyn nodded happily, and she turned to Matt, her smiled fading slightly. "I'm sorry if I upset you the other day, dear boy. The knowledge of one's birth is very important."

To Matt's surprise, he felt a smile creep onto his face. "No, I'm glad that you told me. It saved my life." Matt paused acutely aware of his friends looking at him. "It's just strange that it's been part of me my whole life and I've never known until now."

Galen put a hand on Matt's shoulder and Matt felt the many unspoken words in the gesture. Ellyn smiled dreamily and picked up her knitting again, humming to herself. Catherine led them from the room.

"She's always been like that, insightful and focused one moment and lost in her happy thoughts, the next," Catherine said apologetically.

Emmon and Arden laughed.

"So, what would you say about taking a walk with me?" Galen said.

Catherine looked pleased. "I'd like that. I'll get my cloak."

The teenagers were now battling to hide their laughter.

"Ah, I believe Torrin wished to see us in the port, Matt," Lucian said with a smile.

"Oh, right, um, we'll go then," Matt said, moving to the door with the others close on his heels.

They ran down a side street unable to contain their laughter. Even Hal was clutching at his sides.

"I never thought I'd see the day when I saw a woman make Galen blush," Lucian chuckled. "I'm not exactly sure he's accepted it either."

They continued down the street, heading to the port so they would stay out of Galen's way. The port was as quiet and empty as the streets. They walked to the dock where the *Lady Gemma* was tied. The sailors still moved up and down the ramp, but they were unusually quiet. When they spotted Matt and the others, they shouted out greetings.

"Hey, Matt!" Torrin called from above.

He ran down the ramp, his face bright.

"What's going on, Torrin?"

"You'll have to call me First Mate Torrin, from now on," he answered proudly. "I've been promoted."

He grew serious as he explained that Hanson, the former first mate, had been killed in battle. Matt was saddened, but could not help a smiling at Torrin's excitement.

"I'm happy for you, Torrin!"

"Are you still telling everyone you see, Torrin?" Captain Nick said from behind him.

Torrin turned smartly to face Nick and said cheerily, "Of course not, Captain. Just saying hello."

Nick smiled knowingly and turned to Matt and the others. "A fellow named Tad wants to see you, Hal, and Galen, too, wherever he is. He mentioned something about honorary positions on the guard or something like that."

Hal stood up very straight and nodded briskly. "Thanks, Nick. I'll see you all around."

Hal ran off faster than Matt had ever seen him move.

"I hope he doesn't interrupt Galen and Catherine," Arden said as Torrin and Nick turned back to the ship.

"He won't," Matt said. "Knowing Hal, he'll go ahead and get his 'honorary position' and conveniently forget to tell Galen until a day later."

They continued to walk down the canal, enjoying the sound of the waves against the rocky shoreline. Matt gripped his staff, feeling comforted by its reassuring strength.

"What happens now?" Matt said, thinking aloud. "We won a battle, but where do we go from here?"

He looked at Lucian.

"No one can know for certain," Lucian said. "Malik is unpredictable. Not even the wisest understand him."

"Well, I know now what happened to him in the beginning," Matt said suddenly. "I know what happened when he first got the Stones of the Elements."

Matt was not sure what made him bring it up, but he had been thinking about Malik's disastrous experience with the Stones ever since he had made it out of the mountains with the staff. Emmon and Arden were looking at him curiously and Lucian's gray eyes gleamed.

"What do you mean, Matt?" Emmon asked.

"After I fought of the fog, yesterday, I told you that the Stones joined into this staff," Matt said uncomfortably. "Well, that isn't all that happened."

He took a deep breath. "I held all three of the Stones together and then...everything went wrong. They sort of blended together like they were the elements themselves. I don't really understand it. It was like the Stones were trying to join *into* me.

"At first, I couldn't stop it, but then I remembered what had happened to Malik and how he became disfigured because the Stones joined improperly. I...I fought it, and the Stones' magic pulled back, like they were retreating, and then they joined into this staff instead."

Matt looked up at his friends. Arden put a hand on his arm.

"I think that's what happened to Malik. The Stones joined *inside* of him," Matt continued. "So when he was almost destroyed by Cosgrove, then the Stones must have broken apart again because Cosgrove and Pryor hid them separately. But Malik still has power, doesn't he? So…"

"So he must have managed to keep some of what the Stones gave him," Emmon finished.

Matt nodded. "That's what I think."

"And Malik still wanted the Stones," Lucian said slowly, "so that he could gain all that they had to offer." He smiled suddenly. "But you have destroyed his plan, Matt. Now you, his arch enemy, have the Stones and can wield them at will."

Matt didn't answer, staring unseeing at the ocean.

"What will he do now that I have the staff?" Matt asked Lucian. "You must have some idea what he's planning?"

Lucian shook his head slowly. "Like I said, Malik is unpredictable. With the power of all four elements you truly have become his mortal foe." He sighed. "But there is one thing that Malik has always desired. Something that I don't think he has stopped wanting, or ever will, as long as he has the chance to possess it. It will also make him strong and unending."

"What?"

"The Immortality Scroll."

"But the legends say it was lost in the fire. Does it even exist anymore?" Matt said hopefully.

"I don't think he knows. But I don't think it is ever far from his mind. That was always his goal. Complete domination and eternal life."

"What can *we* do about that?" Matt said.

Lucian fixed him with an unwavering gaze. "There are always steps to be taken, Matthias. Beat Malik to it. Force him to give up."

"So go after the Scroll?"

"Yes. Not to use it, but to tear down Malik's morale. It is the only move that we can make."

Matt nodded. Lucian seemed to recognize his reluctance and said with a smile, "But for now, Matthias, I think a good meal is in order."

"Come on, Matt," Arden said, taking his hand and guiding him down the canal and back to the city.

They were soon laughing and Matt felt as though an enormous weight had lifted from his shoulders. He allowed Arden to pull him into a run and they raced down the pier, and then all the way back to Catherine's street where they finally stopped, gasping for air between fits of laughter. They walked toward the tiny house where they found Galen and Catherine walking to the door.

"Where have you all been?" Galen said smiling.

"How was your walk Galen?" Arden said cheerfully, ignoring his question.

Galen smile grew wider. They others followed and Catherine laid food on the table in her little kitchen. They enjoyed themselves for many hours, laughing and eating as much as they could.

Hal showed up later in the afternoon, looking incredibly proud of himself and wearing a silver pin on his shirt. Galen teased him relentlessly, until, finally, Hal was forced to take it off because he could not bear the ribbing. Evening finally came, and reluctantly, they turn to leave.

As they walked out the door, the cold pierced their cloaks. Fat, white, fluffy flakes fell from the dark sky.

"It's snowing!" Arden yelled.

Catherine smiled. "It only snows about twice a year in Aresburg."

They stood in the deafening quiet of the snow for many minutes, and then slowly, they made their way through the streets back toward the inn. As they passed the archway that led into the city, Matt gave Arden's hand a squeeze, and he broke away from the group.

"I'll see you all in a bit," he said, disappearing through the archway.

He walked out into the quiet fields and reached into his pocket to call Samsire, but the alorath was already flying toward him, as if he had known Matt was coming. He landed lightly, but did not say a word. He bent his huge head down and leaned it against Matt. They both stared out into the plains, now covered in snow.

Matt rolled his staff in his numb fingers. It seemed like they had been fighting Malik for so long now.

"We have to finish this, Sam."

The alorath made a low sound in the back of his throat. "I know. It won't be easy. Malik won't go down without a fight."

Matt smiled at the alorath. "Just a little ray of sunshine, aren't you?"

Samsire nudged Matt playfully with his head, knocking him to the ground. Matt plunged his fingers into the snow and threw a snowball at the alorath's head. Sam growled in mock indignation.

"You deserved that," Matt muttered, getting to his feet and brushing off his front.

"Admit it. You missed me while I was away," Sam rumbled.

Matt grinned. "Unfortunately, yes. But only because I need you to eat my enemies."

He placed a hand on the alorath's shoulder. It was the beginning of an unknown ending. But it was an ending they would face together.

LaVergne, TN USA
18 February 2011

217022LV00001B/7/P